the perfect ruse

(a jessie hunt psychological suspense—book 25)

blake pierce

Blake Pierce

Blake Pierce is the USA Today bestselling author of the RILEY PAGE mystery series, which includes seventeen books. Blake Pierce is also the author of the MACKENZIE WHITE mystery series, comprising fourteen books; of the AVERY BLACK mystery series, comprising six books; of the KERI LOCKE mystery series, comprising five books; of the MAKING OF RILEY PAIGE mystery series, comprising six books; of the KATE WISE mystery series, comprising seven books; of the CHLOE FINE psychological suspense mystery, comprising six books; of the JESSIE HUNT psychological suspense thriller series, comprising twenty-eight books; of the AU PAIR psychological suspense thriller series, comprising three books; of the ZOE PRIME mystery series, comprising six books; of the ADELE SHARP mystery series, comprising sixteen books, of the EUROPEAN VOYAGE cozy mystery series, comprising six books; of the LAURA FROST FBI suspense thriller, comprising eleven books; of the ELLA DARK FBI suspense thriller, comprising fourteen books (and counting); of the A YEAR IN EUROPE cozy mystery series, comprising nine books, of the AVA GOLD mystery series, comprising six books; of the RACHEL GIFT mystery series, comprising ten books (and counting); of the VALERIE LAW mystery series, comprising nine books (and counting); of the PAIGE KING mystery series, comprising eight books (and counting); of the MAY MOORE mystery series, comprising eleven books; of the CORA SHIELDS mystery series, comprising eight books (and counting); of the NICKY LYONS mystery series, comprising eight books (and counting), of the CAMI LARK mystery series, comprising eight books (and counting), of the AMBER YOUNG mystery series, comprising five books (and counting), of the DAISY FORTUNE mystery series, comprising five books (and counting), of the FIONA RED mystery series, comprising five books (and counting), and of the new FAITH BOLD mystery series, comprising five books (and counting).

An avid reader and lifelong fan of the mystery and thriller genres, Blake loves to hear from you, so please feel free to visit www.blakepierceauthor.com to learn more and stay in touch.

ISBN: 978-1-0943-8135-0

BOOKS BY BLAKE PIERCE

FAITH BOLD MYSTERY SERIES

SO LONG (Book #1)
SO COLD (Book #2)
SO SCARED (Book #3)
SO NORMAL (Book #4)
SO FAR GONE (Book #5)

FIONA RED MYSTERY SERIES

LET HER GO (Book #1)
LET HER BE (Book #2)
LET HER HOPE (Book #3)
LET HER WISH (Book #4)
LET HER LIVE (Book #5)

DAISY FORTUNE MYSTERY SERIES

NEED YOU (Book #1)
CLAIM YOU (Book #2)
CRAVE YOU (Book #3)
CHOOSE YOU (Book #4)
CHASE YOU (Book #5)

AMBER YOUNG MYSTERY SERIES

ABSENT PITY (Book #1)
ABSENT REMORSE (Book #2)
ABSENT FEELING (Book #3)
ABSENT MERCY (Book #4)
ABSENT REASON (Book #5)

CAMI LARK MYSTERY SERIES

JUST ME (Book #1)
JUST OUTSIDE (Book #2)
JUST RIGHT (Book #3)
JUST FORGET (Book #4)
JUST ONCE (Book #5)
JUST HIDE (Book #6)

JUST NOW (Book #7)
JUST HOPE (Book #8)

NICKY LYONS MYSTERY SERIES
ALL MINE (Book #1)
ALL HIS (Book #2)
ALL HE SEES (Book #3)
ALL ALONE (Book #4)
ALL FOR ONE (Book #5)
ALL HE TAKES (Book #6)
ALL FOR ME (Book #7)
ALL IN (Book #8)

CORA SHIELDS MYSTERY SERIES
UNDONE (Book #1)
UNWANTED (Book #2)
UNHINGED (Book #3)
UNSAID (Book #4)
UNGLUED (Book #5)
UNSTABLE (Book #6)
UNKNOWN (Book #7)
UNAWARE (Book #8)

MAY MOORE SUSPENSE THRILLER
NEVER RUN (Book #1)
NEVER TELL (Book #2)
NEVER LIVE (Book #3)
NEVER HIDE (Book #4)
NEVER FORGIVE (Book #5)
NEVER AGAIN (Book #6)
NEVER LOOK BACK (Book #7)
NEVER FORGET (Book #8)
NEVER LET GO (Book #9)
NEVER PRETEND (Book #10)
NEVER HESITATE (Book #11)

PAIGE KING MYSTERY SERIES
THE GIRL HE PINED (Book #1)
THE GIRL HE CHOSE (Book #2)

THE GIRL HE TOOK (Book #3)
THE GIRL HE WISHED (Book #4)
THE GIRL HE CROWNED (Book #5)
THE GIRL HE WATCHED (Book #6)
THE GIRL HE WANTED (Book #7)
THE GIRL HE CLAIMED (Book #8)

VALERIE LAW MYSTERY SERIES
NO MERCY (Book #1)
NO PITY (Book #2)
NO FEAR (Book #3)
NO SLEEP (Book #4)
NO QUARTER (Book #5)
NO CHANCE (Book #6)
NO REFUGE (Book #7)
NO GRACE (Book #8)
NO ESCAPE (Book #9)

RACHEL GIFT MYSTERY SERIES
HER LAST WISH (Book #1)
HER LAST CHANCE (Book #2)
HER LAST HOPE (Book #3)
HER LAST FEAR (Book #4)
HER LAST CHOICE (Book #5)
HER LAST BREATH (Book #6)
HER LAST MISTAKE (Book #7)
HER LAST DESIRE (Book #8)
HER LAST REGRET (Book #9)
HER LAST HOUR (Book #10)

AVA GOLD MYSTERY SERIES
CITY OF PREY (Book #1)
CITY OF FEAR (Book #2)
CITY OF BONES (Book #3)
CITY OF GHOSTS (Book #4)
CITY OF DEATH (Book #5)
CITY OF VICE (Book #6)

A YEAR IN EUROPE

A MURDER IN PARIS (Book #1)
DEATH IN FLORENCE (Book #2)
VENGEANCE IN VIENNA (Book #3)
A FATALITY IN SPAIN (Book #4)

ELLA DARK FBI SUSPENSE THRILLER
GIRL, ALONE (Book #1)
GIRL, TAKEN (Book #2)
GIRL, HUNTED (Book #3)
GIRL, SILENCED (Book #4)
GIRL, VANISHED (Book 5)
GIRL ERASED (Book #6)
GIRL, FORSAKEN (Book #7)
GIRL, TRAPPED (Book #8)
GIRL, EXPENDABLE (Book #9)
GIRL, ESCAPED (Book #10)
GIRL, HIS (Book #11)
GIRL, LURED (Book #12)
GIRL, MISSING (Book #13)
GIRL, UNKNOWN (Book #14)

LAURA FROST FBI SUSPENSE THRILLER
ALREADY GONE (Book #1)
ALREADY SEEN (Book #2)
ALREADY TRAPPED (Book #3)
ALREADY MISSING (Book #4)
ALREADY DEAD (Book #5)
ALREADY TAKEN (Book #6)
ALREADY CHOSEN (Book #7)
ALREADY LOST (Book #8)
ALREADY HIS (Book #9)
ALREADY LURED (Book #10)
ALREADY COLD (Book #11)

EUROPEAN VOYAGE COZY MYSTERY SERIES
MURDER (AND BAKLAVA) (Book #1)
DEATH (AND APPLE STRUDEL) (Book #2)
CRIME (AND LAGER) (Book #3)
MISFORTUNE (AND GOUDA) (Book #4)

CALAMITY (AND A DANISH) (Book #5)
MAYHEM (AND HERRING) (Book #6)

ADELE SHARP MYSTERY SERIES
LEFT TO DIE (Book #1)
LEFT TO RUN (Book #2)
LEFT TO HIDE (Book #3)
LEFT TO KILL (Book #4)
LEFT TO MURDER (Book #5)
LEFT TO ENVY (Book #6)
LEFT TO LAPSE (Book #7)
LEFT TO VANISH (Book #8)
LEFT TO HUNT (Book #9)
LEFT TO FEAR (Book #10)
LEFT TO PREY (Book #11)
LEFT TO LURE (Book #12)
LEFT TO CRAVE (Book #13)
LEFT TO LOATHE (Book #14)
LEFT TO HARM (Book #15)
LEFT TO RUIN (Book #16)

THE AU PAIR SERIES
ALMOST GONE (Book#1)
ALMOST LOST (Book #2)
ALMOST DEAD (Book #3)

ZOE PRIME MYSTERY SERIES
FACE OF DEATH (Book#1)
FACE OF MURDER (Book #2)
FACE OF FEAR (Book #3)
FACE OF MADNESS (Book #4)
FACE OF FURY (Book #5)
FACE OF DARKNESS (Book #6)

A JESSIE HUNT PSYCHOLOGICAL SUSPENSE SERIES
THE PERFECT WIFE (Book #1)
THE PERFECT BLOCK (Book #2)
THE PERFECT HOUSE (Book #3)
THE PERFECT SMILE (Book #4)

THE PERFECT LIE (Book #5)
THE PERFECT LOOK (Book #6)
THE PERFECT AFFAIR (Book #7)
THE PERFECT ALIBI (Book #8)
THE PERFECT NEIGHBOR (Book #9)
THE PERFECT DISGUISE (Book #10)
THE PERFECT SECRET (Book #11)
THE PERFECT FAÇADE (Book #12)
THE PERFECT IMPRESSION (Book #13)
THE PERFECT DECEIT (Book #14)
THE PERFECT MISTRESS (Book #15)
THE PERFECT IMAGE (Book #16)
THE PERFECT VEIL (Book #17)
THE PERFECT INDISCRETION (Book #18)
THE PERFECT RUMOR (Book #19)
THE PERFECT COUPLE (Book #20)
THE PERFECT MURDER (Book #21)
THE PERFECT HUSBAND (Book #22)
THE PERFECT SCANDAL (Book #23)
THE PERFECT MASK (Book #24)
THE PERFECT RUSE (Book #25)
THE PERFECT VENEER (Book #26)
THE PERFECT PEOPLE (Book #27)
THE PERFECT WITNESS (Book #28)

CHLOE FINE PSYCHOLOGICAL SUSPENSE SERIES

NEXT DOOR (Book #1)
A NEIGHBOR'S LIE (Book #2)
CUL DE SAC (Book #3)
SILENT NEIGHBOR (Book #4)
HOMECOMING (Book #5)
TINTED WINDOWS (Book #6)

KATE WISE MYSTERY SERIES

IF SHE KNEW (Book #1)
IF SHE SAW (Book #2)
IF SHE RAN (Book #3)
IF SHE HID (Book #4)
IF SHE FLED (Book #5)

IF SHE FEARED (Book #6)
IF SHE HEARD (Book #7)

THE MAKING OF RILEY PAIGE SERIES

WATCHING (Book #1)
WAITING (Book #2)
LURING (Book #3)
TAKING (Book #4)
STALKING (Book #5)
KILLING (Book #6)

RILEY PAIGE MYSTERY SERIES

ONCE GONE (Book #1)
ONCE TAKEN (Book #2)
ONCE CRAVED (Book #3)
ONCE LURED (Book #4)
ONCE HUNTED (Book #5)
ONCE PINED (Book #6)
ONCE FORSAKEN (Book #7)
ONCE COLD (Book #8)
ONCE STALKED (Book #9)
ONCE LOST (Book #10)
ONCE BURIED (Book #11)
ONCE BOUND (Book #12)
ONCE TRAPPED (Book #13)
ONCE DORMANT (Book #14)
ONCE SHUNNED (Book #15)
ONCE MISSED (Book #16)
ONCE CHOSEN (Book #17)

MACKENZIE WHITE MYSTERY SERIES

BEFORE HE KILLS (Book #1)
BEFORE HE SEES (Book #2)
BEFORE HE COVETS (Book #3)
BEFORE HE TAKES (Book #4)
BEFORE HE NEEDS (Book #5)
BEFORE HE FEELS (Book #6)
BEFORE HE SINS (Book #7)
BEFORE HE HUNTS (Book #8)

BEFORE HE PREYS (Book #9)
BEFORE HE LONGS (Book #10)
BEFORE HE LAPSES (Book #11)
BEFORE HE ENVIES (Book #12)
BEFORE HE STALKS (Book #13)
BEFORE HE HARMS (Book #14)

AVERY BLACK MYSTERY SERIES
CAUSE TO KILL (Book #1)
CAUSE TO RUN (Book #2)
CAUSE TO HIDE (Book #3)
CAUSE TO FEAR (Book #4)
CAUSE TO SAVE (Book #5)
CAUSE TO DREAD (Book #6)

KERI LOCKE MYSTERY SERIES
A TRACE OF DEATH (Book #1)
A TRACE OF MURDER (Book #2)
A TRACE OF VICE (Book #3)
A TRACE OF CRIME (Book #4)
A TRACE OF HOPE (Book #5)

PROLOGUE

Kim Carrigan shuffled out of the bedroom in her robe and slippers, making her way to the kitchen as quickly as she could without risking slipping on the hardwood floors.

It was early June, well past Memorial Day, and the unofficial start of summer. But there was still a surprising crispness in the air for Los Angeles at this hour of the morning, and she intended to combat its effects with a hot mug of coffee.

If things had gone according to routine, her husband, Greg, would have brewed a full pot before he left for the gym. He was an early riser, usually up, out of the house, and starting his workout before she rolled out of bed. But he always made time to prep her coffee before he left so that she would awaken to the smell of the ground beans percolating.

Kim wouldn't have that pleasure this morning as she was still getting over a cold and had a stuffy nose, so she'd have to wait until she was actually in the kitchen to end the suspense and find out if Greg had come through. She shuffled down the hall a little faster as her anticipation grew, not that there was ever any real doubt. She couldn't remember the last time her husband had forgotten to fill the pot.

Gregory Carrigan had his faults, including stubbornness, terrible taste in music, and an extra serving of personal vanity—one large enough that it made him get up every morning at five to keep those abs washboard tight, even though he was already healthy, successful, and married to a catch, if she allowed herself a moment of vanity.

But if those were Greg's biggest flaws, Kim thought she was doing pretty well. Her husband was also kind, thoughtful, pretty funny, hardworking, and super into her. She couldn't really complain. She was about to pass into the kitchen when she stopped and glanced at her herself in the reflection of the window, wondering if she was doing her part to keep up, to make sure he stayed super into her.

She thought she was getting by. She went to the gym, too, just not before the sun rose. She wasn't all rippling muscles, but she still looked good in jeans and a tight top. Most importantly, she'd never heard him complain, not that he ever would.

At thirty-three, she was two years younger than Greg, but secretly, she'd always felt like she was the older half of the couple. He bounded places; she ambled. He expounded on ideas; she offered notions. He always seemed to be moving at one and a half speed while she was going at three quarters.

But not this morning. As she stepped into the kitchen, she noted that it was even colder than usual. Whether she could smell it or not, she would really need that coffee to warm her up. Luckily, she saw it percolating on the counter, steam coming up from the spout and condensation settling along the sides of the carafe.

She was about to pour herself a cup when she saw the reason for the chill in the air. Looking across the kitchen, she noticed that the breakfast room sliding door, which opened onto the patio, was wide open. Glancing across the room to where the security alarm panel rested on the wall next to the light switch, she saw that it was green, meaning that it was off.

That was extremely odd. Greg always left for the gym through the garage. He had no reason to open the sliding patio door in the morning. And he always turned the alarm back on as he departed. He didn't like the idea of her being alone and asleep in the house without it. She could count the number of times he forgot to re-activate it on two fingers. But that didn't explain the patio door. And the chances that he would remember to brew her coffee but forget the other stuff were remote at best. It was around that time that she went from being confused to scared.

As her breathing quickened, she quickly rushed over to the patio door and locked it, then darted over to the wall panel to re-activate the alarm. She stood by the panel for a moment, listening intently, but only heard her own rapid heartbeat and the ticking of the kitchen clock.

After a few seconds, she decided to text Greg at the gym to get an explanation, even though he was mid-workout, but remembered that her phone was still on her bedside table. The idea of walking back down the hall to the bedroom was suddenly unsettling. She wondered if she'd acted too quickly by locking the door. What if someone had already snuck in? Maybe, despite the cold, despite being in just her robe and slippers, she should just leave and go to the neighbors' house.

Then she had an idea. The carafe of hot coffee, just a few feet away, might serve as a dual weapon. If there was someone in the house, she could toss the hot liquid at them and smash them with the glass. Without hesitation, she stepped across the room and grabbed the plastic handle, pulling the carafe out of its cradle and popping off the plastic top so that she could fling the entire contents at anyone who might come her way. Standing in the middle of the kitchen, she did a slow turn, looking for anything out of the ordinary. There was nothing.

Her eyes fell on the land line at the far corner of the breakfast bar. She hadn't actually picked up that phone in months, but right now it could be her best friend. She didn't need a pre-programmed contact list or voice activation right now. All she needed was three little numbers: *911.*

Her eyes still darting everywhere, she moved over to the phone and picked up the handset. She switched the coffee carafe to her left hand and pushed the "talk" button to get a dial tone on the phone. But nothing happened. She tried again and still got no response. Then she looked at the back of the cradle and saw the cord that was normally connected to the phone's base was missing. It had been disconnected.

She was just processing that fact when she saw movement out of the corner of her eye, coming from the door near the security panel. Turning quickly, she dropped the handset and swung the coffee pot in that direction, even before she could see what was coming at her. The pot smashed into the oncoming presence but that didn't stop it.

She didn't get a good look at her attacker, just that the person was wearing black and had on a ski mask with holes for their eyes, nose, and mouth. The person didn't cry out in pain at being smashed by glass or hot coffee. Instead, they wrapped one of their arms around Kim's neck and began to squeeze forcefully.

Kim wasn't a big person, about five-foot-three and 125 pounds, and trying to push the person in black away from her was nearly impossible, especially as she struggled to breathe and felt panic starting to overtake her. She reached out for the handset on the breakfast bar, hoping to use it to smash the attacker's head, but her fingers fumbled as she grasped at it, and it fell to the floor.

She heard pieces of the plastic shatter as it landed, but the sound was muffled and distant. She wasn't sure if that was because of the attacker's arm wrapped around part of her ears or because she was starting to lose consciousness. Fearful that it was the second one, she lashed out, trying to poke the assailant in the eyes with her thumbs and fingers, but the angle was awkward, and she was getting weak fast. Her legs were quivering, and her vision was beginning to blur.

She made one final attempt to jab back with her elbow, hoping to hit her attacker in the gut hard enough to break free, but even to her, when contact was made, it felt limp, like a soggy noodle. And that was Kim Carrigan's last conscious thought—of her arm as a wet noodle, flopping listlessly in the air—before coming to unwanted rest.

CHAPTER ONE

Jessie Hunt sat quietly in the passenger seat, sipping her coffee, happy to let Ryan deal with the hazards of morning rush hour.

One theoretical advantage of working at the same police station as her LAPD police captain was that if their shared commute got really bad, he could always turn on the siren and beacon light. Of course, that wasn't really Captain Ryan Hernandez's style, and he'd never used it for personal benefit. So, they usually plodded along with everyone else.

Another theoretical advantage of commuting to work with her husband was that if they ever arrived late to Central Station, her boss couldn't bust her for it, because he *was* her boss. Then again, as the dedicated criminal profiler for Homicide Special Section, LAPD's most celebrated investigative unit, she didn't really have to punch a clock anyway.

The truth was that most of HSS's cases—typically investigations with high profiles or intense media scrutiny—involved multiple victims or serial killers and usually required long hours with few breaks, so showing up a bit late on a quiet Tuesday morning wasn't the end of the world. Not that they were going to be late. Jessie glanced at the car's clock. It was 7:48 a.m. right now, and she guessed that they'd still make it to work before eight.

"So, did you get a chance to think about it anymore?" Ryan asked hesitantly from the driver's seat.

Jessie looked over at him and felt a mix of affection and frustration. She knew exactly what he was referencing. Last night he had delicately broached something that he had only mentioned once prior to their getting married two and half months ago: the idea of her changing her last name.

"I'm not asking you to do it," he had said over dinner, "I'm not even asking you to consider doing it. I'm just asking you to consider considering it."

He had looked almost apologetic as he took a bite of the leftover lasagna, which he stared at aggressively while he waited for her answer.

"I thought you didn't care about that," she had said. "Back when we were engaged and you mentioned it, you said you could take it or leave it. Has something changed?"

He had shrugged sheepishly. "My mother brought it up last week," he admitted. "But with everything going on with your health concerns and recovery, I didn't want to throw another thing at you until I thought you could handle it. I figured you seem pretty calloused up now, so I'd broach it."

"I didn't even know you were talking to your mom these days," she had said. "Why does she care anyway?"

"I think it's because the anniversary of my father's death was a few weeks ago, and the family name was on her mind, so she reached out."

"I'll consider considering it," she had told him last night, effectively ending the conversation.

If she was honest, she hadn't given it a second thought since then, but now it was the next morning and he was bringing it up again, ever so diffidently. Even as he glanced over at her, she could sense his apprehension. There was something sweet about a six-foot, 200-pound, powerfully built police captain looking so meek. His warm, brown eyes were wide, and his short, black hair made him seem even more emotionally naked than usual. He was equal parts sexy and adorable.

And yet she was irked. Did he really want her to become Jessie Hernandez or Jessie Hunt-Hernandez? Or was he just doing this to satisfy his mother, who Jessie had never met and who he'd never expressed any interest in placating before? In fact, he hardly ever spoke of her. To the best of Jessie's knowledge, she'd been a disengaged parent who had largely disowned him when his first marriage fell apart. She hadn't even been invited the wedding.

"No," she said, after taking her time with another gulp of coffee, "I haven't had time to think about last name changes, Ryan. Is it really that pressing?"

"No, of course not," he said quickly. "I didn't mean to push."

A car one lane over cut in front of him, and he had to hit the brakes forcefully to avoid rear-ending them. He honked at them long and hard but didn't take any further action. Pulling them over would just make them later for work.

Jessie wondered what this was really about. Beyond that, she was annoyed that he was adding it to her pile of "big stuff to deal with." He may have thought that her pile of thick life files was a little lower these days, but he was wrong.

On paper, it may have seemed like things were getting easier, and maybe technically, in some ways, they were. After all, her younger half-sister, Hannah Dorsey, had just graduated from high school. And considering Hannah's situation when Jessie had assumed legal guardianship of her less than two years ago, it was amazing that she was a functional human being, much less a high school graduate.

When Jessie first met her, the girl was tied up in a chair, being forced to watch as her adoptive parents were murdered by a serial killer. Together, she and Jessie had managed to overcome and kill the man, who happened to be Jessie's father. Only later did they learn that he was also Hannah's.

Jessie took her in, and despite the trauma that the girl endured and her subsequent, intense desire to numb that pain by inflicting suffering on other violent perpetrators, Hannah had worked hard to curb her urges, find some inner peace, and still graduate with honors. So, that was one life file that Jessie could almost take off the pile. Almost.

And as Jessie celebrated her thirty-first birthday last month at a low-key dinner with Ryan, Hannah, and her best friend, Katherine "Kat" Gentry, Jessie had admitted aloud to them that another thick file could be at least partially removed from the large pile. Her health was improving.

It was only ten weeks ago that crazed, obsessive killer Andrea "Andy" Robinson had kidnapped her on her wedding night and nearly blown her up in a mine explosion. The incident had left her with cracked ribs, a badly bruised ankle, a fractured wrist, and a severe concussion. All but the last one had completely healed.

She could now do her morning run without any twinges of pain in her ankle or soreness in her chest. As far as work went, she hadn't had any major, physical altercations with any suspects since a woman who had been poisoning rich, Beverly Hills women attacked her six weeks ago, but she was confident that she could handle herself if she had to.

But it was that last medical issue, the concussion, that still loomed over her, a life file so thick as to deserve its own cabinet. It consumed more of her waking hours than she cared to admit, which was why throwing last name change suggestions at her was so irritating.

Even now, as Ryan weaved in and out of traffic, she couldn't stop herself from thinking back to her appointment last Thursday with Dr. Varma. Ryan had held her hand the whole time as Priya Varma, one of the most renowned neurologists on the west coast, met with them for the fourth time in eight weeks.

As at all the other appointments, her staff conducted a series of tests that ranged from showing her images on screens and asking her to identify them, to using playing cards as part of a memory game, to testing her limb strength, vision, and hearing. After that, Dr. Varma joined them and reviewed the tests silently, even gravely, before finally looking up.

"As per usual," the doctor had said, not wasting time with silly greetings, "we'll have you go for an MRI after we're done here. In the meantime, let's review your status."

Jessie was mildly curious to see if Dr. Varma would simply skip ahead to ask how things had been going since they last saw her, but as with all the prior appointments, she insisted on starting fresh.

"So, your issues with memory, concentration, and headaches became pronounced after the mineshaft incident in late March when a grenade exploded in close proximity to you and the mine collapsed around you, correct?"

Dr. Varma, statuesque and attractive in a taciturn way, had repeated the litany of events as if it was a grocery list.

"That's right," Jessie had said.

"But you indicated that you may have also bumped your head multiple times when you were unconscious in the trunk of her car while traveling on the mountain road to get to the mine."

"Also true," Jessie had confirmed.

"And you've indicated that in apprehending past suspects as part of your job over the last two years, you've suffered myriad injuries that including being knocked out on several occasions."

"When you put it that way, it sounds kind of bad," Jessie had muttered jokingly.

Varma hadn't laughed. Neither had Ryan, who squeezed her hand as if to silently beg her not to quip. It was easy for both of them to be so serious. Their brains weren't potential scrambled eggs. Hers was. If this was how she wanted to cut the tension for herself while she waited for the doctor's feedback, then she'd damn well do it. The doctor thumbed through the file again.

"I've reviewed the preliminary results of the in-office studies from today compared to your previous visits," Varma had said, "and you've made discreet but measurable progress in every metric, just as you have on all your prior appointments. Your strength function seems to be close to a hundred percent. Memory and concentration aren't to that level, but both are trending upward, which is what we're looking for.

These are good indicators, and we'll see what the final results reveal when they come back in the next few days. And obviously, we'll need to see if the MRI confirms what we're seeing here in the office."

"That's great news," Ryan had blurted out, far louder than he clearly intended.

"So, what does this mean?" Jessie had asked, more measured. "I don't hear you saying I'm all better, Doctor."

"Because that's not what I'm saying," Varma replied simply. "My suspicion is that you've suffered multiple concussions in recent years, and this is just the first one that was formally diagnosed. The trend lines are looking positive right now. But I want to review the images to confirm them. Even if they do, that's not positive proof. I understand that you still get headaches?"

"Yes," Jessie had conceded, "but they're not as intense as they were."

"Do they ever make you lose vision? Feel unsteady or nauseated? Have you ever thrown up as a result of one?"

"Not lately," Jessie had answered, though that depended on the definition of the word "lately." One headache about a week ago had coincided with some queasiness, but she'd also spent twenty-nine straight hours working just before the feeling and was inclined to attribute it to that, so she decided not to mention it.

"All right," Varma had said. "You've got the MRI this afternoon. We'll reach out to you to discuss the results sometime next week. They should go a long way to helping us determine next steps."

"Next steps?" Jessie had asked.

Yes," Varma had replied, "as in, whether your injury is temporary, and if you can continue as is, or if it's advisable for you to curtail your work in a profession where you risk additional potential head trauma that could do lasting damage to your brain."

They hit a pothole, and Jessie nearly lost her grip on her coffee as she snapped out of her thoughts and back into the moment.

"You okay?" Ryan asked.

"Yeah," she said. "We're still expecting those MRI results from Dr. Varma this week, right?"

"Yeah," he said as he pulled onto Wall Street, where the Central Station parking garage was located. "Any day now. Why?"

"I'm just tired of having this hanging over my head."

He nodded sympathetically and seemed about to say something when his phone rang. "It's Chief Decker," he said, pulling over to the side of the road just before the garage entrance. "I better take it here, so I don't lose the connection underground."

He answered the call and put it on speaker.

"Hi, Chief," he said. "How can I help?"

"Captain Hernandez," replied someone who was definitely not their former captain and now interim LAPD Chief Roy Decker, "this is Lydia from Chief Decker's office. I'm afraid he was just called in to testify before the City Council, but he asked me to convey a priority request to you."

"Of course," Ryan said. "What's the request?"

"Apparently the wife of a local news anchor was found strangled in their home about forty-five minutes ago. He believes this is an ideal case for HSS and asked you take ownership of it immediately. I have the contact information for the sergeant on the scene. Shall I pass it along?"

Ryan looked over at Jessie, and she knew he was thinking the same thing that she was: their quiet Tuesday morning had come to an unceremonious end.

CHAPTER TWO

Jessie waited for her partner to arrive.

As she stood in Ryan's office, anticipating him bringing in Detective Sam Goodwin, she tried to relax. While she and Goodwin had interacted multiple times in the two months since he'd joined the unit, they'd never been paired together on a case.

She'd only heard good things about his intelligence and dedication but working with someone new for the first time was always a little nerve wracking. It was especially so when she wasn't certain that her brain was operating at full capacity, a fact no one in the unit officially knew but Ryan. She didn't want to have a mental hiccup while questioning a suspect, with him standing beside her.

Of course, that was out of her hands. What was in her control was how she presented herself to him at their first meeting as partners. So, feeling mildly ridiculous about it, she opened the small coat closet in the corner of Ryan's office and looked herself over in his narrow, full-length mirror.

As far as she could tell, she looked like she did most other workdays. She was dressed in comfortable, gray slacks and a thin, long-sleeved, green shirt that matched her eyes. She wore brown sneakers that could pass as loafers but would work if she had to chase down a suspect. Her shoulder-length, brown hair was loose now but would end up in a ponytail the second they got to a crime scene. At five-foot-ten and 145 pounds, she was tall, lean, and imposing enough to make most people she questioned think twice before getting physical.

She didn't know why she felt the need to make a good impression on the new guy. She was the unit veteran with multiple serial killer takedowns. He was the newbie, fresh from vice. Maybe it was because she felt vulnerable after everything she'd been through recently. Maybe it was that she didn't want Goodwin to view her as a figure in need of sympathy. Whatever the reason, she just wanted to look professional and competent. And as she closed the coat closet door, she assured herself that she did.

A moment later, Ryan entered with Goodwin right behind him. The captain—her husband and boss—motioned for both of them to take seats in the rickety chairs opposite his desk. As Jessie settled in, she took note of Goodwin.

At thirty-three, the man was sinewy and tall, easily six-foot-two, with a bird's nest of irrepressible, brown hair. He wore a corduroy, sport coat over a checkered shirt and black tie, making him look like either a young, absent-minded professor or the past-his-prime bassist in a band that played Americana music.

His looks belied his reputation. He had served eight years as a uniformed officer, followed by three as a detective in Vice Division's Exploitation and Investigative Section, which focused on human trafficking, exploitation of minors, and prostitution connected to organized crime. He may not have formally handled homicide cases prior to joining HSS, but Jessie knew that he'd seen ugly things.

"How's it going?" he asked as he sat down beside her.

"Good," she said, reaching out to shake his hand, "glad to finally be working a case with you."

"The honor's all mine," he replied, and she got the sense that he meant it.

"Sorry to interrupt the mutual admiration society," Ryan said, sitting behind his desk, "but time is short on this one. I want to give you two the basics and then get you on your way. Since this case involves a media member, we can expect local press to swarm the scene momentarily, and I'd like you to be on the premises before they get there."

"Go ahead," Jessie said, even though she'd already heard some of the details he was about to share.

"Right," Ryan replied. "So, about an hour ago, Greg Carrigan, the midday and afternoon news anchor for Channel Six, called 911 to report the death of his wife, Kimberly. They live in Hancock Park. Officers secured the scene. Initial reports on the cause of death suggest strangling. The crime scene unit is there now. The medical examiner is on the way. Local detectives were called back when Carrigan's name came up. Chief Decker requested we take the lead. The officer in charge on the scene right now is Sergeant Alton Brunson. He's waiting for you and will provide additional details upon your arrival. That's about all I have. You should head out."

Goodwin immediately popped up. Jessie took her time easing out of her chair. The update had been so brief that she hardly saw the need to have them sit in the first place. They were almost to the door when Ryan stopped them.

"One last thing," he said. "Chief Decker didn't give us this assignment directly. His assistant did. That's because Decker was testifying to the City Council this morning. The subject was the after-action report into the Operation Z attack in April that killed nearly thirty people. As you are already well aware, that attack could have resulted in thousands of deaths if not for the efforts of the team here at HSS. But the chief is going to get some hard questions from the Council this morning, right as they're deciding whether to replace him or if his interim chief title should become permanent. The best thing we can do to help him is make sure any new headlines coming out about HSS are positive. I know you guys aren't media crisis managers; you're crime solvers. So, do what you do best. Close cases. Catch killers. Hopefully, it will all work out for the best."

Both Jessie and Goodwin nodded their assent. Jessie kept the primary thought that was bouncing around in her head to herself.

No pressure, boss.

***

Sam Goodwin offered to drive, and Jessie didn't fight him.

The Carrigan house was only fifteen minutes away, and considering the urgency involved, this time they did use the siren and beacon. It was only when they got close to the neighborhood that Goodwin shut it off for fear of attracting the attention of any nearby TV trucks.

As they slowed to something close to the speed limit, Goodwin turned to her. "Do you have a particular approach that you prefer to take with cooperating law enforcement, witnesses, etc." he asked. "I don't want to step on any toes."

Jessie shook her head. "Thanks for asking, Goodwin," she replied, "but you're the lead detective, so feel free to take the lead. I'll pepper my questions in when I deem appropriate. In general, when it comes to witnesses and potential suspects, I like to observe their body language when my partner asks them probing questions, then maybe jump in with follow-ups. I hope that's cool with you."

"Your methods seem to have worked pretty well for you in the past," he said, "so I'm not inclined to balk at them. I will balk at one thing though."

"What's that?"

"It's Sam. If you call me Goodwin, I inevitably think I'm going to the principal's office."

"Okay, although it's hard to imagine you *ever* getting sent to the principal's office, *Sam*," Jessie said, making sure to emphasize the requested name. "And of course, it's Jessie for me."

"You might be surprised by my youthful indiscretions, Jessie," he said. "There was one time, when I was fourteen, that I snuck into the school after hours …"

He continued to talk but Jessie didn't hear the words. A light switch clicked off in her head at the word "fourteen," then switched on again, only this time her brain was consumed with the image of a different fourteen-year-old—a girl with blonde hair, a crooked smile, and piercing, blue eyes.

She knew who it was, even if she'd only ever seen pictures of the girl at this age. It was Andy Robinson, long before she became the murderer that Jessie caught two years ago. It was before she was incarcerated in a psychiatric prison unit, before she manipulated her way into parole, kidnapped Jessie, tried to hold her in a mine in the Arizona desert, and blew the both of them up when that failed.

This was the Andy Robinson who spent her pre-teen summers visiting her cousin in Arizona. It was the girl who went on a hike with her uncle and was led into the mineshaft, which she would later take Jessie to, where that uncle would brutally rape her and threaten to kill her and her family if she ever revealed the truth to anyone.

While Sam Goodwin's voice murmured in the background of Jessie's mind, in the foreground, Andy's crooked smile turned to a frown of sadness, and they both knew why. While keeping her captive in the that mineshaft, Andy had revealed the truth about her rape and about how she hoped to one day bring her uncle back to the mine to torture and kill him as repayment. But he died of a heart attack before she could. She admitted to Jessie that his premature death made something inside her snap.

Later, when Jessie attempted to escape, she brought up what had happened to Andy in the hopes of creating a connection that would aid her cause: she tried to convince Andy that she was sharing her *own* most secret, vulnerable self—and that she might be open to an intimate life together in that mine—all in order to get her to call off the Operation Z attack and let her go.

It hadn't worked. Andy had seen through it. And worse, Andy had viewed it as a betrayal of trust. She accused Jessie of using her childhood trauma as a psychological tool to manipulate her.

In the end, Andy had died in the mine collapse, but her charge had lived on: that Jessie had used her revelation of her most painful secret—being raped as a young girl—as a tactic to get what she wanted. Jessie had fought the allegation in her mind ever since.

But in the weeks since then, her longtime psychiatrist, Dr. Janice Lemmon, had been suggesting that she ask herself a different question entirely. Not if she had manipulated Andy's pain for her own advantage, but even if she had, was that wrong? Was it morally defensible to make tactical use of anyone's personal childhood horror, even a killer's, if it served a larger good. She knew Dr. Lemmon's answer to that question, but she wasn't so sure of her own.

As Jessie considered the question anew, Andy's fourteen-year-old face morphed into that of a different thirteen-year-old girl. This one had short, spiky, jet-black hair and wore dark eye makeup. Jessie knew her immediately too. It was Harley Reid, the daughter of retired and recently deceased detective Callum Reid, who had died in the mine collapse while helping to save Jessie and gather crucial information that stopped Operation Z.

Harley's face was stoic, even as black, mascara-stained tears streamed down her face. This was how Jessie remembered the girl when they'd presented her, along with her younger brother and their mother, with a medal of honor for his service in the wake of Operation Z. The girl had never said a word, barely even looked at her. But just as with Andy, Jessie could feel the judgment radiating off her, sending waves of shame straight toward her, ones she couldn't ward off.

"Jessie?"

"What?" she said.

"You sort of drifted there," Sam said. "I guess I need to work on my tales of youthful misdeeds. I would have thought that hiding three garter snakes in my Algebra class the night before the final in order to delay the test a few days was a solid story, but you couldn't have looked more bored. Either I need to up my game, or you've done some way worse stuff."

"That's totally on me," she said apologetically. "Remind me never to have coffee after five at night unless I'm planning to stay up *all* night. It was a rough one, and my attention span is paying the price. Please don't take offense."

"None taken," he said as he pulled up in front of a large house. "I can't promise everyone will be so accommodating though. We're here."

Jessie got out, hoping she'd sounded convincing, and tried to shake the cobwebs out of her head. She would have done so literally if she hadn't been worried that it would have done damage to her fragile brain. Less than ten minutes in the car with her new partner and she was already spacing out, losing track of conversations, and fixating on the accusatory teenage faces of dead killers and of orphaned girls who didn't know she existed. Suddenly, she found herself doubting if Dr. Varma's claims of "discreet but measurable progress" could be trusted.

She had to set all that aside if she was going to do her job right. Her partner was counting on her. If Ryan was to be believed, so was Chief Decker. Most importantly, there was a dead woman inside that house who was counting on her to reclaim something in her name. If not peace, then at least justice.

She slammed the door shut and started toward the house.

CHAPTER THREE

Jessie knew this neighborhood well.

It was the same one that Andy Robinson had lived in, along with many other wealthy Angelenos. Hancock Park was unconventional, with small, cottage homes sitting right next to three-story, Tudor-style mansions. The Carrigan home was somewhere in between.

It was Colonial Revival in spirit, with a gabled roof and portico, but it wasn't overly ostentatious. Around here, that probably still meant it cost around six million dollars. Jessie and Sam quickly walked past the crime scene unit truck and medical examiner's van, then moved into a jog when they saw a TV truck round the corner and head in their direction.

They darted under the police tape, flashed their IDs to the officer at the front door, and stepped into the foyer, where Jessie pulled her hair back into her work-mode ponytail. Multiple voices could be heard in the distance. They followed the sound, down a long, pillared hallway to the kitchen, where a sizable crowd was assembled.

Officers stood guard at each entrance to the kitchen and breakfast room area. One was right beside them, near the hallway from the foyer. Another stood by a hallway that seemed to head back toward the bedrooms, and a third stood next to a sliding door leading out to a patio.

It looked like the CSU team was packing up. The medical examiner, who was typing notes into her tablet, also seemed to be wrapping up. Jessie was quite familiar with her. Dr. Cheryl Gallagher wasn't a barrel of laughs, but she was professional and rarely made mistakes.

She was standing beside the body of the victim in the corner of the breakfast room, whose bare feet Jessie could see from where she stood. She looked away quickly, not out of squeamishness, but because she preferred to see the victim for the first time without any context other than the one that she created for herself. She didn't want people standing beside the dead woman or offering their perspectives. She wanted to see everything fresh, so that the potential for fresh insights was less likely to be corrupted by the views of others.

An officer standing close to Gallagher had been staring at her and Sam since they walked in and now made his way over. Jessie suspected that he was Sergeant Alton Brunson. Black, bald, and in his early forties, he was about the same height as Sam Goodwin. But he had about fifty pounds on Jessie's new partner, and with his near-uniform-bursting chest, he looked like he might fare well in a head-on collision with a pickup truck.

"I'm Sergeant Al Brunson," he said, extending his hand, "I recognize you from my TV screen, Ms. Hunt. That must make you Detective Goodwin."

"Nice to meet you, Sergeant," Sam said, returning the handshake. Jessie did the same.

"As you can see, the science-type people are finishing up here, so you'll have the room to yourself momentarily," Brunson said. "Can I answer any questions for you in the interim?"

Sam looked over at Jessie, who nodded that he should proceed as he saw fit.

"Do you have a rough timeline yet?" he asked.

Brunson pulled out a small notepad and flipped a few pages back.

"We're still locking all this down," he said, "but we've been able to confirm a fair bit so far through Secure Home Services, or SHS, the security company for the house. The husband, Gregory Carrigan, says he turned on the alarm last night a little after 11 p.m. That matches the log that SHS gave us: 11:14 p.m."

"Sorry to interrupt," Jessie said, "but where is Carrigan now?"

"He's in his study," Brunson said. "After doing a preliminary interview, we put him there while the crime scene people did their work. He knows you'll be coming in to talk to him momentarily."

"How did he seem?" she asked.

"He looks to be holding up okay, all things considered," Brunson replied. "I think being a news reporter and having been to crimes scenes as part of his job, he's not as shell-shocked as the average person. I mean, he's broken up but functional."

"Thanks, sorry," Jessie said. "Please continue with the timeline."

"So, SHS has the system being disarmed at 5:44 a.m. this morning, which is when Carrigan said he turned it off before leaving for the gym. It was re-armed again at 5:45, which he said he did so that it would be on when his wife was alone in the house. That's where the confusion comes in."

"How so?" Sam asked.

"He said all the doors were still locked, but the alarm wasn't on when he got home," Brunson explained. "That was unusual because his wife usually left it on after she woke up until he got home from the gym. He said that after he found her in the breakfast room and called 911, he started to question himself, wondering if he forgot to reset the alarm when he left—if maybe someone had jimmied a lock and snuck in."

"But based on the data you got from the security company, he didn't forget," Sam said.

"Nope," Brunson said. "So, he was wondering the same thing that we are: how did the killer get into a locked house with an alarm on?"

"What about his gym alibi?" Jessie pressed. "Any chance Carrigan came back later and de-activated it himself?"

"We checked with them," Brunson said, shaking his head. "Members scan a barcode on their phones when they arrive, which he did at 5:57 a.m. We also had an officer go down and check their security cameras. The video footage matches. It shows him walking in at that time."

"And leaving when?" Jessie wondered.

"Carrigan told us he left just before 7 a.m., and our officer found video of him walking out of the lobby at 6:53 a.m. So, his story holds up pretty well. He also gave us the name of a workout buddy, who we're tracking down now. But there's more."

"What?" Sam wanted to know.

"The security system was de-activated at 6:12 a.m.," Brunson said. "And Carrigan told us that his wife sets her alarm for 6:30 a.m. He said that she never gets up before then."

"So," Jessie mused, "if she was loathe to turn off the security system until her husband got back, and she wasn't even up at the time it was turned off, that means our killer likely turned it off somehow. And yet, they didn't go straight to her bedroom and kill her while she was sleeping. They waited at least twenty minutes until she was in the kitchen area."

"There's even more to it than that," Brunson said. "According to the data from SHS, it looks like the killer, after getting in and turning off the alarm, left the sliding patio door open. At 6:44 a.m., the door is closed and locked, and the alarm is re-activated."

"You think that's Kim Carrigan coming into the kitchen, seeing the open door, locking it, and activating the alarm?" Jessie asked the sergeant.

"I do," he said. "That's reinforced by the fact that the alarm is deactivated one final time at 6:49 a.m."

"When the killer left for good," Sam suggested. "Which suggests she was killed in that five-minute window."

"It makes sense," Brunson said.

Jessie nodded in agreement. "I assume you've already asked SHS for a list of employees who have access to the Carrigan's code," she asked.

"We have," he replied, "but they assure us that, by design, no one at the company has access to the customer's code. They can turn the alarm off in an emergency using a default code but that shows up in the system. Apparently, whoever turned it off and on this morning used the Carrigans' code, which would suggest it wasn't an inside job."

Jessie's attention was piqued by Dr. Gallagher, who closed her tablet and started to move toward the other kitchen exit. She wasn't sure if the medical examiner was oblivious to her presence or trying to avoid her, but she wasn't getting out of here without answering a few questions.

"Hold on one second, Sergeant," she said, before calling after the M.E., "Dr. Gallagher … Cheryl!"

The medical examiner, who was almost out the door, stopped in her tracks. Her spine straightened as she visibly bristled at the use of her first name. When she turned around, the forced smile on her face was as tight as the bun her blonde hair was tied in. She made a fuss of readjusting her white lab coat and walked over, making up for her small size with quick, forceful strides.

"I was just headed off to the lab to prep my preliminary report, Ms. Hunt," she said sharply, before unconvincingly adding, "but I'm happy to share anything that might be of use now."

"That would be great, Cheryl," Jessie said, finding herself unable to stop from poking the doctor slightly, whom she knew hated being addressed by her first name. But the woman had just tried to sneak out without giving them any details at all, so a little poking was deserved. "I think Detective Goodwin and I would love anything you could offer in the way of time and means of death."

Gallagher looked like she wanted to go with her typical "I can't say anything this early in the process" line, but the request was so basic that even she knew she couldn't get away with that kind of claim. Her shoulders slumped and with a look of resignation on her face, she answered, "I arrived on the scene just after 8 a.m.," she said. "CSU was already hard at work. Based on my initial data, I'd peg the time of death as less than two hours prior to that, but my understanding is that your security system data may prove more useful than that."

"If it bears out, it looks like she was killed between 6:44 and 6:49," Sam said.

"Well, that's certainly within my two-hour window," Gallagher said tartly.

"And the method of death?" Jessie asked, choosing to ignore the M.E.'s tone. "Is strangling accurate?"

"As always, I can't be definitive until after the autopsy," Gallagher said, "but it's a solid guess. Bruising around the neck is consistent with that, as is the petechial hemorrhaging in the eyes. I should know more in a few hours. Can I go?"

Jessie waved her arms elaborately, like a matador inviting a bull to pass by. She got what she needed, and there was no need to keep Gallagher around any longer, especially in this mood.

"Is she always like that?" Sam asked, once she had left.

Brunson grunted softly under his breath but said nothing, letting Jessie explain.

"She's always testy," Jessie told the detective. "But she was in rare form today. Let's not let that distract us."

"From what?" Sam asked.

Jessie pointed at the two members of the crime scene unit crew who were standing patiently in the corner of the breakfast room with a body bag.

"They're done with their work," she said. "Once we've looked at the body, they can take her, so let's get to it."

Sergeant Brunson waved off the officer by the sliding glass door and stayed where he was as Jessie and Sam walked around the breakfast room table to get a clear view of Kim Carrigan. No one was within fifteen feet of them.

Jessie closed her eyes for a few seconds, then opened them quickly, trying to picture the moment when Kim Carrigan realized she was in danger and tried to save herself. She looked at the woman, lying on the floor, wearing boxer shorts and a Weezer t-shirt. A robe was still half draped over one shoulder. She had a single slipper on one foot. The other was in the kitchen by the coffee machine.

Kim was an attractive woman with angular features, longish, dirty-blonde hair, and hazel eyes that were currently dotted with red. She was on the shorter side and looked to be in good shape, though not a maniac about it like some folks who lived around here. There were no obvious signs of plastic surgery.

Jessie knelt down beside her and moved her robe over so that it covered her exposed legs. It didn't impact the evidence as CSU had already done their work, and there was no harm in giving the woman a little dignity. Jessie hoped that wasn't all she could provide her with. Kim Carrigan had lost any chance at a future, but there was still an opportunity to get her justice.

She took note of the cordless phone shattered on the ground near Carrigan's feet and wondered if Kim had used it to try to call for help and lost her grip. Or maybe she'd attempted to use it as a weapon to smash her assailant with. Then she glanced at the broken glass and coffee on the ground nearby and the plastic carafe handle still gripped in the woman's hand.

"You think she was pouring coffee when she was attacked?" Sam asked.

"No," Jessie said. "There's no mug out on this counter or anywhere else. Plus, she's nowhere near the coffee machine, and she's still holding the carafe handle. I think she tried to use the carafe to defend herself. She must have hit her attacker with it, sending the glass and coffee across the room. I see some as far away as the far wall. She fought hard with what she had until she couldn't fight anymore."

She looked up at Sam, whose face was deathly white.

"Are you all right?" she asked.

"I'm still adjusting," he admitted. "I used to deal with cases that involved human exploitation. It was horrible but most of the victims had been suffering for a while by the time we got to them. I haven't gotten used to victims who wake up one morning, slide into their slippers to get their coffee thinking it's a normal day, and end up lying cold on the floor minutes later with a coffee pot handle in their hand."

"Good," Jessie said forcefully, standing up. "Don't ever get used to it. That's what keeps you sharp."

"What do you mean?" Sam asked, slightly taken aback by the intensity of her tone.

"Kim Carrigan isn't just a case file," Jessie reminded him. "She's a woman who liked coffee and Weezer; a woman who had a husband who had to find her like this. As raw as you feel, imagine what he's going through and hold on to that, because we're going to talk to him right now."

CHAPTER FOUR

Jessie stayed a few steps behind the others.

As she and Sam followed Sergeant Brunson, who led them down the hallway they had yet to pass through, she took a moment to compose herself. Her words to Sam Goodwin had a twin purpose: to give him a reality check and maybe to inspire him a little.

But they'd also gotten her a bit riled up, and that was no way to be when meeting with the spouse of the deceased. She needed to calm herself before coming face to face with the victim's husband, especially when he was a news anchor who, despite his grief, would be more on guard than most.

The hallway floor was hardwood and creaked softly as they passed a guest room and stopped at a closed door. At the end of the hall was an open door that Jessie surmised led to the Carrigans' bedroom. Jessie tried not to think about how Kim Carrigan would never rest her head in there again. Brunson knocked softly on the office door, before opening it and muttering something. Then he turned to Jessie and Sam.

"He's in there with a support officer," he said. "You good?"

Jessie looked over at Sam. He nodded. "We're good," he said.

They stepped inside. The lights were on but dimmed. Gregory Carrigan wasn't seated at his desk but on a small loveseat off to the side. He was sprawled out, and his head was sitting in his hand, which was resting on the arm of the seat. He didn't look up when they entered.

The support officer, an older man with thinning hair and a sour bearing that suggested he might not be great at offering support was sitting in the single chair opposite Carrigan's desk with a weary expression. He started to get up to leave, but Jessie motioned for him to stay. She wanted to keep any familiar face around, even if it was only recently familiar and not especially comforting.

Carrigan's office was smaller and less self-absorbed than one might have expected from a news anchor. There were a few local Emmys shoved in the back corner of a corner shelf and two framed photos on the wall.

Upon closer inspection, Jessie realized that Carrigan wasn't serving in a reportorial capacity in either one. In the first, he and Kim were posing in front of Sleeping Beauty Castle at Disneyland. In the other, they were at Dodger Stadium, standing giddily alongside legendary announcer Vin Scully. Otherwise, there were no indications that he was a media figure or even from Los Angeles. Everything else in the office, from the books to the pictures to the tchotchkes on the desk, could have belonged to an accountant in Toledo.

"Mr. Carrigan," Sam said, his voice somehow equally determined and sympathetic, "I'm Detective Sam Goodwin from LAPD's Homicide Special Section. I'm here with our criminal profiler, Jessie Hunt. We're here to investigate your wife's death."

At the mention of Jessie's name, Carrigan looked up. Jessie, who wasn't a regular viewer of local news, was still well aware of him. He was good-looking in an unintimidating way, with a big forehead, slightly oversized ears, thick, wavy, brown hair, and big eyes that were the same hazel color as his wife's.

Normally, he also had a winning smile to go with all that but not today. He stared at Jessie impassively for a second, though with obvious recognition. Then he lowered his head again. When he spoke, his voice was soft and low, and he sounded like he was reciting words from a textbook.

"Homicide Special Section is an elite unit that specializes in cases that have high profiles or intense media scrutiny, often involving multiple victims and serial killers," he muttered, before looking up again and clearing his throat. "I'm assuming that there is no serial killer component and that HSS is here because the victim was married to someone with a 'high profile' and that this case will likely generate 'intense media scrutiny?'"

"That's correct," Jessie answered, seeing no reason not to be forthright.

"And is there any particular reason for your involvement, Ms. Hunt?" Carrigan asked, with a slight edge in his voice. "It wouldn't be because Interim Police Chief Decker is, at this very moment, defending his record in regard to Operation Z and might want his top profiler on a potentially explosive case to ensure that it doesn't cause him more political headaches?"

"Mr. Carrigan," Jessie said, taking a step forward and staring at the man with unblinking eyes, "I'm going to be straight with you. My job is to go where I'm told, to catch killers, and close cases. But off the record, it would be pretty naïve of me to suggest that your theory is ridiculous."

"We're off the record?" Carrigan said, his eyebrows raised.

Jessie ignored his comment and pressed ahead, making sure to keep her tone politely professional despite his challenge. "Luckily, I don't have to worry about the politics involved. All I have to do is find out what happened to Kim. And I'm assuming that because of what you do for a living, you know my track record when it comes to this sort of thing. I'm also assuming that when you set aside the reporter in you for a second, you'll be glad that I was assigned—for whatever reason—to Kim's case." She stopped for a moment, long enough for her heart to soften her words. "I'm sorry that she was taken from you. I'm sorry your life with her—and the future you had planned—was stolen from you. You know better than most that I genuinely understand what that feels like. And I'm here, along with Detective Goodwin, to catch the person who did this to you. But to do that, we could really use your help. Can you help us, Greg?"

She watched him closely as she waited for his response. At first, his face retained the same emotionless expression from when they'd first entered the office, but after a few seconds, his steely reserve seemed to melt away. His jaw softened, and his eyes began to glisten.

"I've reported on so many of these stories," he said, his voice raw with emotion. "I never thought that I'd be living one of them. I know it's cliché to say it, but I never thought this would happen to me, to us."

Sam, who had been leaning against the door, stood straighter at that comment. Jessie could tell he wanted to ask something but didn't want to interrupt the connection that she'd developed with Carrigan. She tried to hint that it was okay.

"No one ever does," she said softly. "That's why we're here—to ask the questions you would never think to because you're just not in that headspace, right Detective Goodwin?"

"Right," Sam said, pausing for a second before registering that she was giving him an opening. "For example, Mr. Carrigan, you said you never thought this would happen to you. But we really need you to think—have you had any negative experiences lately? Maybe a viewer who called in upset about a story you did? Or the subject of a piece who threatened you after the fact?"

Carrigan thought for a second, then shook his head.

"I can't recall anything lately," he said. "I used to get some hate e-mails back when I worked the evening and late-night newscasts. They were heavily 'if it bleeds, it leads.' But since I moved to middays and afternoons last year, that really dropped off. We do a lot more human-interest stuff during the daytime. I can't recall the last time I heard anything more negative than 'I wish that piece was longer' or 'that recipe was harder to make than it seemed with your chef.' It's been almost exclusively positive."

Sam nodded sympathetically. "I know you've gone over this already, but do you mind if we review the timeline of events from this morning again?"

Carrigan agreed to. As he went over his description of his moment-to-moment movements, which matched up with Sergeant Brunson's notes from earlier, Jessie had a thought about another possible motive. She waited until Sam was done to broach it.

"Mr. Carrigan," she said, "you told us that you don't believe anyone wanted to hurt you, but what about Kim? Did she mention any recent arguments with co-workers? An altercation at the supermarket? An online dispute that got out of hand perhaps?"

He shook his head far more vehemently than he had when asked about any conflicts of his own.

"No way," he said emphatically. "If you knew Kim, you'd understand that she just wasn't that way. Everyone loved her. She didn't get into arguments in supermarkets or online or anywhere else like that. And her co-workers adored her."

"What did she do?" Sam asked.

"She was a special education teacher at a public elementary school," he told them, a smile breaking across his face at the thought of it. "She didn't really need the job anymore. We've been doing pretty well for the last few years. But she was committed to the work, and she cared about the children so much. She'd been there for seven years and loved seeing how much these kids could develop from kindergarten to fifth grade. It defined her and—"

He stopped suddenly.

"What?" Jessie asked.

"I just realized that I haven't called the school to tell them," he said. "I wouldn't even know where to start."

"We'll take care of that, Mr. Carrigan," Sergeant Brunson said quietly. "We'll give them the information they need. You can call them with a more personal message when you feel up to it."

Carrigan nodded again. He seemed on the verge of fading off into his own thoughts. Jessie tried to pull him back. "Did anyone other than you or Kim have access to your security code?" she asked.

"No," he said, eager to focus on a specific question. "We never had anyone house-sit. We don't have pets, so there was no pet-sitter to give it to. We rarely had people stay with us and never gave them the code."

Jessie looked over at Sam to see if he had any more questions. He shook his head that he didn't. She nodded that he should wrap up.

"Okay, listen, Mr. Carrigan," he said, with an impressive reassurance in his voice, "we promise to do our best for Kim. We're going to follow up on every lead and see where they take us. We'll keep you informed as best as we can. That's our job. Your job is to take care of yourself. That's not easy. But the support officer here has resources available to you that may help."

Jessie, less than confident that the sour-faced officer would be much help, decided to offer her two cents.

"Mr. Carrigan—Greg," she added, getting his full attention with the first name. "I'm going to give you some unofficial advice that you won't find in the brochures but that I've learned the hard way. You're a public figure. This story is going to be catnip to people. There are already TV trucks camped out in front of your house, maybe even from your own station. If you haven't gotten calls from your producers, you will soon. They will pressure you to go on the air, to tell your story, to make it personal. After this first wave of grief, you may even have the urge to pursue the case on your own, to use those reporter's instincts to get justice for Kim. Ignore all that."

"What?"

"Don't go on the air. Don't take those calls from your producers. Don't take calls from any 'work' friends for the next forty-eight hours. They won't mean to use what you say for a story, but in the end, they won't be able to help it. Other than calling human resources to say you're taking some personal time, go silent. Anything else you say will get turned into tabloid fodder. Don't mention HSS's involvement in the case. Don't mention me. That will only jack up media interest. Plus, the more press attention this gets, the more that helps the perpetrator. The less the killer knows about our investigation, the more likely we are to catch them. It's going to be hard, but the best thing you can do right now is stay quiet, unless you're talking to us. Can you do that?"

"I can try," he said hesitantly.

"Please do," she said. "In fact, if you have a beach house or a mountain cabin, I'd stay there for a few days. Just make sure to give us the address and remain reachable."

They left him in the study and returned to the kitchen, where they found that Kim's body had been removed, as had the glass debris and the coffee. If someone walked into this room now, they'd never know that a murder had been committed here.

Jessie heard a small cough behind them and turned around. Sergeant Brunson was standing behind them. Something about the anticipatory tension of his posture told her that he had news.

"What is it, Sergeant?' she asked.

"This just came in," he told them, holding out his phone. "It's footage from the Ring camera at the Carrigan's front door. "Somehow it didn't get logged in the first pass."

He hit play, and Jessie and Sam looked at it together. The timestamp said 6:11 a.m. The sun had fully risen now, and the light created a bit of a glare on the camera. At first, the screen showed nothing unusual, but then a figure shot out of the bushes off to the right and quickly approached the front door. The person was dressed in dark colors, wearing a ski mask and gloves, but because of the glare and the distortion of the camera, it was hard to determine much more than that.

Suddenly, the right hand of the figure came up to reveal they were holding something that looked like a bottle. A moment later, a thick spray came from the bottle, completely covering the Ring camera lens. After five more seconds, the video cut out.

"The video ran longer, but it was just more blackness," Brunson told them. "Needless to say, this footage was from one minute before the security system was de-activated. We're having CSU check the Ring camera to find out what was sprayed."

Sam sighed heavily before speaking, "So, we have a killer who arrived at the house in a ski mask, wearing gloves, equipped with a spray to make the exterior camera ineffectual, and broke into the house at a time when they knew the victim's husband would be out. This wasn't just a crime of opportunity."

"No, this was well-planned," Jessie agreed. "And on top of everything you said, there's still the fact that the killer got their security code when everything suggests that the only two people in the world who knew it were Greg and Kim Carrigan. If we're going to find out who did this, we must find out *how* they did that."

CHAPTER FIVE

If this guy was having an affair, he was the most boring cheater of all time.

Hannah Dorsey might only be eighteen and even though she'd been apprenticing as an assistant to a private detective for less than two weeks—first during Spring Break and now in the first week of summer—even she knew that this dude was no lothario.

This was her second consecutive day following Lyman Feller for Gentry Investigations, the detective agency run by Kat Gentry, who happened to be the best friend of her older sister, Jessie Hunt. And so far, Feller had given no indication that he was engaged in marital infidelity or had any interest in the subject.

He'd spent most of yesterday in his downtown Los Angeles office, where he served as the business manager for several giant shopping plazas. Hannah and Kat had alternated duty keeping an eye on his fifth-floor office from the public "leisure lounge" of the hotel directly across the street, while the other stayed in the car on the street below in case he made an unexpected change in plans.

But Lyman Feller, a fifty-seven-year-old man with bad posture, thinning, gray hair, and a permanent, distracted expression, *never* made an unexpected change in plans. Even when he left his office, it was to do standard, boring stuff, like what he was engaged in now: meeting with the on-site manager of a shopping plaza, walking slowly past each store, making notes on a clipboard, presumably determining the future fate of an establishment with the stroke of a pen.

"What's he doing now?" Kat asked through Hannah's AirPods.

"He's spending this fine morning standing at a coffee bar," Hannah replied from a courtyard table fifty feet away from Feller, "sipping at a drink with way too much whipped cream and talking animatedly to a woman with an aggressive perm, while pointing at a store that sells souvenirs and leather goods. He doesn't seem to like the store. Remind me again why we think this guy is secretly harboring a mistress?"

"It's not that *we* think he is, Hannah," Kat corrected. "It's that Mrs. Rhona Feller thinks he is. And Mrs. Feller is paying us $500 a day, plus expenses, to either confirm or invalidate her suspicions. So, that's why we'll continue to follow him, whether we think that Lyman is the cheating type or not. Remember, sometimes it's the least likely suspect who lulls us into complacency before doing his dirty deeds. Stay vigilant."

"I'm trying," Hannah assured her.

She really was trying. Plus, she knew better than anyone that Kat was right. The last time they worked a case together, over Spring Break, a seemingly boring one about car insurance fraud turned out to involve the abduction of a child for sex trafficking. So, she wasn't inclined to assume anyone was what they seemed.

At least today she wasn't stuck in the car all day like she was that time around. For the car insurance case, she had been trapped in Kat's Subaru for hours at a time. This time around, she'd been outside, able to walk around. She knew she couldn't complain—not if this was what she really wanted to do.

Of course, not too long ago, it hadn't been what she wanted to do. It had only been a few months since she'd made a radical, life altering choice. Up until then, she'd been on a very different path. She was planning to go to culinary school with the goal of becoming a chef. That goal was threatened by the possibility that she might not graduate from high school at all.

Everything seemed up in the air when she checked herself into an in-patient psychiatric and rehabilitation facility, not for drinking or drugs, but because of an unquenchable desire to inflict harm, even kill, people she viewed as wrongdoers. She'd done it once before, shooting and killing a serial killer who threatened Jessie, Ryan, and herself after he'd already been taken into custody. The rush from that experience was something she found herself chasing ever since and feared she couldn't control.

But after she solved the murder of a fellow patient at the center, something in her had changed. Once she left, she realized that while she still loved cooking, it was no longer what she wanted to do with her life. She wanted to catch bad people, to bring them to justice. She wanted to channel her thirst for vengeance in a healthy direction, like Jessie had done.

She knew that her big sister still had darkness in her, a remnant of the horrors she'd suffered both as a child and as an adult. But Jessie had found a way to use that darkness to make the world a better place.

Rather than giving in to the shadows that constantly encircled her, she made them work for her.

So, Hannah told Jessie and Ryan that she wanted to pursue a career in criminal justice in some capacity, though she wasn't sure if that would be as a police detective, an FBI agent, or heaven forbid, a criminal profiler. She got Jessie's permission to "intern" with Kat at the detective agency over Spring Break and during the summer. Despite her month in "rehab," she didn't just graduate from high school, she graduated with honors. And she was accepted at Cal State Fullerton, where she would begin classes in the fall.

"He's moving again," she said as Lyman Feller took his overly whipped coffee drink and led the overly permed shopping plaza manager down the outdoor plaza path, pointing out some signage that troubled him.

Hannah stood up and ambled causally behind the pair, pretending to be just another eighteen-year-old girl who was more focused on her phone than on the events around her. Glancing at her reflection in a shop window, she thought that she mostly fit the bill.

Unlike when she was heavily made up and could easily pass for twenty-five, she actually looked her age today. She had intentionally dressed down for the day, wearing blue jeans, a casual, unbuttoned, white shirt over a black tank top, and black Converse sneakers. Her shoulder-length, blonde hair was loose under the baseball cap she wore, and her green eyes—the same as her sister's—were hidden behind her sunglasses. At five-foot-nine, she was the same height as the man she was following.

She feigned interest in the water fountain near Feller and the permed lady and stood in front it as if she was going to take a selfie with it in the background. Then, making sure that she wasn't in the frame, but they were, she snapped a few photos, just in case. Who knows? Maybe the overly permed lady was Feller's mistress.

Even as she shook her head at the silliness of her current assignment, Hannah couldn't help but marvel at her current options, at how much her life had changed for the better considering where she was just two short years ago.

Back then, her whole world had just fallen apart, and a woman named Jessie Hunt, who she would only later learn was her half-sister, helped her put the pieces back together. She still had nightmares about the night they met, about the serial killer called The Ozarks Executioner, who she later learned was her and Jessie's shared father, who abducted her and her adoptive parents, then tortured and killed them while making her watch. She still remembered Jessie finding her in that state and the two of them, still strangers to each other, engaging in a battle to the death with their own father, which they somehow won.

Lyman Feller and the permed woman rounded a corner, and Hannah followed them, trying to keep her focus on her target and not her memories of the wonderful couple who adopted her as a baby and were rewarded for it with violent murder. The thought reminded her of another dead parent, one who passed much more recently, and the children he left behind.

She thought of Callum Reid, the retired HSS detective who had been a guest at Jessie's wedding when she was abducted by Andy Robinson. She remembered how Callum, without hesitation, had joined Hannah and Kat as they began an unsanctioned search for Jessie that ultimately led to her discovery in a mine in the Arizona desert.

She remembered how Callum had gotten stuck on the wrong side of a giant chasm in the collapsing mine and sacrificed himself to make sure a burner cell phone was retrieved, a phone that later proved crucial to saving hundreds of lives. She remembered seeing Callum smile sadly at her just before the ground gave out beneath him and how he disappeared into the earth, never to be seen again.

It was the same sad smile she'd seen on the face of Eli Reid, Callum's ten-year-old son, when the retired officer was posthumously awarded with the department's Medal of Valor. Callum's widow, Tanya, had shown gracious strength. His daughter, Harley, however, had barely managed to look up the whole time. Those kids seemed so lost.

She remembered how she had felt after losing her own parents, and she was already in her late teens at the time. The thought of these two, losing their father when they were so young, right after he'd left the force and just settled into being the kind of dad who could hang around the house and not get called into work in the middle of the night, was almost too painful to accept. She remembered looking over at Jessie during the ceremony and seeing the same thing in her eyes: the desire to ease the pain of these children, and the knowledge that she could not.

Lyman Feller stopped walking again. A shop owner had come out, and he was now in a heated three-way discussion with the guy and the permed manager. Hannah was too far away to hear what they were saying and doubted that it was relevant to their investigation anyway.

She looked down at her phone again, playing the part of the disinterested teenager. Only this time, something on her screen actually caught her eye. A local news headline made reference to a missing teenage girl. What sparked Hannah's interest more than usual were the parallels between the girl and herself.

Sasha Wexler was eighteen and had just graduated from high school. She was supposed to attend a local community college in the fall. There wasn't much in the way of biographical detail on the girl, other than that she was supposedly well-liked and that there was no indication that she was having personal conflicts with anyone in her life. The photo of her looked like it was pulled from the senior yearbook. Sasha was attractive in a sullen, "win me over" kind of way with long, brown hair and matching brown, mournful eyes.

The police said she hadn't been heard from since last night, that she'd disappeared out of the blue after not returning home from meeting up with her boyfriend at a local hangout. Her phone was found in a trash can in a quiet neighborhood not far from the hangout.

There was no video from nearby homes or businesses showing what happened. According to authorities, there were no suspicious texts or calls from her to anyone. There had been no ransom calls. Authorities suspected an abduction but not for money. They didn't sound optimistic about her being returned unharmed, if at all.

Hannah knew that a case like this was not just none of her business, but it was also well outside her wheelhouse. She had neither the experience nor the skillset to pursue something like this on her own. And yet, as she watched Lyman Feller continue to wave his hands histrionically about some issue he had with a downtown mall stationary store, she made herself a promise: once she had a spare moment, even if it wasn't until the end of the day, she was going to look into this.

She was going to find out what happened to Sasha Wexler.

CHAPTER SIX

It was Jessie's idea, but she had to give Sam Goodwin some credit for taking it to the next level.

She was certain that the key to figuring out who had killed Kim Carrigan was determining how the killer had gotten access to the couple's alarm security code. So, after they returned to the Central Station detectives' bullpen to review the evidence they had so far, she'd suggested they look through the records of Secure Home Services to find other recent, similar instances of customers who had filed complaints about their codes being accessed without explanation.

They'd found a few, but none that resulted in violence. Even less helpfully, each incident was ultimately easily explained. That was when Sam offered his idea.

"What if we expanded the search to other security companies who serve the area?" he suggested. "Maybe we pick a radius of three miles around the Carrigan house to start and see if anything similar comes up."

Jessie felt like an idiot for not thinking of the proposal herself. She wondered if not having come up with it was just a result of fixating on her own plan or some vestige of her concussion symptoms. Either way, it was a good call.

"That's great," she said. "Maybe we ask Jamil and Beth to help us narrow down the options."

"Let's do it," Sam agreed, standing up.

They walked past the empty desks of the other HSS detectives—Karen Bray, Jim Nettles, and Susannah Valentine—who were all out on assignment and down the hall to the HSS research department, which was comprised of Jamil Winslow and Beth Ryerson, both only twenty-four years old.

They poked their heads in to find both researchers typing away while staring at computer monitors. Jamil, the head of the department of two, was hunched over in concentration, his fingers flying across the keyboard.

Jamil Winslow was not what one might picture when imagining the research leader of the LAPD's top investigative unit. Short, black, and incredibly skinny, despite taking on an aggressive workout regimen lately, with thick glasses and no sense of fashion style, Jamil was quite literally a genius. He was capable of filtering through massive databases, sorting surveillance video into manageable buckets, or making complex financial records understandable—all seemingly in the blink of an eye.

Jessie and Ryan had met him languishing, unappreciated, in the Manhattan Beach Police Department staff office while they were working a case there a couple of years ago. His experience with them had inspired him to follow them to LAPD, where he'd become HSS's sole researcher, and then its department head after he was permitted to hire one additional staffer.

He had selected Beth Ryerson, who couldn't have been more different from him. Over six feet tall, with brown hair that she liked to keep in a ponytail, Beth was a former college volleyball star at UC-Santa Barbara. Unfussily attractive, she never wore makeup and was perpetually chill, a total contrast to Jamil's constant, jittery intensity. But her relaxed demeanor hid a sharp mind. No one had the computer brain that Jamil did, but she was adept with all the databases, and her more casual, confident vibe often helped center her boss, letting him direct his focus more constructively than he otherwise might.

In recent months, it had also become clear to Jessie that Jamil had a big crush on Beth, which he was trying hard, and failing, to keep hidden. What was less clear was how Beth felt about him. It was obvious that she adored him as a person, always talking him up to the detectives and higher-ups and bucking him up when he got down on himself. She was also fiercely protective of him whenever anyone was critical of him, which usually only happened when someone outside HSS expected major miracles from a guy who provided minor ones every day.

But Jessie still couldn't get a bead on whether her affection extended beyond professional respect and personal friendship into something closer to romantic reciprocation. In terms of keeping her relationship intentions private, Beth was the genius of the department.

"Hey guys," Sam said, interrupting the symphony of typing, "can Jessie and I bother you with an issue we're having?"

Both researchers spun around in their chairs. Beth wore her usual broad smile. Jessie noticed that Jamil didn't have his typical look of eager anticipation at a coming challenge. Instead, he appeared worn down, trepidatious, borderline surly.

"What's up?" Beth asked sunnily.

"We're looking for any complaints from customers about security alarm codes being hacked in recent weeks, specifically within a three-mile radius of this address," he said, handing it over. "We've already checked out SHS, but we were hoping you could help us get through to the other companies that serve the area."

"We're particularly interested in incidents that involved violence," Jessie added, "in which a customer claimed someone knew their code, accessed their home, and then attacked them. If there are associated police reports, all the better. We're sending you the incident and case file this is connected to for context."

"I don't know," Jamil said unenthusiastically, turning his attention back to his own screen. "Detectives Bray and Valentine have us searching homeless shelter camera footage for a potential fugitive. This might have to wait."

Jessie was taken aback by both his tone and his reluctance. She couldn't remember Jamil Winslow ever actively objecting to a request from her, much less in such a disinterested manner. She caught a glimpse of Beth, who frowned ever so briefly, before her usual smile returned.

"I can take care of that, Jamil," she said. "It's really a one-person job. Why don't you focus on this alarm security code thing for now. The footage will still be waiting for you when you're done."

"I guess so," Jamil said unenthusiastically. "Send me the file, and I'll start a search. Did you already submit requests for data from the companies?"

"No," Sam said. "We just thought of the idea. I can do that now."

"I'll take care of it," the head researcher told him sharply, before turning his attention back to his screen. Apparently, the conversation was over. Jessie looked over at Beth, who had a pained expression on her face, but clearly didn't feel like she was in a position to leave the room for a heart to heart right now.

"Thanks," Jessie said. "Keep us posted."

She and Sam left the room and headed back down the hall to the bullpen.

"What was all that about?" Sam asked. "I know Jamil can be a little socially awkward, but he was downright prickly in there."

"I don't know," Jessie said, her pace quickening with each step. "But whatever it is, it's going to have to take a backseat to solving this case. Right now, my sole focus is on finding out who choked the life out of Kim Carrigan."

CHAPTER SEVEN

Jessie couldn't help but be impressed.

Whatever was bothering Jamil, it wasn't affecting his work. They'd only been back at their desks for ten minutes when he pinged them both with a message, along with an attached file. The message was curt and to the point: *still looking but think this will be useful.* Once they opened the attachment, they saw that he was right.

The document was a police report from three nights ago for a death that had been ruled accidental. A woman named Eleanor Hill had apparently fallen down the stairs in her house and broken her neck. There was no sign of a struggle or forced entry into the home. Cheryl Gallagher, who was also the medical examiner on that case, made no mention of strangling. The security system was still on when the woman's husband, Sean, and their two children arrived home and found her dead at the bottom of the stairs.

In fact, at first it was hard to understand why Jamil had flagged the case at all. That is, until they got to the statement of the live-in housekeeper, who had her own small, self-contained apartment adjoining the back of the house. Sam noted that the woman had a more provocative view.

"According to Marjorie, the housekeeper, while the rest of the family was spending the night with Sean's sister's family in Temecula, Eleanor was enjoying a solo evening at home," he said. "But Marjorie swore that around 9 p.m., she heard the alarm get deactivated, followed by voices that sounded louder than anything that would typically come from the television. Then she heard a thud, after which the voices stopped, and the alarm was reactivated. The detectives handling the case asked Marjorie why, if she was so concerned, she didn't go check on the situation."

Jessie had been scanning ahead in the report, so she already knew the answer to that question.

"You want to know what her official response was?" Jessie asked.

"What?"

"This is a direct quote," Jessie said. "*Miss Eleanor was clear that this was to be her night alone. I wanted to respect that. I did text her to make sure there was no problem, but she didn't answer. I thought she might be annoyed that I was bothering her. I thought maybe she had too much to drink and slipped, maybe a friend came over and they had a loud conversation. But that seemed weird because she said she wanted alone time. I don't know. It wasn't really my business, and I didn't want to be nosy. Still, I never considered that something like this had happened.*"

She looked up at Sam and could see that he was as stunned as she was.

"Apparently, the detectives on the case weren't as troubled by the discrepancies as Marjorie was," Sam noted, "because according to their final report, they chalked the inconsistencies up to a combination of Marjorie mishearing things, the loud television, and Eleanor likely turning off the alarm to go outside, then turning it on again once she returned to the house."

Jessie felt frustration starting to bubble up inside her. "Yeah, well, they conveniently ignored several facts," she said pointedly.

"Like what?"

"First, that Marjorie insisted that the alarm was reactivated *after* the thudding sound, which was presumably Eleanor falling down the stairs to her death. Second, that according to their own report, the television wasn't on when the rest of the Hill family came home, suggesting the loud talking might have come from somewhere else."

"But absent a smoking gun that indicated something other than an accident," Sam noted, "they only had conjecture to work with. Clearly, they were happy to drop the whole thing and move on."

"Well, we're not going to drop it," Jessie said. "I think that maybe we should pay our warm and cuddly medical examiner friend Cheryl Gallagher a visit and see if she has any additional thoughts on the matter that didn't make it into her final report."

"You think she left something out?" Sam asked, surprised.

"I think that if it was clear that the case wasn't going anywhere, she might have kept some inconvenient conclusions to herself. It can't hurt to ask. So, let's go ask."

***

When they arrived, Gallagher was in the lab, and she didn't seem to be in any better of a mood than she had been at the Carrigan house. She looked up as they walked through the door and immediately frowned.

"I told you that I'd update you after the autopsy was complete," she said caustically. "Coming down here to pressure me won't expedite the process."

"That's not why we're here," Jessie said, walking over and dropping the Eleanor Hill file on the metal table in front of Gallagher. "Do you remember this case?'

Gallagher opened the folder and thumbed through it. Jessie could tell from the way the woman's back immediately straightened while looking at the photo of Hill's body at the bottom of the stairs that she remembered everything.

"What about it?"

"The detectives on the case ruled it an accidental death, likely due to slipping on the stairs, maybe a result of alcohol in her system," Sam said, unnecessarily repeating details for the M.E.'s benefit. "Do you stand by that analysis?"

"I signed off on the case, didn't I?" Gallagher said, turning away as she answered so that neither Jessie nor Sam could see her expression. She pretended to be fixated on something on her computer screen.

"That's not the same the thing, Cheryl," Jessie said, again calling Gallagher by her first name to keep from getting comfortable, just as she had at the Carrigan house. "We get that there might not have been anything definitive that would allow you to actively object to closing the case. But was there anything that gave you pause?"

"Why are you asking?" Gallagher asked, her back still to them.

Sam looked over at Jessie hesitantly, clearly unsure how forthcoming they should be. She pointed at herself. In a situation like this, where they were asking Gallagher to go out on a limb, they would have to be equally forthright, and the honesty would have to come from Jessie, who had more experience with the M.E. than he did.

"We think Eleanor Hill's case may be connected to Kim Carrigan's," she said bluntly. "We think there's a chance that someone may somehow be getting access to women's homes via their alarm security system secret codes and attacking them when they know the women are alone. Hill's housekeeper thought she heard multiple voices that night when the rest of the family was gone. And she thought she heard the alarm being reactivated again after the loud thud that could have been Eleanor 'falling' down the stairs."

Gallagher turned around but her face was still inscrutable. "Go on," she said.

"Right now," Jessie said, emboldened, "we have one confirmed attack in a home and one seemingly unconnected accidental death in another home two miles away, two and a half days earlier. But if we can find evidence that the first death might not have been an accident at all—that perhaps it was an attack too—then that potentially validates the theory that the alarm was reactivated by someone else *after* Eleanor's death. And if that's the case, then that means that we have two murders committed by someone with access to home security codes, targeting women who were home alone. It means we have a potential serial killer on our hands. So, what can you tell us?"

Cheryl Gallagher stared at Jessie silently for a good five seconds. Then she stepped over to the Eleanor Hill case file and opened it to page three. She pointed at the field marked 'BAC.'

"Hill's blood alcohol level was .07," she said. "Clearly, she had a few drinks, and that percentage indicates some degree of impairment. But we're not talking slurred speech, massively impaired judgement, or severely reduced muscle coordination. Could she have had some mild impaired judgement and slight reduction in muscle control and reaction time? Sure. Could that have led to her slipping on the stairs and falling all the way to bottom, breaking her neck? Conceivably. But the way it's written up in the report—as if she was likely in a drunken stupor and a massive tumble was an inevitability—that's the detectives' conclusion, not mine."

Jessie studied Gallagher's face. The woman's lips were twitching, as if she was aching to say something more but couldn't quite bring herself to volunteer it.

"I feel like you have more to share, Cheryl," she prompted.

Gallagher sighed heavily, then motioned for both Jessie and Sam to come around the metal table and join her at the computer screen, where she punched several keys violently. A tab came up marked "Hill, Eleanor—photo images." Gallagher opened the folder and clicked on the seventh photo, which showed bruising on the woman's back, neck, shoulders, and arms. Next to Jessie, Sam winced audibly.

"What should we be noticing here?" she asked. "Isn't this all just bruising as she went down the stairs?"

"Most of it," Gallagher said as she zoomed in on one portion of Eleanor Hill's upper left arm. As the image got bigger, Jessie heard herself gasp. She pointed at the screen.

"Those bruise marks are different," Sam noted, seeing it now too. "They look like … fingers?"

"They look like someone had a tight grip on her upper arm," Jessie agreed. "Maybe just before she yanked herself free, maybe so hard that she went tumbling down a flight of stairs."

She looked over at Gallagher.

"That thought had occurred to me," the medical examiner said quietly.

"I assume that area of her arm was tested though," Jessie said, "for fingerprints, skin, DNA?"

"For all of that," Gallagher told them. "There was nothing, though the indentation pattern in her skin could suggest gloves. I never pursued that because, well, the detectives said the death was accidental, and I didn't have anything definitive to contradict them, so there didn't seem to be anything to pursue."

"Well, there might be something to pursue now," Jessie said. "Do you think you could test for a match between those indentations and the ones on Kim Carrigan's skin?"

"Of course."

"Thanks," Jessie said excitedly. "Please let us know right away if you find one. If there is, that will give us a lot more juice to pour additional resources into the investigation. It's one thing to pursue the killer of a local TV anchor's wife, but if this is part of a pattern, we need to know. There might be other potential victims out there right now."

"Great, that's just what your boss needs," Gallagher muttered under her breath.

"What do you mean?" Jessie asked, confused.

The medical examiner glanced over at Sam with consternation, then back at Jessie. It was clear that she wanted some privacy.

"Detective Goodwin, can you warm up the car?" Jessie asked. "I just have to address one or two more issues with Dr. Gallagher here."

"Not a problem," Sam said, pretending not be offended that he was being kept out of whatever was about to be discussed.

Once he was gone, Jessie turned back to Gallagher and shrugged. "So?'

"You really ought to watch your boss's back," Gallagher said under her breath.

"Ryan?" Jessie demanded, her heart starting to pound. "I mean, Captain Hernandez?"

"No," Gallagher said, annoyed, "your big boss, Chief Decker."

"What are you talking about?" Jessie demanded.

"The last thing he needs is another high-profile case to blow up in his face right after the whole Operation Z debacle."

"Debacle?" Jessie pressed, feeling her blood pressure rise. "That Operation Z attack was planned for months by Andy's Robinson's final acolyte, Zoe Bradway. She intended to poison everyone in an entire movie multiplex. I know that lots of people died, and that was terrible, but it was twenty-seven when it could have been thousands. Bradway is locked up in a psychiatric prison for the rest of the millennium. All things considered, we averted a catastrophe of far worse proportions than what occurred."

"I know that, and you know that," Gallagher hissed, "and so do all the members of the City Council that have been interrogating Decker all morning. But that doesn't mean that some of them aren't after his head anyway. They want someone who is more pliable, who isn't so "independent" of their influence, and at least one of them is willing to squeeze some city employee peons to get rid of him."

Suddenly, Gallagher's unusually surly behavior from earlier this morning made a lot more sense.

"And you were one of those peons," Jessie said. "What kind of pressure did you get?"

"I was asked to offer testimony that he favored HSS to the exclusion of other units and that he pushed me to direct easier cases to the unit to improve your stats."

"Is any of that true?" Jessie asked, trying not to be defensive even though she found the idea absurd.

"No," Gallagher told her, sounding offended at the suggestion. "But because I deal with a lot of HSS's cases, I guess they thought they could put pressure on me to shade the facts. I got a call this morning from a councilmember on the way to the Carrigan house suggesting that my future might depend on how 'helpful' I was."

"What did you say?" Jessie asked.

"I told the guy to take a flying leap into the Pacific."

"And that was why you were so salty when you saw me."

"I wasn't salty!" Gallagher protested.

Jessie decided to let that one go. "Who called you?" she asked.

Gallagher shook her head.

"You've got enough on your plate," she said. "If I need your help with that, I'll come to you. But you just let the chief know, if he doesn't already, that the long knives are out. He needs to keep his guard up. Decker is a good man and a good leader. A lot of us want that interim title gone."

"I'll tell him when I get a chance," Jessie assured her. "But neither of us can worry about that right now. You've got to try to match some skin indentations, and I've got somewhere to be too."

"Where are you going?" Gallagher asked.

"To the Hill House. Apparently, it's gone from the scene of an accident to the scene of a murder."

CHAPTER EIGHT

Jessie knew which house it was from half a block away.

As they pulled up to the home of Sean and Eleanor Hill, they eased past the driveway, where four cars were parked. Three more were lined up in front of the house. It was clear that friends and family have rallied to help recently widowed Sean and his children in their time of need.

"Remember," Jessie said after Sam had parked, "no one here suspects foul play. We need to try to get our answers without raising any alarm bells. The last thing this family needs is to add doubt to their tragedy. Until we know more, we have to be very careful about what we say."

"Got it," Sam said.

They got out of the car and headed for the front door. Like the Carrigans, the Hills lived in Hancock Park, but farther south and east, in a marginally fancier area, if that was possible. Here, there were no cottages. All of the houses were large. Many were gated with tall hedges designed to keep lookie-loos away.

The Hills' house was Tudor-style but on steroids, almost like the residential version of an accordion, only expanded far wider than what seemed architecturally possible. As they walked up the entry path, Jessie wondered how a family of four could have possibly filled the giant space.

Sam knocked on the door rather than ringing the bell. While they waited, Jessie noticed that just above the front door was a large, tinted, decorative window in the shape of a sunrise. She imagined that when the real sun shined through, it created an impressive kaleidoscope of colors. Within seconds, the door was opened by a pleasant-looking blonde in her mid-thirties wearing a long, floral dress. She smiled cautiously.

"May I help you?" she asked, as her eyes darted to their empty hands, apparently noting that they hadn't brought any food for the grieving family.

"Yes, ma'am," Sam said in the familiar, warm, reassuring voice he seemed able to turn on whenever they were in delicate situations. "My name is Sam Goodwin. This is Jessie Hunt. We're with the Los Angeles Police Department. We're sorry to bother you during such a difficult time, but we need to speak with Mr. Hill."

Jessie suspected that Sam had cultivated his practiced tone through years in the vice unit, where he regularly had to tell families about the deaths of their daughters, often under unimaginably horrific circumstances. If he couldn't make the news any less painful, at least he could make the breaking of it a little more humane. Despite his best efforts, the woman's face fell.

"Come in," she said in a hushed voice. "I'm Marilyn, a friend of the family. I'll put you in one of the front sitting rooms away from the children. Then I'll get Sean. Follow me."

Once inside, Jessie saw the alarm panel on the wall across from the door and wondered if that was the same one the killer had used to deactivate the system when he first came in the house. Before she could point it out to Sam, Marilyn was leading them down a long hallway, past several rooms, one of which housed a grand piano.

In the distance, Jessie could hear the squeals of multiple children, maybe as many as half a dozen. As they moved down the hall, they passed a series of family portraits showing the Hills over the years. The first was an engagement photo, then a wedding picture, then a portrait with a baby, and so on.

Jessie lost track of the number as they passed each one, but there were easily more than ten. By the last one, the older child, a boy, looked to be about eight, and the younger one, a girl, to be around five. She could see how their features matched their parents. The boy had his father's reluctant smile and gray eyes, and the little girl had the same shade of blue in her eyes as her mom.

Jessie knew that their mother was thirty-five when she died but seeing her dead body in photos was far different than watching her age over a decade in lovingly curated portraits. It was like walking through a mini time machine, seeing Eleanor Hill go from a wide-eyed newlywed with long, brown hair and an unfurrowed brow to a still lovely, but perhaps more weary, now shorter-haired, tired-eyed woman who was fighting to hold back the furrow. Just that short walk made Jessie feel the family's ache and stirred her desire to find some justice for the woman staring back at her.

Marilyn finally stopped at a small alcove that was easy to miss. It had just a loveseat and one leather chair. It was clear why she'd led them there. She must have hoped that in such an easily hidden spot, they wouldn't be noticed by the kids or anyone else for that matter. Jessie didn't mind.

"I'll get Sean and be right back," Marilyn said.

Jessie sat down on the loveseat. Sam looked unsure whether to join her.

"It's okay, Detective," she said. "When Hill arrives, he's probably going to want the chair opposite us."

Sam nodded and was just about to join her when a little kid tore around the corner, slammed face-first into his backside, and plopped onto the ground. It was a boy of about seven. He looked briefly stunned. Jessie thought he might be about to cry, but he popped right up, scurried behind the loveseat, put his finger to his lips, and gave them both an elaborate "shush!"

"What the—?" Sam started to ask.

"Ready or not, here I come!" came another young female voice from another room, making it clear what was going on.

They could hear squeals and giggles from nearby rooms, and soon the little boy behind the loveseat found it hard to contain his own snickers. The sound of them echoed from the alcove out into the hall, and within seconds, a head peeked around the corner. With her brown hair and blue eyes, Jessie recognized the little girl from the portraits. She looked at Sam standing awkwardly in front of her, then at Jessie, and was seemingly untroubled by their presence. She knelt down, peered below the loveseat, smiled, and then stood up again.

"I recognize your socks, Jaden Moran," she said in a schoolmarm-y tone. "You're out!"

"Oh man," Jaden said, standing up.

"Go back to home base," the girl said. "I still have three more people to catch."

As Jaden shuffled out, the girl fixed her attention on Jessie.

"I know who you are," she said confidently. "I've seen you on the TV."

"Hi, my name's Jessie. This is my friend, Sam."

"I'm Charlotte," the little girl said. "Are you here to talk to my daddy about my mommy? She died and went to heaven while we were in Temecula."

Jessie fought to push words past the lump that had suddenly formed in her throat. "We are," she said.

“That’s what I see you doing on the TV,” Charlotte said, “helping with people who died. My mommy was watching you too. She said that they call this the City of Angels, and that you are one of its angels.”

All at once, Jessie found that she couldn’t speak. She knew that if she tried, only sobs would escape her lips, so she looked desperately over at Sam for help. He seemed to understand and turned back to Charlotte.

“Your mommy sounds like she was a very nice lady,” he said quietly.

Before he could continue, a phalanx of kids rounded the corner, apparently alerted to the presence of new people by Jaden Moran. They began peppering Sam with questions. Jessie recognized one of them, standing silently toward the back, as Charlotte’s older brother, Charlie.

He reminded Jessie of another boy, though she couldn’t remember who. Then it hit her. With his black hair and sad, shy smile, he looked like he could have been related to another son of a fallen parent, Eli Reid, Callum Reid’s younger child.

She pictured the other boy back at the ceremony to honor his dead father, trying to put on a brave face for his mother and sister as they were awarded Callum’s posthumous Medal of Valor, which was somehow supposed to substitute for losing his dad. She remembered Eli trying his hardest to hold it together even as his older sister, Harley, couldn’t bear to look up. She remembered looking over at Hannah at one point during the ceremony, seeing tears in her little sister’s eyes, and realizing for the first time just how much Callum’s death— sacrificing himself to save countless others— had affected her too.

They had all lost their parents young. Jessie had. Hannah had. Now, so had the children of Eleanor Hill. But at least these two kids had one parent left and apparently unlimited financial resources at their disposal.

Yes, the Reid children had their mother, Tanya, but they didn’t live in Hancock Park in a giant Tudor mansion. Their mom was a legal secretary, and their father, even before his death, was a retired cop. Their future was anything but certain. That ate at Jessie.

Marilyn re-appeared to save Sam. This time, she was accompanied by Sean Hill, who was only somewhat recognizable as the man from the portraits. He had the same black hair and gray eyes, the same square jaw and sharp nose, but he looked gaunt and haunted. His jeans seemed to cling to his waist for dear life, and his sweatshirt looked like it might consume him. Though she doubted the most recent family portrait was more than six months old, he looked like he'd aged five years since then.

"Kids, out!" Marilyn instructed forcefully. "Adults are talking in here."

The children scurried out, all except for Charlotte, who moved over to her father as he settled into the leather chair opposite them.

"Look, Daddy," she said, taking his hand in hers, "it's the angel Mommy talked about from the TV."

"Yes, sweetie," Hill said softly, giving his daughter a kiss on the forehead before Marilyn escorted her out as well.

Once the voices had faded into the distance, Sam spoke, "We're sorry to bother you at such a difficult time, especially after you've already spoken to our colleagues," he said, "but we just had a few more questions for you. We'll try to keep them brief."

"Was Ellie murdered?" Hill asked abruptly.

"I'm sorry?" Sam said. "What makes you ask that?"

Hill sighed heavily. "I have to ask," he said, his voice raspy from exhaustion. "My housekeeper has been crying for the last two days, insisting that someone was in the house, and no one will take her seriously. The police report by your so-called colleagues says Ellie was sloppy drunk when she hasn't had more than three glasses of wine at one time since college. And now, I'm sitting across from a criminal profiler who handles serial killer cases when I was told my wife's death was an accident. So, it would be weird *not* to ask the question, right?"

Sam looked over at Jessie, not sure how she wanted to proceed. She had insisted before they came in the house that they not reveal that they suspected foul play, but Hill seemed to have figured them out before they'd asked a single question.

For the first time today, Jessie briefly wished she'd been paired with a different partner. Though her concussion issues hadn't been a major problem so far today, she was still reeling from the whole "angel" thing, coupled with the echoes of guilt about Callum Reid's fatherless children. It would be nice to have a partner who could take point in a moment like this. But that wasn't possible, so she did it.

"Mr. Hill," she said, leaning forward, "the truth is that we just don't know. Initially, your wife's death *did* seem like an accident. But Detective Goodwin and I are investigating a murder that has some suspicious similarities to what happened to her. We can't get into all the details, but it involves an alarm system deactivated by someone other than a family member, and a victim who was killed when the murderer knew she would be alone in the house. With that context, your housekeeper's statement, and some other information we've gleaned, we wanted to revisit the circumstances of Ellie's death. It may not ultimately lead to anything. But just in case, can you tell us: is there anyone who might have wanted to hurt her? Had she mentioned feeling unsafe lately? That she felt as if she was being followed? Anything out of the ordinary?"

Hill shook his head. "None of that," he insisted. "Everything seemed normal. And I can guarantee you that if she was concerned, she wouldn't have wanted to spend the night at home alone. She would have come with us to my sister's. Hell, we only moved to L.A. six months ago. She barely had time to even get a sense of what she should be scared of."

"Is it possible that anyone has a vendetta against you?" Sam asked.

"Never say never," Hill conceded, "but I do international corporate mergers. It's lucrative, but it's pretty dry stuff. Plus, I'm part of a team of five that's part of a larger group of thirty within a 300-person firm. It's hard to imagine why anyone would target me individually or how harming Ellie would accomplish that. My last major merger wrapped up three weeks ago, and my team was only in the early stages of prepping the next one."

Charlotte stepped into the alcove again. She had a worried look on her face.

"Daddy," she said, "I'm sorry to bother your talking, but Charlie threw up again. He ran to his room. I think he might need you."

Hill's face briefly contorted in anguish before he got control of it.

"Okay sweetie, thanks," he said, scooping her up in his arms as he addressed Jessie and Sam. "I've got to deal with this. He's having a really rough time. If you have other questions, call me. And if you get definitive confirmation that this was … intentional, please give me a heads up. I want to know that. I'm sorry I couldn't be more help."

And then he was gone. Sam and Jessie stood up.

"What do you think?" he asked.

Jessie stepped out of the alcove and looked down the long hallway toward the front door. It was easily fifty yards away.

"I don't think I can prove anything yet," she said. "But Ellie Hill doesn't strike me as the kind of person who ever came close to getting shit-faced enough to topple down a flight of stairs."

Sam nodded in agreement. "And this doesn't feel like the kind of home that one invades on a whim, without prior knowledge about how to access it," he said.

Jessie didn't want to get ahead of herself, but she had done this job long enough to sense where things were going.

"We'll need to wait for Dr. Gallagher's skin analysis to draw any firm conclusions," she said. "Two things might be possible at the same time: Ellie Hill's death may have been an accident, but it feels like the accident interrupted a murder in progress. Now, we just need to find the murderer."

CHAPTER NINE

Sam tried not to let himself get overwhelmed.

As he drove back to the station from the Hill mansion, he listened as Jessie told Jamil and Beth the parameters she wanted included in a search for potential suspects.

"We need someone who moved to the area recently," she said. "Let's make it in the last six months and within a three-mile radius of both homes. We're likely talking male, but don't rule out women. They should have some history of work in technology, security, maybe an electrician—that universe. And their record should include a history of violence or at the very least, stalking, peeping, that kind of thing."

By the time they arrived at the HSS research office fifteen minutes later, a list of potential suspects was waiting for them. Unfortunately, it was twenty-three people long. That was when the sense of getting overwhelmed started to kick in. He was still getting used to the different pace from vice. Things could get intense there, too, but there wasn't the constant sense that even reviewing paperwork was a life and death endeavor that required uninterrupted focus.

But he pretended that he was fine and quickly agreed when Jessie recommended that they split up the list. Once that was done, they began to methodically make their way through it. A half hour into the process, they got a call from Dr. Gallagher confirming what they'd already suspected: the indentations on the skin of Eleanor Hill's upper arm matched the indentations on Kim Carrigan's skin.

"They were both made with the same brand of glove," Gallagher told them over speaker.

"Which strongly suggests that they were killed by the same person," Jessie noted. "The odds that two women in the same neighborhood had their security systems disabled and were attacked by different people wearing the same brand of gloves, in June in Los Angeles, seem pretty remote, don't you think?"

"I do," Gallagher agreed. "Unfortunately, that's as much help as the gloves will offer. I checked, and that brand is sold in pretty much every department store in Southern California."

“That’s okay,” Jessie said, impressively undeterred. “At least now we definitively know we’re dealing with a two-time killer. That’s a person with a pattern. And patterns can be predicted, which means we have a shot at stopping them before they kill again.”

“Should we reach out to Sean Hill?” he asked once they’d hung up with Gallagher. “He wanted to know when we knew something definitive.”

“I’d like to hold off for now,” Jessie replied. “Right now, all we can tell him is that his wife’s death wasn’t a true accident, and that the person responsible is still out there. With a little luck, maybe when we call him, it will be to tell him we have that person in custody.”

Sam wished he could be as optimistic. As he pored over the potential suspects, he worried that he was missing something important. It took a while to definitively eliminate someone on the list, whether by verifying that they were back in prison, had moved away, or were simply working the night shift at the time of the murder.

They had gone through eighteen of the suspects when he came across the first one that he couldn’t conclusively eliminate. His name was Jacob Greeley.

Thirty-eight years old, Greeley was a temporary street lighting technician for the Los Angeles Bureau of Street Lighting, contracted out by the city through a hiring firm. His work history listed time as an electrician and, briefly, working for a security company installing alarm panels. Those jobs had been back east in North Carolina, where he’d lived until moving here four months ago.

The substation that Greeley worked out of was in the mid-Wilshire district, which regularly serviced Hancock Park. He lived on North Las Palmas Avenue in Hollywood, which was just a few blocks north of the Carrigans’ place, although once one crossed the dividing line of Melrose Avenue, the level of luxury dropped precipitously.

Sam also noted that Greeley had conveniently left off his resume what Jamil and Beth had not missed in their research: his criminal record. Back in North Carolina, he had several convictions for assault, one in a bar and another in a football stadium parking lot. But the one that got him sentenced to real time was for beating up his live-in girlfriend. She ended up in the hospital, and he ended up in prison, where he served fourteen months. After his release, he spent three years on probation. The day that ended, he moved to California.

“Take a look at this,” Sam said, sliding Greeley’s file over to Jessie.

She scanned it quickly, then looked up. "This is the best hit I've seen yet," she noted. "Nothing I've reviewed has come close. Great catch. Let's see if any of these last four on the list have potential. But at least we know we have one person we can visit."

Sam knew he was the lead detective on the case but couldn't help feeling a little kick of giddiness at getting an "attaboy" from Jessie Hunt. For much of the morning, she's seemed a little distant, in her own head, and he'd been starting to wonder if it had something to do with him. But getting her unadulterated praise for his work smoothed over all that insecurity.

He felt a little silly needing it in the first place. After all, he was a thirty-three-year-old man, older than Hunt herself. He'd been on the force for over a decade. She'd been a criminal profiler, and often a part-time consultant at that, for barely two years. And yet he still found himself looking up to her, seeking her approval, hoping that his interrogation methods and investigative analysis met her rigorous standards.

It was all a little ridiculous, and yet he couldn't help himself. After all, she'd earned the respect she got. This was a woman who had survived more horrors in her first thirty years than most people could endure in ten lifetimes. Sam remembered when he first read about her, wondering how she wasn't permanently institutionalized.

It was bad enough that when she was six years old, her father, who was secretly a serial killer, murdered her mother in front of her in a remote, snowed-in cabin in the Ozarks. But then he'd left her there, tied up, alone with the body, where she was trapped for three days before two hunters found her.

That alone would be enough to do in most people. But years later, she ended up unknowingly marrying a sociopath who surreptitiously poisoned her when he discovered she was pregnant because he "wasn't ready" to be a parent, causing a miscarriage. She only learned that fact later, when she uncovered the other crimes he was responsible for, including murdering his secret mistress and trying to frame Jessie for it. And then, when Jessie uncovered his plan, trying to kill her as well. Luckily, she outwitted him, and he ended up in prison.

It was later, as she was trying to put her life back together and began to consult as a criminal profiler for the LAPD, that her long-missing, serial killer father returned to her life. In short succession, he murdered her adoptive parents, then tried to kill her and a teenage girl that turned out to be her half-sister, Hannah. The two of them, unaware of their familial connection, managed to turn the tables on him but not before he'd slaughtered Hannah's adoptive parents too.

And yet Jessie plowed ahead, assuming guardianship of her half-sister. And just when that seemed to be going well, her ex-husband was released from prison on a technicality and immediately sought revenge. He first killed Jessie's profiling mentor, Garland Moses, then tried to do the same to her, Hannah, and Ryan Hernandez, who was then Jessie's boyfriend. They ultimately ended his reign of terror, but only after he'd stabbed Hernandez, leaving him in a coma for weeks and causing injuries that required months of rehabilitation.

There were other, equally terrifying incidents, including a run-in with an elderly serial killer and with another one who viewed Jessie's father as his personal hero. And then there was her most recent trauma: being kidnapped on her wedding day by brilliant but obsessively unhinged Andy Robinson, who had tried to make Jessie into some kind of private love slave, permanently trapped in a mine in Arizona.

Just thinking about all that made Sam want to curl up in the fetal position. In fact, he recalled that he'd done exactly that when he was twelve and learned that his seventeen-year-old sister, Charlene, who'd run away from home six months earlier, had been found dead in a cheap motel room, beaten up by a man she'd been paid to have sex with but had somehow disappointed. That was the reason he eventually became a vice cop, something he'd never shared with anyone at HSS, mainly because her loss still haunted him, and he didn't think he could talk about her without breaking down.

And yet here Jessie was, not just upright and walking, but somehow married and having raised a damaged young woman into a functional adult. More than that, mere weeks after nearly getting blown up in that Arizona mine, she was still coming to work every day. She was still trying to get justice for other victims, trying to get answers for a husband who thought he was just starting his life with his wife, trying to find peace for a suddenly single father trying to comfort a little boy who couldn't stop throwing up and a little girl who thought the profiler was an angel.

Sam thought that if he was going to have a little hero worship and someone to model his own recovery on, he could do worse than Jessie Hunt. Still, he couldn't let that get in the way of the job he had to do. And he did his best to put it out of his head as he reviewed the last two files on his list. When they both proved fruitless, he looked up at Jessie, who was already done with hers.

“No other prospects?” she asked.
“None that are especially promising,” he admitted.
“Me either,” she said. “You know what that means.”
“I should get the car keys?”
Jessie nodded.
“It’s time we had a friendly chat with Jacob Greeley.”

CHAPTER TEN

There was no light in the room other than the glow from the multiple computer monitors on the desk.

The man sitting in front of them didn't seem troubled by the darkness. In fact, he found it comforting. He did his best work in the darkness.

He studied one of the monitors especially closely. It was footage that he'd collected lately, and though he'd reviewed it many times in the last few days, it had taken on special urgency now that his most recent "visit" was complete. This was his new, top priority.

He looked at the details of the location, trying his best to memorize them. He wouldn't have access to this footage when he was in the field, and it would be very dark. He'd have to depend on his memory, his meticulous planning, and what he liked to call his "steel will," a cold ruthlessness that he'd cultivated over the years and had only recently allowed full rein.

But he was confident that it would work out. After all, that steel will had worked for him this morning as he had calmly choked the life out of Kim Carrigan. Admittedly, his will had been less resolute a few nights earlier with Eleanor Hill when his brief hesitation had led to her breaking free of his grip.

But even then, that situation had ultimately resolved itself when she broke her neck falling down a flight of stairs while trying to escape. He didn't get the satisfaction that came from directly causing her end, but he consoled himself with the knowledge that had he not visited her that night, she would be alive right now. It wasn't the same rush that he got this morning or that he'd get again in the near future, but it was something.

He heard a noise beyond the wall, outside the room, and glanced behind him. He thought he'd locked the door but from where he was, and with the dim light, he couldn't be certain. Quickly, he got up, removed the obstruction, and hurried over to double check. Though it was his preference, he couldn't always guarantee that he would have the entirety of this room exclusively to himself, so he had to be careful.

The task at hand required complete privacy, but he couldn't risk raising suspicion by having the door locked all the time. That would lead to questions that he wasn't prepared to answer.

The door *was* locked, as he knew it would be. He was foolish to have doubted himself in the first place. He would never be so reckless as to allow for the possibility of someone walking in while he was planning his next visit. Especially not now when that visit was so very soon.

CHAPTER ELEVEN

Jessie and Sam pulled into the small parking lot for the Bureau of Street Lighting substation.

Jessie hoped they'd have better success here. Greeley hadn't been at his Hollywood apartment, which wasn't really a surprise. She and Sam both wished he'd been there so that any potential confrontation could have avoided putting anyone else at risk. Now, they had to track him down at a place of business, where anything could happen.

As they walked up to the entrance, Jessie again cursed the ancient Los Angeles municipal services phone tree system. Despite their best efforts, they'd been unable to get hold of an actual person who could tell them where Greeley might be right now. They didn't know if he was in the substation, on a job, or if he had the day off and had gone to a movie.

They'd briefly considered trying to get permission to access his phone data, but that would have required getting Jamil's help, and Jessie wasn't inclined to deal with his surliness right now. Besides, it would be hard to justify such a request unless they'd first at least tried to locate Greeley via traditional shoe leather methods.

They got to the substation front door and found it locked. Sam banged on it for a good thirty seconds before a portly, middle-aged guy in an orange vest with yellow stripes meandered over and stared at him through the square glass window in the door, making no attempt to let them in. Jessie admired Sam's restraint as the detective calmly held up his badge and ID. The portly guy reluctantly opened the door.

"You really roll out the welcome wagon," Jessie said sarcastically as they stepped inside the small entry vestibule, unable to bite her tongue.

"We don't get a lot of visitors," said the guy unapologetically, who had on a nametag that read "Morse, J." "That's why our reception area isn't brimming with hospitality items."

Morse wasn't kidding. Reception amounted to three folding chairs against one wall and a small desk with a fourth folding chair against another. The facility had two hallways extending away from the vestibule like a "V."

"We'll let it slide," Sam said. "Just tell us where we can find Jacob Greeley."

Morse sighed heavily. "Let me check our high-tech system to determine his current location," he said, walking over to the small desk.

He opened the top drawer and pulled out a clipboard with a gridded sheet of paper on top.

"He's listed as on-site here at the substation for the afternoon," Morse said, looking at his watch. "And seeing as how Greeley likes to take a late lunch and it's after 2 p.m., I'd say he's either in the lunchroom at the end of this hallway or chowing in the A/V room at the end of that hallway, even though he's not supposed to be."

"Why is that?" Sam asked.

Morse looked at him like he was idiot, detective or not. "Because consuming food or beverages is prohibited in the A/V room, what with all the audio and visual equipment and whatnot. But Greeley doesn't seem to give a damn about that kind of thing. He locks the door, so he won't get caught in the act and then shoves everything in his bag. Real tricky, that fella. Anyway, those are your options. Now, if you don't mind, I have about a dozen field assignments to parcel out for tomorrow. May I please return to my duties, or do you need something else?"

"I think we're good," Jessie said, before adding. "Aren't you curious why we're looking for Greeley?"

Morse shook his head. "Not really," he told them as he opened the door to what looked like a broom closet. "The guy's an asshole who always looks like he's trying to swallow his temper. I assume he eventually forgot to swallow it and punched the wrong guy or stabbed the wrong guy or shot the wrong guy. But if you end up arresting him, let me know so I can bump him from tomorrow's schedule."

He shut the door, leaving them alone in the hallway.

"Now that we're done with Mr. Charming, which do you want to try first?" Sam asked. "Lunchroom or A/V room?"

"Based on Morse's description of Greeley's proclivities," Jessie said, "I think we should go with A/V first. That's down the left hallway, right?"

"Yep," Sam said.

Jessie noted that he stepped in front of her, taking the lead as they moved down the hall. It occurred to her that this was their first real moment of potential danger today, and she wasn't sure whether to be flattered or offended by his insistence on putting himself in more direct harm's way. She wondered if he'd taken point of his own volition or if Ryan, still concerned about her fitness to return to duty, had privately instructed him to do so. Either way, she said nothing.

They moved down the hall quietly, both unsnapping the holsters of their weapons as precautions. When they reached the door marked "A/V," Sam looked over to make sure that she was ready. With her hand resting on her holster, she nodded that she was.

Sam knocked on the door. Because this wasn't a private residence, he didn't feel any obligation to identify himself as law enforcement. There was no answer. He reached for the door handle and turned. It gave way, and he pushed the door open, moving to the left, out of view. Jessie darted to the right, then peered in. The A/V room, apart from the equipment, including multiple computers and television screens, appeared empty.

Sam took a cautious step inside to make sure. Jessie waited by the door, covering him. As her partner peered around corners, she studied the room. There was a bank of large servers along one wall, behind a long desk with multiple computers. Overhead were CCTV monitors, all on mute, all showing different street intersections. The room was dark and musty smelling.

As Sam checked against the far wall, Jessie heard a creaking sound behind her and spun around, pulling her gun out of her holster at the same time. The door across the hall, which had a symbol on it, opened, and out walked none other than Jacob Greeley.

Jessie recognized him immediately from his file photos. Heavyset, he had a thick, dark beard and shaggy, brown hair that looked like birds had settled in it. He had patchy, pale skin and dark eyes, which were currently wide with shock, mainly because Jessie was pointing a gun at him. He put his hands, which were still dripping with water after having just washed them and given them a cursory drying, high in the air.

"What the hell?" he muttered.

"Detective, I found him," Jessie called out, before addressing Greeley. "Hi, Jacob, you're a hard guy to track down. I'm Jessie Hunt with the LAPD. Do you mind if we have a little chat?"

Greeley's eyes were still wide but after a gulp, he managed to find his voice. "Do you mind not pointing the gun at me?" he asked.

“She’ll put it down once I’ve had a chance to search you,” Sam said, rushing out of the A/V room and starting a pat down. Once he was done, he looked over at Jessie.

“All clear,” he said.

Jessie holstered her gun.

“Is anyone going to tell me what this is about?” Greeley demanded.

Just then, a door in the hallway opened and another guy in an orange vest walked past all three of them into the bathroom.

“Do you want to have that conversation here or outside?” Sam asked.

“Is my job in danger?” Greeley wanted to know.

“That depends on what you tell us,” Jessie replied.

“Outside then,” he said.

They all walked out and stood next to Sam’s car in the parking lot. Before they could ask him any questions, he launched into a tirade of his own.

“This isn’t fair, you know. I did my time. I made it through probation. I followed all the rules. I got permission to come out here. I’m just trying to get a fresh start, and now I’m getting harassed. When do I get to put my past behind me and start living my life again? When do I get to stop paying for old crimes?”

Jessie was unimpressed. “I guess that depends on how old those crimes are, Jacob.”

Greeley screwed up his face in confusion. Whether it was manufactured or genuine, she couldn’t tell. “What does *that* mean?” he demanded.

“How about you answer our questions first, Jacob?” Sam requested with a forcefulness that was absent in their other exchanges today.

“Wait, am I under arrest?” Greeley demanded. “Should I be asking for a lawyer?”

“Have you heard us arrest you, Jacob?” Sam asked. “Is that how you want this to go? Because as an ex-con, I’m guessing that being cuffed and taken down to the station in front of the co-workers that are starting to peek through the office blinds over there wouldn’t be ideal for your future job prospects. So, we’ll try this again. Are you willing to answer our questions?”

As Greeley leaned against the hood of Sam’s car, his shoulders slumped.

“This is a bunch of crap,” he muttered under his breath before adding, “what do you want to know?”

"Can you account for your whereabouts at 6:45 this morning?" Jessie pressed, not giving him a second to reconsider.

"This morning?" he said, squinting though there was no sun in his eyes. "My shift started at 7 a.m., and my first assignment this morning was up near The Magic Castle on Franklin, so I'm guessing I was driving that way around that time."

Jessie looked over at Sam. This wasn't going well. The Magic Castle was in the opposite direction from the Carrigans' house. If Greeley's claim could be verified and he actually showed up at the job site at 7 a.m., that would make it almost impossible for him to have killed Kim Carrigan. Just getting from their house to the Magic Castle would take fifteen minutes. Add in choking her, resetting the alarm, getting out of the house, in the car, *and* driving up, and it was probably closer to twenty minutes.

"Can anyone verify that you arrived at 7 a.m.?" she asked.

"Just the half dozen guys I handed out doughnuts to," he said huffily. "I was on breakfast duty today, so I had to pick them up, along with a big to-go coffee carrier. If the doughnut guy is late, people notice."

Jessie's heart sank as Sam pressed ahead. "We're going to need names and contact info for all those people," he said. "What about last Saturday night around 9 p.m.—where were you then?"

Greeley seemed to sense that the intensity of their questioning had softened and so did his corresponding diffidence. "I don't know man," he said flippantly, "that was days ago."

Sam Goodwin took a step forward and stood straight so that all six-foot-two of him hovered over Greeley, who was giving up about five inches and all other kinds of physical prominence.

"Try to remember," the detective growled quietly.

This was the first time Jessie had seen Goodwin really make use of his size for intimidation purposes and was briefly surprised that he was even capable of such a thing. Greeley didn't have the same reaction. Sheepishly, he pulled out his phone and scrolled through it. After a few seconds, he smiled.

"I remember now," he said. "I was watching the Dodgers game against the Mets at a bar over on Highland. I was psyched because I had a bet on the Dodgers to lose, which they did. I made $150."

"Are you sure it's such a good idea for you to be hanging out in bars, what with your criminal history?" Jessie asked.

It was a cheap shot, and she knew it, but she was frustrated. Greeley looked like he wanted to offer a comeback but wisely held his tongue.

"We'll need the name of the bar and any receipts that prove you were there," Sam told him, quickly short-circuiting any further conflict as Jessie stepped off to the side.

"Yeah, sure, I can send all that to you guys now, same with the contact info," Greeley said, sensing that he was almost off the hook. "What's this all about anyway?"

"You don't worry yourself about that," Sam said, then joined Jessie while they waited for Greeley to collect the necessary information. "Thoughts?"

"Same as you're probably having," she said. "All that hard work down the drain. Our best lead a dead end. This guy's not our killer. He's just a jerk and abuser who's new to town."

"Maybe we missed something with one of the other people on the list," Sam offered hopefully. "We can go back through them again to see if we have better luck the second time around."

"Maybe," Jessie agreed unconvincingly.

Sam returned his attention to Greeley while she stared up at the sky, blue and cloudless, hoping it might offer some clue going forward. But it just mocked her, offering another perfect Southern California afternoon but no help in finding their killer.

Suddenly, a thought popped into her head, and she realized that maybe sunny SoCal hadn't failed her after all.

"Let's wrap this up," she called out to Sam, "I've got an idea."

CHAPTER TWELVE

Jessie didn't say anything until they were back at the station.

That was partly because she wanted to formally eliminate Jacob Greeley as a suspect first. But there was another reason too. She was doubting herself.

Her idea was dependent on her recall from an interview they'd done earlier, and she wasn't sure if that recall could be trusted. She wanted to review her notes to make sure her memory was accurate.

She thought that when they'd talked to Sean Hill, he'd said that they'd only moved into their huge, Tudor mansion six months ago. But she worried that she was getting the timing confused with Jacob Greeley, who'd supposedly come to L.A. just four months ago.

All the dates were becoming muddled in her head. Whether that was concussion-related or just due to the sheer volume of dates being thrown her way, she wanted to make sure she had her ducks in a row before presenting her idea to Sam.

But sure enough, according to her notes, Hill had said they'd moved to Los Angeles six months ago. That meant she could proceed with pursuing her theory. Sam was getting a snack in the break room, but not wanting to waste time and annoyed at her own self-doubt, she got up from her desk to go see Jamil and Beth.

She was just heading down the hall when Detectives Karen Bray and Susannah Valentine arrived from the opposite direction. They were both smiling broadly. In front of Bray, cuffed and morose-looking, was a swarthy-looking guy that Jessie assumed to be the fugitive they'd been searching homeless shelters for.

"You two look happy," she noted.

"Successful morning," Karen said happily before turning to her partner. "I can take him to booking if you like."

"Thanks," Susannah said.

"Why aren't you booking him too?" Jessie asked.

"Oh, when we caught him, I ended up having to tackle him. We rolled around a bit, and he clearly hadn't bathed in a while. So, I was going to go wash up really quick. Maybe change into something less offensive to the nostrils."

"But do any of your extra clothes include skin-tight pants and too-small sweaters?" Jessie teased.

Susannah Valentine liked to make a habit of wearing outfits that showed off her impressive curves. There was a time when it had annoyed Jessie, but during a spirited heart to heart while working a case together a few weeks back, Susannah had revealed to her that she intentionally chose her exhibitionist attire as a reaction to an assault she'd suffered when she was younger. It was her way of saying "screw you" to a world that wanted her to feel ashamed of herself. Ever since then, Jessie's attitude had changed, but that didn't stop her from tossing the occasion playful barb the detective's way. Susannah gave her a mock-offended frown.

"As a matter of fact, they do," she retorted playfully. "You don't think my extra outfits would ever just include sweats, do you?"

"No, I most certainly do not," Jessie said truthfully.

"How's it going for you?"

"Not great so far," Jessie admitted, "but hopefully looking up. I may have just stumbled on a new lead."

"I wasn't just talking about the case, Jessie," Susannah said, tapping her skull.

Susannah Valentine had seen some of the side effects of Jessie's concussion, including some forgetfulness and confusion, when they worked their case together, though she had kept it to herself.

"I know you weren't," Jessie said. "But the answer is the same: things are hopefully looking up."

Susannah held up her hands to indicate that she was backing off. "Okay," she said. "Let me know if that changes."

"I will," Jessie promised before continuing down the hallway to the research office. To her surprise, the door was closed. She pushed it open to find the room was far darker than usual. Beth was nowhere in sight, but Jamil was at a computer terminal, his back to her, typing away furiously. She was about to call out to him when she heard an unsubtle cough to her right and looked over. Beth was standing there, holding two cups of coffee.

"I was just coming to ask you guys a question," Jessie told her, "but I wasn't sure it was cool to go in. It looks like Jamil's turned the place into some kind of secret lair or something."

"Oh yeah," Beth said, turning pink, "he's kind of going through a phase, I guess."

"I've been meaning to ask you about that," Jessie started to ask, but seeing Beth shift uncomfortably from foot to foot, she decided now might not be the time to broach what was clearly an uncomfortable subject for the young woman, "but it can wait. I have something more pressing for you."

"What's that?" Beth asked, seemingly relieved.

"Can you check on when Gregory and Kim Carrigan bought their house?"

"Sure," Beth said. "If you get the door for me, it'll just take a sec."

"You sure I'm allowed to come in?" Jessie half-joked as she opened the door.

Beth laughed uncomfortably but didn't say anything as she stepped inside and walked over to her computer. She handed Jamil a coffee, put hers down on her desk, and began typing. Less than a minute later, she grabbed a page off the printer.

"The Carrigans bought their place eight months ago," she said.

Jessie felt a tingle at the base of her skull. She didn't want to get over-excited, but it looked like they had a new lead to pursue.

"What was the name of their real estate agent?" she asked.

Beth scanned the page.

"Vera Steele," she said. "You think she had something to do with this?"

"I don't know about that," Jessie said. "But I think that both victims buying their houses in the last few months feels more than just coincidental, and I'm betting that Vera is just the person we need to talk to to get to the bottom of all this."

Just then, Sam Goodwin walked in. His mouth was full, and he was holding a bag of pistachios. Both women stared at him.

"What did I miss?" he asked.

"I'll explain in the car," Jessie said.

CHAPTER THIRTEEN

It was mid-afternoon when they pulled up in front of Vera Steele's realty office.

Jessie was relieved to see the light on. She'd called ahead to make sure the woman would be there and was assured she would be, but one could never be sure. Maybe there was an emergency open house or something.

They were approaching the door of the office, located in a strip center on a chichi stretch of Larchmont Boulevard that also housed an artisanal cheese shop and baby clothing boutique, when it was opened by Steele herself.

"Please come in," she said excitedly, waving them through the door and motioning for them to take seats in the flamboyant, gold-painted, high-backed, velvet-cushioned chairs along the side wall. On a small table between the chairs was a sampling of cheeses, likely from the shop next door, and some kind of sparkling beverage.

"Don't worry, it's just cider," Vera said, sitting in an equally plush, but slightly smaller chair across from them. "I know you're on duty."

Much like her chair, Vera Steele was quite something. She looked to be about forty, but her makeup was styled like that of someone two decades older. She wore a magenta business bodycon sheath dress with a neck bow knot. Her black hair was tied in an elaborate bun that extended three inches above her head. And she wore five-inch heels that made Jessie's feet ache just looking at them. Even with the shoes and the hair, she still only came up to Jessie's nose, which meant that without them, she probably topped out at under five feet tall.

"Thanks for making the time," Jessie said. "We promise not to take up too much of it."

"Are you kidding?" Vera asked. "It's not every day that I get a call from Jessie Hunt asking for my help. I had a first-time meeting scheduled with a couple, and I immediately postponed it. No potential commission is better than this."

Jessie was willing to put up with the woman's celebrity fixation for two reasons. First, as the Carrigans' real estate agent, she really could have valuable information. And second, they had vetted her on the way over. Steele had been out of town at a conference from Friday until this morning, so she could be eliminated as a suspect. They didn't have to worry that they were sharing details with the killer.

"Well, I'm afraid this may not be as exciting as you might hope," Jessie told her. "We're really just looking for someone to guide us through the ins and outs of the Hancock Park real estate market players. We'll need some names associated with a few sales. But more important than any information you give us, what we're counting on most from you, Vera—may I call you Vera?"

"Of course!" Vera said gleefully.

Jessie felt Sam Goodwin flinch beside her but pretended not to notice.

"What we need most from you, Vera, is discretion," Jessie said, her tone low and confiding. "This involves a case that we're pursuing, and we need to know that what we discuss with you won't end up on the evening news. For the purposes of our inquiry, you're almost an ad hoc investigator, which essentially requires you to swear confidentiality going forward."

"This is about Kim Carrigan, isn't it?" Vera whispered breathlessly, barely able to contain herself.

Jessie looked around the office, as if she was checking to see if there was anyone else around. Of course, she'd already done that the moment she'd entered the place and knew that, besides Vera, it was empty.

"Vera, before I share any further details, can the LAPD count on your total discretion in this matter? The chief of police won't authorize me to coordinate with civilians who are unwilling to agree to these terms."

"Of course, of course," Vera said impatiently. "You can count on me. Lips sealed!"

Jessie doubted that the realtor's promise would last the rest of the week, but she suspected that it would at least keep her from going to the press for a day, which was all she could realistically hope for.

"In that case, yes, we are investigating the Carrigan death," she said. "We know you were the agent representing the seller. What we need from you is a comprehensive list of everyone associated with that sale: the sellers, the Carrigans' realtor, the loan officers, title company reps, escrow reps, home inspector, any lien holders, basically anyone associated with the sale who could have had access to the home at any point."

For the first time since their arrival, Vera's smile faded.

"That could be a long list," she said.

"That's why we need you," Sam added. "We need the people who would have actually had reason to be on the premises, maybe someone who might have access to the keys at or before closing, maybe even access to home security information. For example, you know who just answered phone calls for the home inspector and who actually came out to the house, that kind of thing. We need the list narrowed down."

"Okay, I can do that," Vera said, warming to the idea that only she had the skill set to make this happen.

"We're also going to ask for that information for a few other sales which you may not have been involved with, just for comparison's sake," Jessie added, handing over several additional addresses as if they were just Lucky Strike extras. "Do you think you can provide details on those, even if you weren't part of those transactions, or is that too much for you?"

"Not a problem," Vera said. "Even if I wasn't part of the sale, I'll likely know everyone involved. I've been working this market for a decade, Jessie. If I don't know someone, they're not worth knowing."

"I'll bet," Jessie said, popping a piece of cheese in her mouth. "This is delicious by the way."

The truth was that they only needed the information from one other recent home purchase—the Hills', but they gave Vera two more sales in addition to that to throw her off the scent. It was one thing to let her blab a little to friends about her tangential involvement in the Carrigan case, but if she put together that Eleanor Hill's death might somehow be connected and shared that with the press, that was a different matter.

So far, all the news today had been about Gregory Carrigan's devastating personal loss. But if word got out that his wife's death was part of a deadly pattern, they'd have a media firestorm on their hands well beyond what they were already dealing with.

"Let me go to the back office," Vera said. "I'll pull up these other sales and see what dots I can connect."

She darted off with unexpected speed. Once she was gone, Jessie turned to Sam. She felt guilty about the request she was about to make but did it anyway.

"Do you think you could call Sean Hill?" she asked.

"Sure," he said, munching on a piece of cheese of his own. "Why?"

“We promised that we’d let him know if we had any updates,” she reminded him. “Ever since Cheryl Gallagher definitively confirmed that both Ellie and Kim Carrigan had glove marks on their skin, we’ve been treating these deaths as connected, committed by the same killer. He deserves to know, and not from some news report where a chatty real estate agent is interviewed because she connected one dot too many. And to be honest, that’s just not a conversation I’m up for right now.”

“I get it,” Sam said, standing up. “I’ll go outside and call him right now.”

“Thanks,” she said. “Sorry to make you do the dirty work.”

“Don’t worry about it,” he replied. “I just hope that when it comes to this case, that’s the last call we have to make like this.”

He stepped outside, leaving Jessie alone in the now silent office, seated in her gaudy chair, next to the tray of cheese and the flutes of sparkling cider, whose bubbles were slowly petering out.

She admired Sam’s optimism and hoped that his wish—that his call to Sean Hill would be the last one they’d have to make to the loved one of a dead victim—would come true. But she knew better than to count on hope.

She’d seen too much to bet on wishes. Whoever had attempted to kill Eleanor Hill and succeeded in murdering Kim Carrigan had a taste for it now. And they were unlikely to just quit. They were probably out there right now, plotting their next attack. And unless she found a way to stop them, another call like the one Sam was making right now was inevitable, and probably very soon.

That couldn’t happen. Ryan had assigned this case specifically to them for a reason. Lives were at stake. Chief Decker’s future was potentially at stake too. They needed to come through.

***

An hour later, Jessie sat on the edge of her chair and waited, trying not to look as anxious as she felt.

She and Sam had returned to Central Station with the thumb drive full of data that Vera Steele had provided and promptly handed it over to Jamil and Beth. Jessie had learned long ago that, while she could pore over the information provided and eventually, probably draw the right conclusions from it, Jamil Winslow had the ability to do the same thing faster and with more accuracy.

That's why she and Sam had been sitting quietly for the last twenty minutes as the two researchers typed away, occasionally talking to each other in a shorthand she didn't understand. Eventually, she realized that she'd been clenching her jaw for so long that it had started to ache, and she stood up to get some coffee. Sam did the same.

"We'll be right back."

Beth gave a half-hearted wave of acknowledgement. Jamil didn't even offer that. When they stepped outside, Sam pulled the door closed.

"Is this typical for them?" he asked. "I don't know how long to expect this to take."

"Me either," Jessie conceded. "It's not searching an entire database of felons, so I would have thought it wouldn't be *that* complicated, but then again, they don't typically deal in real estate matters. It's a whole separate set of parameters. It may just be taking longer to set up the system that they want to use. Regardless, I would never bet against Jamil Winslow."

"I keep hearing that," Sam said as they started down the hall, "And my limited experience with him seems to back it up, but he seems a little off his game today."

Jessie nodded reluctantly. Sam had noted the same thing earlier.

"Yeah," she said. "I don't know what's up with him. He seems to be running a little ragged. Maybe he just a had bad night of sleep."

"You could check with Beth," Sam suggested.

"I could," Jessie acknowledged, "but I don't want to press her. It's not really her responsibility to answer for him. After all, he's technically her boss, not the other way around."

Sam seemed satisfied enough with that answer and dropped the issue as they headed toward the break room. Jessie was glad he didn't push because if she was honest, she was more worried than she let on. Ever since she had first met him, Jamil was most clearly defined by one trait: his eagerness and enthusiasm to solve the puzzles he was given. But lately, he didn't seem to take any joy in his work. He was hardly recognizable.

They were almost to the end of the hall when they heard Beth's voice.

"Come back!" she shouted. "He's cracked it!"

They sprinted back down the hall and into the research office, where Jamil had pushed his chair back away from his monitor. Normally, he would have projected his findings onto the wall so that they were easier to read, but he made no attempt to do that now, so Jessie and Sam crowded around his screen.

"You want to tell us what we're looking at, Jamil?" Jessie asked.

Jamil sighed wearily, then launched into an explanation, "Out of the twenty-five people who touched the Carrigan home purchase file and the thirty-four who were involved in the Hill purchase file, there was an overlap of nine people who dealt with both purchases," he said, his voice never changing from a flat monotone. "But after additional review, only three of those people would have ever had cause to actually be on the physical property of either home at any point, and only one person would have cause to be at both homes. That person was the loan officer for both the Carrigans and for the firm that handled the purchase for the Hills. His name is Gene Coleman. He works for WMC, or Wilshire Mortgage Corporation."

"That's great," Sam said. "Any chance you checked to see if Coleman has a record?"

Jamil nodded unenthusiastically in Beth's direction.

"Right, I did," Beth volunteered. "Other than a DWI nineteen years ago when he was twenty-six, the guy is clean. No record of violence. No stalking. No restraining orders."

"Good to know," Jessie said. "Of course, that doesn't mean it's not him. It could just mean he's never been caught."

"Agreed," Sam said. "Until we get a chance to evaluate him up close and personal, we shouldn't jump to any conclusions."

"Well," Jessie said, pointing at the screen, which had all of Coleman's contact information, "there's no time like the present."

They started for the door, but before they left Jessie turned around.

"Thanks guys," she said to Jamil and Beth. "That was great work."

Beth smiled broadly at her. Jamil didn't even look up.

CHAPTER FOURTEEN

Hannah knew it was a bad idea.

As she sat on a bench in the small West Los Angeles parkette, staring at the house directly across the street, ignoring the sound of the squealing toddler who was being pushed on the swing a few feet behind her, she asked herself for the half dozenth time whether she should leave.

She looked at the time on her phone. It was 5:04, exactly one minute later than the last time she'd looked. Right now, she should be at home, relaxing on the couch, taking advantage of the fact that Kat had let her off work early and neither Jessie nor Ryan would be at the house for a few more hours. She could kick back and chill, choose whatever show she wanted to watch, and even put her bare feet on the coffee table.

When she and Kat had learned from Rhona Feller at 4 p.m. that afternoon that her husband Lyman would be taking her to the symphony that evening, it meant that he would definitively *not* be cheating on her, at least not that night. It also meant that they wouldn't have to follow him once he got home. Kat generously offered to tail him to his house and let Hannah cut out early.

So, why had she, instead of going straight home, walked to a local coffeehouse, and started poring over every detail she could find about Sasha Wexler, the eighteen-year-old who had gone missing the previous night? Why had she read every news article she could locate? Why had she scoured the web for any background information she could glean. Why had she gone through every social media post from Sasha that wasn't private?

She knew the answer, of course. It was because Sasha reminded her of herself, or at least of the version of herself she could have become if she'd continued to "lose" herself, before finding a path to survive the madness of this world.

But that was just projection. There was no evidence that Sasha had "lost" herself other than the mournful, lost look in her eyes in all her photos and the fact that she was quite literally missing.

Sasha could be perfectly happy right now. Just because her phone was found in a trash can on a residential street didn't mean she'd met with some horrific end. At this very moment, she could be on a bender at a friend's house or at Disneyland or at the beach or partying at a club in Cabo San Lucas. All of that was possible, but Hannah's personal experience told her that it wasn't the most likely scenario.

Which was why she was sitting in the parkette across the street from the house, debating what to do next. She'd taken a rideshare over here after reading Sasha's posts. Many of them were standard teenage fare, the sort of thing any eighteen-year-old girl who hadn't seen her parents slaughtered or gotten a troubling thrill from shooting an elderly serial killer might write.

Others were dark and disturbing, discussing experiences with drugs and sex that sounded unsatisfying at best, and sometimes closer to soul-deadening. Her relationship to her parents seemed to be largely non-existent. Her circle of friends had shrunk dramatically over the course of her senior year. If she was to be believed, she barely managed to graduate. To top it all off, just yesterday, in the hours before she went missing, her boyfriend broke up with her.

That boyfriend, whose name was Keanu Mendoza, lived in the house across the street from where Hannah currently sat. And whether or not to talk to him was the internal debate that had been consuming her for the last several minutes, as the toddler on the swing squealed even louder in the background behind her.

Sasha's last post had come across as extremely bitter about Keanu dumping her. Worse, she sounded broken. Hannah wasn't the only one who thought so. So had the police, who, according to news reports, had already interviewed him both at his house and at the police station. Interestingly, she couldn't find any law enforcement representative who referred to him at any point as a "person of interest."

That led her to believe that they had moved away from him as a suspect, which meant that he ought to be an ideal person for her to talk to. He should have information to share but theoretically, not be a threat to her safety. That was important, because if Jessie and Ryan found out about this freelance investigation idea of hers, she could at least legitimately claim that she had made sure not to put herself in harm's way, something she had promised them she would no longer do.

So, now she just had to decide if she was going to really do this. Was she going to insert herself into a police investigation of a missing teenage girl she didn't know, when she had no inside information, no personal stake in the outcome, and no justification to get involved other than boredom with her day job and a tangential sense of connection to the girl in question? She realized that the question had already been answered for her by the fact that, even without her mind ever officially making a choice, her feet apparently had.

She realized this because those feet were currently walking across the street, stepping up onto the curb, and walking along the path toward Keanu Mendoza's front door. Her feet then made the decision to stop, and—even as her heart felt like it might pound right through her chest and fall out on the ground in front of her—her right hand made the choice to ball itself in a fist and knock on the front door. And when the door opened, revealing a tired-looking woman in her early forties who was clearly Keanu's mom, her voice, despite almost giving out on her, made the decision to speak.

"Hi," she said, surprised at how her tone was suddenly younger and sadder than usual, "my name's Hannah Dorsey."

"I'm sorry, Hannah," the woman said, starting to close the door. "We've had a long day, and whatever it is, we're really not interested."

"Please," Hannah pleaded, hearing her voice crack slightly, "Just hear me out. I was friends with Sasha, and I just finished being questioned by the cops. They were pretty intense with me. Then, when they were done, they just kind of tossed me away like I was trash they weren't interested in anymore. Right now, I feel kind of raw and helpless and when I talked to my folks, they—no offense—but they didn't get it at all. I don't know Keanu, but I heard they questioned him in a really … aggressive way too. I just—I was hoping that I could talk to someone who'd been through the same thing as me, that maybe it would help calm my nerves a little bit. I took a half-hour rideshare to get here. I know I shouldn't have just shown up but—you know what? This is stupid. Never mind. I'm sorry. I should go. I didn't mean to bother you. Have a good night."

She turned and started to head back down the path. She'd made it five steps when Keanu's mom stopped her.

"Hold on," she called out. "Give me a minute. Let me see if he's up to talking."

***

Three minutes later, Mrs. Mendoza ("call me Carolyn, please") knocked on Keanu's second-floor door. Hannah stood politely behind her.

She had already called up to tell him the situation and after chastising him in a hushed whisper, got his consent to bring Hannah up.

"It's unlocked!" he shouted from inside.

"Go on in," Carolyn Mendoza said with a sweet smile.

"Thank you," Hannah said, opening the door slowly and cautiously stepping inside.

It took her eyes a second to adjust. The overhead light was off, and the room was dimly lit with the kind of string lights people usually hang in their backyards. The walls were covered with posters of 1990s Britpop bands like Oasis, Blur, Elastica, and Suede, for whom Keanu was apparently singlehandedly trying to spearhead a revival from the privacy of his bedroom.

The man of the hour was not on his bed but rather sitting at his desk chair, hunched over, with his chin in his hands. He was staring at her with well-justified suspicion. His dark eyes had shadows under them that were visible even in this low light. His hair was black, just like in the senior year photo she'd reviewed earlier, but right now it was spiky, shooting in all directions, like he'd had a run-in with a downed powerline. He wore ripped jeans and a flannel shirt that appeared to be misbuttoned.

"Who are you?" he asked, moving his hands away from his face and sitting up straight. "Sasha never mentioned anyone named Hannah to me."

"I met her through temple," she said, recalling how Sasha had complained in one of her posts that Keanu hadn't been very supportive when she expressed interest in exploring the Jewish faith she'd lost touch with in the last few years. It was unlikely that he'd know anyone she'd met from that part of her life. "I don't remember ever seeing you there."

"Oh, I wasn't really involved in that part of her life very much," he admitted. "She told me a lot of stories about all the fun she had at some Jewish summer camp she went to near Durango, Colorado, as a kid, but as far as more recent stuff, she didn't share it with me."

"Why not?" Hannah asked, keeping the pressure on so that he'd forget that he'd been asking about how she knew Sasha.

"It just wasn't our thing, I guess," he said awkwardly before abruptly changing the subject, "so, the cops were rough with you, huh? What did they do?"

"They locked me in a room and cuffed one of my wrists to a metal table that was bolted to the floor," Hannah said as she sat down on the corner of his bed, recalling what she'd seen done with some of the people questioned at Central Station, before she decided to embellish the already imaginary story a little more. "They said that they had GPS data that showed us together last week, and they demanded a detailed rundown of what we were doing and what we discussed. They said that any false statement I made could be considered a crime, and since I'm eighteen, I could be charged as an adult and sent to prison if convicted. They threatened to throw me into county lockup downtown at Twin Towers for the night if I didn't cooperate. What about you?"

Keanu's eyes had gotten wider as she went on, which was her goal. She hoped that by making her "interrogation" sound extra-intense, he wouldn't be so precious about guarding his experience.

"I thought I had it bad," he said, "but I guess it could have been worse. They pressed me pretty hard at first about her post saying I broke up with her. I told them that it wasn't true, that she was the one who dumped me. They didn't believe me, no matter how many times I told the story."

"What did you tell them?" Hannah asked. This was the first she'd heard about Sasha ending the relationship.

"Just that she asked me to meet her at Industrial Coffee on Ocean Park Boulevard at 9 p.m.," he explained. "It's this place where we would always hang out. She was waiting for me when I got there. I had only just sat down when she started crying. I could barely understand her at first, and she had to repeat herself for me to understand that she was saying that she had to end things."

"Did she say why?"

"No," he said. "It was totally out of the blue. I had no idea what I did wrong or if it even had anything to do with me. She didn't give me any explanation. Then she left, and a few hours later, she posted that I'd dumped her. I was already crushed. Add total confusion to it. I tried to reach out to her, but she didn't answer my texts, and all my calls went straight to voicemail. Then the cops showed up the next morning to question me."

"First here at the house and then later at the station, right?"

"Yeah," he said. "The first time was mostly polite, but the second time, at the station, was scary. Like I said, they kept making me repeat my story, like they were hoping I'd slip up somehow. I even gave them my phone to show them my texts and calls to her. After that, they let up a little, but they still made me feel like a criminal. And now, none of my friends will return my texts. It's like I'm some kind of pariah. The only people who want to talk to me now are those frickin' vultures from the TV stations, and you, of course. I guess the only good thing is that those texts proved to the cops I was telling the truth."

Hannah felt a flicker of guilt pass through her, knowing that she was not that much different than the vultures he was describing, even if her motives were more sincere. In that moment, she decided that she couldn't continue with the lie any longer. She hadn't planned on it until this very moment, but she was going to come (mostly) clean.

"Those texts aren't why they let up on you, Keanu," Hannah said.

He looked at her, confused. "What do you mean?"

"When you gave them your phone, they probably asked you something about letting them use it to verify your story more generally. Do you recall anything like that?"

"Not really," he said. "It's all kind of a blur right now. I guess they could have."

"Well, whether you gave formal consent for them to search your phone or whether they got a warrant from a judge while they were holding you at the station, they likely searched the GPS data from your phone and found where you were all of last night. I'm guessing you came straight home after Sasha dumped you and stayed here until the police showed up in the morning, and that you had your phone with you the entire time?"

"Yeah," he said, now even more confused looking than before. "Why does that matter? Did they do that to you too?"

"No, they didn't," she said, standing up and taking a cautious step toward him. "Listen, Keanu, the police checked your location data and found that you were home all last night, meaning you were home during the time that Sasha went missing. That's your alibi, so they let you go. They weren't obligated to tell you any of that or apologize to you for how they treated you, so they just sent you on your way, feeling crappy and ashamed and angry. It's upsetting but not all that unusual."

"How do you know all this?" he asked, standing up from his desk chair, his tone now guarded again.

Hannah hadn't realized how tall he was until now. She was five-foot-nine, and he towered over her.

"Because I haven't been completely honest with you," she said, taking a small step back in case he reacted badly to what she said next. "I am eighteen, and just like you, I just graduated from high school, but I don't really know Sasha. I'm actually an assistant private investigator looking into her disappearance. I work for a detective named Katherine Gentry. I'm sorry that I wasn't up front with you, but I knew you wouldn't talk to me if I told you the real reason I was here."

"I can't believe this," Keanu said, slumping back down into his chair. "I can't believe I trusted you and opened up to you, and it was all a lie."

"That's not true," Hannah insisted. "I did lie, yes, but I'm not here for some slimy reason. I'm here to get information that uncovers what happened to Sasha, and you helped with that. I didn't know that she broke up with you. Now I do. For some reason, she did that—despite seemingly being devastated about it—and then posted that you dumped her, all just before she disappeared. That has to be significant."

"How?" Keanu asked, his curiosity outweighing his anger with her.

"I don't know yet," Hannah conceded. "I'm trying to piece together the puzzle of what happened to her. But it's hard when I don't have all the pieces. Just know that the piece you gave me is an important one."

"I just want her to be okay," he said forlornly.

"I know. I'm going to do everything I can to make that happen. The police do a good job, but sometimes they start with a conclusion in mind and put everything they find into that box. I start with an empty box and fill it as I go along."

Keanu nodded. He looked spent. She decided to let him get some rest, but before she left, she couldn't help but offer a little advice.

"Hey," she said, "I'm sorry for being deceptive, but remember, I'm not the only one who's going to do that. You got lucky with me. I'm one of the good guys. Don't assume anyone else is. You said people from the news are calling you?"

He nodded heavily.

"Don't talk to any of them," she warned.

"Why not?"

"At some point, they might be helpful in resuscitating your public image or to assist in a search," she told him, "but right now, with Sasha's situation unknown, their natural inclination is going to be to look for someone to blame. You're an obvious target. Don't do any interviews. It's too easy to say the wrong thing and end up getting demonized. Lie low."

"Okay," he said.

"Same thing with your friends," she warned. "It might actually be a good thing that they're not getting back to your texts. If someone suddenly reaches out, wanting to be your sounding board, be suspicious. They may be looking for a quick payday, hoping to pass along some juicy quotes to a tabloid. If you need to talk to someone, you've got your parents. Lean on them. Your mom seems like a real sweetheart. If things get hairy, secure a lawyer. And you can always call me, whether you have information or just need to talk, okay? I'll give you my number."

Keanu nodded, looking overwhelmed.

"And one more thing," she instructed, "get some sleep. You're going to need it."

CHAPTER FIFTEEN

They were down to their last strike.

Jessie hoped they'd have more success with their last swing than with their first two.

When she and Sam had arrived at the offices of Wilshire Mortgage Corporation, Gene Coleman had already left for the day. So, they tried his house next. When they knocked on his door, it was answered by a very blonde, very pregnant woman in her mid-thirties who turned out to be Gene's wife, Maisy.

"I'm afraid Gene's not home right now," she told them after they introduced themselves. "Maybe you can speak to him at the office."

"We just came from there," Jessie said. "They said he'd likely be home by now."

"I don't know what to tell you," Maisy said, shrugging disinterestedly. "He's out and I have to finish prepping dinner for the other kids."

Sam broke out his warmest, most empathetic smile. "Here's the thing, Mrs. Coleman—we're investigating a home inspector who may have falsified some reports," he lied, his voice convincingly buttery. "We need to talk to everybody who has crossed paths with this guy in the last six months. It's dry stuff, and your husband is the last person on our list. If we can knock out our interview with him today, we can file our report before the end of business tonight and maybe get home to our families in time to put our own kids to bed. That would be the first time for me on a weeknight this month. If you could tell us where to find Gene, we could ask him our questions, which will take all of three minutes, be on our way, and everyone's evening will be a little better. What do you say?"

Maisy, faced with Sam Goodwin's friendly persistence and the sound of whining children in the background, relented. "He usually stops off for a beer on the way home at a bar called The Hound's Tooth. It's on Cahuenga. He'll typically hang out there for about a half hour before heading home. My guess is that if you leave right now, you can catch him. Or I could just call him and tell him to stay put or come home now."

"That's okay," Jessie said quickly. "We find that if folks know that the police want to interview them, even for something as simple as this, they get nervous, and everything flies out of their head. We'd rather just pop in, get his thoughts in the moment, and be on our way. No need to call him."

"Fine by me," Maisy said impatiently. "Can I go now?"

She barely waited for them to say yes before closing the door. Their exchange may have been terse, but it at least gave Jessie confidence that Maisy had no interest in warning her husband about cops planning to call on him.

That swing and miss had led to their current situation, which involved standing cluelessly in the entrance of The Hound's Tooth, trying to adjust to the dramatic shift in light from the sunny early evening they'd just left outside to the intentional gloominess of the bar. The place was lit almost exclusively by neon beer signs, which adorned the walls like paintings in an art gallery.

As they approached the bar, Jessie noted that The Hound's Tooth wasn't exactly hopping. She counted a grand total of five patrons, which was pretty pathetic considering that it was almost 6 p.m., prime post-work drinking time. In fact, there didn't even seem to be a bartender on duty.

"Do you see Coleman?" she asked Sam.

"It's hard to make anyone out in this giant crowd," he said sarcastically, "but no, I don't."

Jessie noticed an older, leathery guy with a shock of white hair, probably in his sixties, sitting alone in a booth in a corner, nursing a whiskey, and eyeing her and Sam. She headed his way. If anyone fit the profile of a regular in this joint, it was him. She hoped he could answer some questions.

"How's it going?" she asked.

"It's a Tuesday in June and I'm still alive," he answered, his voice resembling human sandpaper, "so I can't complain. You?"

"I'd be better if I knew who to ask for a drink?" she replied.

"Raylene's bartending tonight," he said. "She's on her break right now. Regulars can sometimes grab a beer straight from the tap and leave their money on the bar, but I don't recommend that for you. Raylene's gotta vet you first. You'll just have to wait."

"Okay," Jessie said. "In the meantime, my buddy and I are looking for a guy we heard likes to hang out here—Gene Coleman. You know him?"

The old guy smiled, revealing that he'd lost more than a few teeth somewhere along his journey through life. "Sure, I know Gene."

"Did we miss him?" Sam asked.

"Nah," the old guy said, "he just made a visit to the lavatory. I'm sure he'll be out soon. That's his beer on the bar there."

Jessie glanced over and saw the beer, half empty, resting on the bar. Then she looked at Sam.

"You care to wait?" she asked.

"I'd just as soon expedite the process," he said.

"Me too," she agreed.

If Gene Coleman was their killer, she didn't want to chance him getting tipped off to their presence and sneaking out a window.

"Thanks for the information," she said to the old guy as she started toward the back hallway with the restrooms.

"No problem, Jessie," the man said.

Jessie turned around, startled at hearing her name.

"What?" the man said with a half-toothed smile. "You don't think drunks watch the news too? I know a famous investigator lady when I see one. Don't worry, your secret is safe with me."

"Thanks," Jessie said before returning her attention to the back of the bar. Sam joined her as they headed down the hall, which was even more dimly lit than the main bar. As they walked, he leaned over close to her ear.

"Does it ever get old being a celebrity profiler?" he muttered. "Everybody thinking they know you personally because they've seen you on TV?"

"Sometimes," Jessie conceded. "It can be a problem if the wrong person recognizes me. But sometimes it opens doors too. There are folks who would never talk to me if they didn't know who I was. If it helps solve a single murder, then it's a small price to pay."

Sam was about to respond when they both heard a sound that made them freeze. It was hard to identify. To Jessie, it was clearly human, but she couldn't place it. She looked over at Sam, who appeared equally perplexed.

They moved to the end of the hall, where they found three doors. One was to the manager's office. The other two were for gender neutral bathrooms. The sound was coming from one of them. Jessie wasn't sure, but it almost sounded like muffled crying, as if someone had been gagged and was trying to call out for help through the material blocking their throat. She was about to ask Sam if he thought the same thing when she distinctly heard something else.

A male voice grunted the word "hush!"

CHAPTER SIXTEEN

Jessie's hand went to her weapon.

She saw Sam's do the same and knew that they were on the same page.

It seemed unbelievable that Coleman would attack someone in a public place, especially one that he frequented, where people knew his name and face, but it wouldn't be the first time someone's urges overwhelmed their judgment.

"I'll open the door," Sam whispered, "then you go in. I'll be right behind you."

Jessie nodded, unholstering her gun as she forced any thoughts about concussion-inducing confrontations out of her mind. She couldn't think that way if she was going to be worth a damn in a moment like this.

Sam quickly mouthed a countdown from three to one, then turned the door handle. It was locked. He took a step back, then launched forward and kicked it, sending the thing flying open. Jessie rushed in with her weapon ready.

There was no one at the sink or the urinal, but she could see two sets of legs in the one bathroom stall. One person was wearing men's loafers. The other had on women's block-heeled ankle boots.

"Open the door!" she shouted, moving toward the door even as she motioned for Sam to climb onto the urinal where he could look down into stall from above.

"What the hell?" shouted a male voice.

Jessie couldn't tell if he was stalling or genuinely confused, and she didn't care. She rapped on the metal stall door with her free hand.

"This is the LAPD," she barked. "Open the stall door and come out with your hands up right now. Don't make any sudden movements."

Sam had now hopped up onto the top of the urinal and was leaning over to peek into the stall. He peered down, and his eyes opened wide. He turned to Jessie and was about to say something when the door opened.

Standing before Jessie was Gene Coleman, easily recognizable from his various photos. He had thinning, brown hair, brown eyes, pale skin that suggested he spent most of his time indoors, and a slight paunch that had yet to get out of control, but none of that was what grabbed Jessie's attention. Unlike in all the pictures of him that she'd seen so far, right now his pants were down around his knees, and his boxer shorts, which had clearly been pulled up in a hurry, were not fully covering everything that they normally would.

In front of him was a woman in her late thirties with long, auburn-gray hair, currently in disarray, and green eyes that Jessie suspected had broken many hearts over the years. She looked a little like Bonnie Raitt in her early 1990s heyday.

It was immediately clear that the muffled crying sound they'd heard earlier had come from her. But based on her flushed cheeks and her annoyed expression, Jessie doubted that it was a result of any distress. The button and zipper of the woman's jeans were undone, and her shirt was untucked and unbuttoned, revealing her bra. On the floor beside the toilet was an open condom wrapper.

"Raylene, I presume?" Jessie asked, taking a not-so-wild guess.

"Yeah," the bartender said huffily. "You want to tell me what in damnation has the police breaking down bathroom doors in a sleepy little bar and interrupting the activities of two consenting adults?"

Sam hopped down off the urinal and joined Jessie. "You want to take this, or should I?" he asked.

"I've got it," Jessie said, not in the mood to placate either of the people in front of her. "Here's what I'm willing to tell you: first of all, you need to zip up your jeans and button your top. Second, Gene over there needs get all his … loose ends tied up. This isn't a peep show, man. Cover up. Third, your break is over, Raylene. Go back out to the bar. We'll let you know who you can contact about the damage to your door. That's all you're getting in the way of answers right now."

"But that's not good en—" she started to object.

"Gene," Jessie interrupted, sensing that the bartender wasn't fully aware of her lover's domestic situation, "we just came from your house. We can have a group discussion about that experience, or you can convince Raylene to leave us to chat privately."

Gene's eyes almost popped out of his skull.

"Baby, just give me a minute to clear all this up," he pleaded. "I promise I'll be right out."

Raylene threw him a skeptical stare before reluctantly leaving the bathroom. Once she was gone, Sam motioned for him to stand over near the sink. The man did so, pressing his back up against the tiled wall as if it could somehow shield him from what might come next.

With every move he made, Jessie's heart sank a little lower. Gene Coleman's body language did not match that of a serial killer who was worried that he'd just been discovered. It better fit a scumbag who feared his infidelity was about to be revealed. Of course, the two weren't necessarily mutually exclusive, and he could be masking nervousness about one with the other, but that would be an impressive bit of performance. She decided not to waste any time in getting to the point.

"Mr. Coleman," she said, spitting her words more than saying them, "you are obviously a disgusting, repugnant excuse for a human being. The fact that you would choose to spend your precious time after work going to a dive bar to screw the bartender rather than go home to see your very pregnant wife and children tells me everything I need to know about your character."

"That's not fair," Coleman insisted. "I love Raylene. I can't help it if my life got more complicated than I can handle."

"Please shut up until I ask you to speak," Jessie said, ignoring the somersault of nausea in her gut. "It's clear that Raylene doesn't know about your wife. And I doubt Maisy knows about Raylene, or you'd already be in divorce proceedings. And as much as it would fill me with glee to blow up your world, this is your lucky day, assuming you don't mess it up."

For a second, Coleman's face froze like a computer that had stopped working. He didn't seem to comprehend. "What do you mean?" he finally asked.

"If you answer our questions directly, without giving us any trouble, you might get out of this without either of these unfortunate women learning the truth about your piggish nature. Do you think you can do that?"

Coleman, leaping at the chance, nodded vigorously.

"Go ahead, Detective Goodwin," Jessie said, certain that Sam knew where she was headed.

"Mr. Coleman," Sam said, leaning in toward the man menacingly. "Where were you this morning at 6:45 a.m.?"

Coleman closed his eyes tight. His forehead became a mass of wrinkles as he tried to either remember or make something up. "Um, okay. Maisy had an early appointment with the OB/GYN, so I had to drop the kids off at daycare and kindergarten. I think we were finishing up breakfast around that time, or maybe getting in the car?"

"We'll need to confirm that information through your phone's location data and by speaking with people at the daycare and the school," Sam said. "You'll provide us with all the necessary information."

"Of course," Coleman groveled.

"What about last Saturday night at 9 p.m.?" Sam asked. "Where were you then?"

Coleman did the same eyes-closed, head-scrunch routine but came up empty this time. He opened his eyes. "Can I just look at my phone to jog my memory?" he asked.

Sam nodded. Coleman pulled it out and quickly scrolled through a few screens before stopping on one. He didn't seem happy with what he found.

"What?" Sam demanded.

"I don't want to say."

Jessie fought the urge to punch the guy in the stomach. "Mr. Coleman," she growled, "in case you couldn't tell, we're trying to establish your whereabouts at these times to determine if you have a plausible alibi for the period when some serious crimes occurred. If you have a credible way to explain where you were on Saturday night that doesn't involve you committing a felony, I suggest you share it now. No matter how bad it makes you look, I think you'll agree that's preferable to being arrested."

"I was here!" Coleman blurted out unexpectedly.

"In the bar?" Sam asked.

"Yes, but not just that," he said. "I was in this bathroom. I texted Raylene at 9:03 saying I was coming in here and saving her a spot. She said she'd be right there. We stayed in here—in the stall—for about ten minutes. So, that's where I was, in this bathroom."

The guy was sniffling quietly to himself.

"I've seen more dead bodies than I can count in my life," Jessie muttered to Sam, "and somehow, it's this guy that's going to make me physically sick. Can you wrap this up?"

She stepped over to the doorway and stared down the hall, so she didn't have to look at Gene Coleman as Sam spoke to him.

"We're going to confirm that as well," he said. "We may also have additional questions for you, unrelated to your alibi. They could be about your favorite ice cream, or they could be about how the escrow process works on the home mortgages you service. Whatever we ask, we expect immediate, comprehensive answers. Do we understand each other, Gene?"

"We do."

Sam tapped Jessie on the shoulder, and the two of them walked down the hall.

"You okay?" he asked. "I wasn't sure how much of that was you acting and how much was real?"

"To be honest, I'm not sure either," Jessie said. "All I know is that we're walking out of here having caught a philanderer, but we're no closer to catching a killer."

"I think maybe we call it a day and start fresh tomorrow," Sam suggested. "We've hit a wall in terms of leads, and personally, I need to wash the stink of Gene Coleman off me."

Jessie felt the same way. She just wanted to go home, take a shower, relax, and let her brain take a bit of a break. Of course, she knew herself too well to believe that would actually happen. She would stew over this all night until she fell into a fitful, unproductive sleep.

But at least she'd be home, alive, and able to wake up to see a new day tomorrow. That was more than she could say for Kim Carrigan and Ellie Hill.

CHAPTER SEVENTEEN

He rewound the DVR for the seventh time. This time, he was sure.

In the background of the reporter's standup report from this morning outside the home of Gregory and Kimberly Carrigan, two people could be seen passing through a dining room. The camera was too far away to get a good look at their faces, but Mark Haddonfield knew who they were.

One of them, a tall, wiry guy with untamed, brown hair, was clearly Samuel Goodwin, the newest addition to the team of detectives that comprised LAPD's Homicide Special Section unit. Goodwin had come from vice and had a solid reputation. Beyond that, details on him were limited.

Mark Haddonfield would have recognized the other person in the window anywhere. He knew her by her height. At five-foot-ten, she wasn't dwarfed by Goodwin. He knew her by her clothes—comfortable slacks and a professional but loose-fitting shirt that wouldn't be a hindrance if she had to get physical. And of course, he knew her by the ponytail that held her shoulder-length, brown hair in place. When she was working, she always wore it up.

Just to be absolutely sure, he reviewed some other videos of her. A few were from news footage. Others were ones he'd shot himself. In all of them, her stride pattern was the same as when she walked through the dining room of the Carrigan home. It was definitely Jessie Hunt.

And why wouldn't it be? It made perfect sense that she would be assigned to this case. After all, HSS was almost always given the highest profile cases in the city, and the murder of the wife of a popular local news anchor certainly fit that description. And once HSS was tasked with the investigation, Jessie was invariably the first choice as profiler if she was available, which she now seemed to be after a slow recovery from her abduction by Andy Robinson a few months ago.

There was no mention of Jessie in the reporter's story, which wasn't a shock. She'd gotten very good at getting in and out of crime scenes quickly and stealthily so as to avoid press attention, wisely understanding that the bigger the media circus, the harder it would be for her to do her job.

Of course, sometimes the circus got too big for even her to control. Mark had heard about a few tabloid photographers, eager to get salacious images of Jessie off the clock, who'd sneaked onto her property. It hadn't gone well.

Apparently, they had foolishly forgotten that, as the wife of a police captain and the victim of a recent abduction, she might be afforded a little extra protection. They were arrested for trespassing, even stalking in one instance, and thrown into lockups overnight. Some may have thought that was an abuse of power, but Jessie was such a beloved figure in the city that these slime merchants didn't get much sympathy.

That's why Mark never went near her house. Why chance getting picked up by a roving patrol car and being put in the system? It was just too risky. What if HSS's genius researcher, Jamil Winslow, was able to use the arrest, or even a filed warning report, to identify him later on? What if Jessie recognized his name, or more realistically, his face, and made a connection too soon?

No, there were other ways to keep tabs on Jessie Hunt that didn't require making himself vulnerable. Hell, half the time he just had to watch the news. There was always a new, breathless take on L.A.'s most brilliant profiler, saver of lives, hero to a city.

And truth be told, she was his hero too. Or at least, she used to be. After all, that's why he had ravenously devoured every article about her cases while he was at Stanford. It was the reason that, after discovering that she would be taking a lecturer position at UCLA, he excitedly transferred there for his junior year. He intended to take her seminar and absorb every nugget of knowledge she had to share.

Of course, he didn't tell his parents that was why he was transferring. Nor did he did tell them—or anyone else—about his grander plan, for fear that they would dismiss it as unattainable.

Mark dreamed that during one of the seminar sessions, he would raise his hand to answer a particularly difficult question, and that Jessie Hunt would call on him, hear his reply, and be so overwhelmed by his insight that she would invite him to become something of an apprentice. She would train him in the skills of profiling and eventually ask him to become her partner, working as a team to root out the dark heart of evil that lurks among the rest of us, striking out, then receding for a time before attacking again.

But it didn't happen. When he started at UCLA the next fall, her seminar was in such demand that seniors were given enrollment priority. He couldn't get registered for a slot for that quarter or for the winter or spring quarters either.

He resigned himself to the frustrating reality that he wouldn't even be able to study with her in the summer quarter and would have to wait until his senior year to get his chance. But then, without warning, Jessie announced that the spring quarter would be her last for a while—that she was returning to work at Homicide Special Section full-time.

She had forsaken him without ever giving him a chance to win her over, to even meet her in person. Well, that wasn't quite true. They had met once, very briefly, though it hadn't gone exactly as he would have hoped. Mark tried to introduce himself to her months ago, in a campus courtyard, when she was walking with her friend, an intimidating-looking woman he later learned was named Katherine Gentry.

He had approached her while pulling a newspaper with a story about her out of his backpack, hoping she'd autograph it for him. But apparently, after just recently surviving an attack by her ex-husband that left her boyfriend in a coma, she was a bit skittish about people pulling things out of bags unexpectedly, and both she and Gentry drew guns on him.

Once they cleared up the confusion, she was apologetic, but she declined to sign the newspaper because it was an article about how she had killed the notorious serial killer, Bolton Crutchfield. She had claimed that it felt wrong to autograph something discussing a person's death like it was a baseball program. She instead offered to give him a priority pass to her next seminar session and said to come by her office during office hours to get it. Then she'd walked off, oblivious to the genius that had been standing right in front of her.

That would have almost been acceptable if she had come through with the pass. But when he went to her office as she had instructed, she wasn't there. According to the psychology department staff assistant, she was consulting on a case for HSS, even though she was supposedly on sabbatical from the police department.

Worse, the staff assistant said that Jessie had "misspoken," and that she was not authorized to give passes to students for individual seminar sessions; that because of the seminar's popularity, they were doled out via a lottery, and that only seniors were eligible to participate. No amount of pleading on his part made any difference. It was department policy.

He tried to appeal to Jessie directly at her next office hours but again, she was out. As she was the time after that. Eventually, he learned that the department had dispensed with traditional office hours for her because of security concerns, and that she did all of her student meetings over Zoom. Apparently, only students in the seminars got that important update, so he had wasted multiple afternoons sitting on the floor outside the office she never used, waiting for a person who would never come.

And now, after everything he'd been through—transferring schools, jumping through bureaucratic hoops to no avail, sitting on dirty linoleum for hours on end, being ignored except for the one time that he had a gun pulled on him—Jessie was rubbing his nose in it yet again.

Sometime soon, she would solve this Carrigan case and dominate the news cycle. Her face would be plastered on every television screen in the city. She was like an ex-girlfriend who was also a supermodel. No matter where you looked, you couldn't avoid seeing her. How was he supposed to heal?

As it turned out, Mark had found a way. A sly smile crept across his face as he thought about his special little secret, the one he'd been keeping ever since the straw that had broken the camel's back, when Jessie had foiled Operation Z six weeks ago. The truth was that he'd been massaging his resentment ever since Jessie announced she was leaving UCLA. But it was the seventy-two hours of non-stop tributes to Jessie's bravery and fortitude in the aftermath of her kidnapping and near-death that had finally made him stop silently nursing his grievance and come up with a plan.

And that plan would be put into action very soon. He turned off the TV, stood up, and stretched. He caught a glimpse of himself in the mirror on the wall in his tiny university apartment and liked what he saw.

At six-foot-four, he was even taller and skinnier than Detective Goodwin. His frame masked surprising strength. His blond, curly hair and thin, wire-rimmed glasses gave him a soft, academic look that tended to make people underestimate what he was capable of. Most twenty-one-year-olds would be self-conscious about looking so gawky, but for him, it was a disguise, hiding what he didn't want them to see.

He moved over to his desk and the ancient laptop that he'd bought after committing to the project at hand. The laptop had no internet capability and was for all practical purposes, air gapped, which was an extra, perhaps unnecessary, precaution. He reviewed the details of the upcoming course of action and how it fit into his larger plan, which he'd come to refer to as "The Strategy."

As his eyes scrolled over his research, he couldn't help but be impressed with his own work. As someone who already had exhaustive knowledge of most of Jessie Hunt's past cases, it wasn't hard to fill in the blanks. But now, after six weeks of comprehensive deep dives into their minutiae, he felt equipped for everything to come.

He knew every case that Jessie had worked since she joined HSS. He had read the full police reports backward and forward. He knew everything about her partnering detectives on each of them, about all the witnesses, about the suspects who ended up being false leads, about the victims, and about the near victims that Jessie had saved by stopping all those killers.

Starting imminently, his thorough knowledge of all things Jessie Hunt would finally bear fruit. He would show her that she wasn't quite as smart as she believed herself to be. He would show her that she couldn't protect everyone the way she thought she could. He would pull back the curtain to reveal that being close to Jessie Hunt had a dark side that nobody seemed to acknowledge: it put you at greater risk.

He would get the media to start to turn on her. Instead of viewing her as Los Angeles's guardian angel, they would begin to see her as an angel of death. She might offer you temporary salvation from its grasp, but eventually, she would deliver you into its cold embrace. That deliverance would begin with Woody Garnett.

Garnett was one of the many people Jessie had saved from dying at the hands of a serial killer. In fact, he was near-death, stabbed in the stomach with a hunting knife, when Jessie found him in a hotel suite about to be cut down by Harper Grey, a psychiatrist's receptionist, who had snapped and made it her mission to punish people who had wronged their spouses. After outmaneuvering Grey, Jessie managed to keep Garnett alive long enough for the EMTs to stabilize him.

But maybe she shouldn't have. After reading the case file, Mark wondered if Harper Grey didn't have the right idea. Woody Garnett seemed to be a terrible person. Apparently, he announced at the beginning of their final couples' therapy session that he was cheating again, this time with "a long-legged hottie," and that he was dumping his wife after thirty-two years together. Then he just walked out of the session, leaving his wife crying and the psychiatrist to pick up the pieces. If Jessie should have let one of these killers take out anyone, it was Woody Garnett.

That's why Mark was starting with him, someone he could justify removing from the world. After all, he had never killed anyone before. His dream had been to work with Jessie to *stop* killers. He had never envisioned himself becoming one. But she'd pushed him to this. He really had no choice anymore.

Still, despite all the elaborate planning in The Strategy, he knew that none of it would work if he wasn't able to do the deed when the time came. He knew that, at the moment of truth, there would be doubt, and he'd be tempted to turn back. That's why he was making it as easy on himself as possible by choosing the most objectionable person possible to start.

His hope was that, if he could go through with this, it would be like a break in a dam, and that it would get, if not easier, at least less agonizing, with future outings. Because The Strategy required future outings.

Don't get ahead of yourself. That's how mistakes get made. Concentrate on the task at hand.

Mark did just that, focusing on the details of the plan for a while longer, then closed the laptop. Only then did he allow himself a moment to glimpse a possible future. He wondered, when it was done, if Jessie would make the connection right away, or if it would take further prodding from him.

He'd always dreamed of being in the room with her to see how her brain operated when she hunted a killer. How ironic, now that he was the killer she'd be hunting, that he couldn't be anywhere near her. He wouldn't be able to see if she was really as clever as they all said.

The only way to know for sure would be to observe the results. He had a sneaking suspicion that she'd be a disappointment, that she'd gotten too full of herself. She needed to be brought down a peg or two. And he was the man to do it.

For her own good.

CHAPTER EIGHTEEN

Jessie couldn't decide what to blame.

Was her exhaustion causing the headache, or was the pounding in her skull making her whole body heavy with weariness?

As she entered her mid-Wilshire house through the side door connected to the garage, she set aside the question and focused on solving the most pressing issue. She moved into the kitchen, poured herself a glass of water, popped an 800mg ibuprofen, swallowed it, chomped down a few crackers to fight off any potential stomach upset, and sat down at the breakfast table to regroup.

The house was quiet. She had assumed that getting home after 7 p.m. that at least Hannah would be home, if not Ryan. But she was the first back. She pulled out her phone and was about to text her sister to see where she was when she heard a car pull up out front. A few seconds later, the front door opened, and Hannah walked through.

"Hey," Jessie said, "how are you?"

"Okay," Hannah said, looking pretty tired herself. "You?"

"Long day. Kat didn't want to stop in?"

Hannah shook her head. "That wasn't her. I took a rideshare back," she said. "Our supposed cheater is taking his wife to the symphony tonight, so Kat said she'd tail him back to his house and I could skip out."

"Oh," Jessie said, getting the odd sense that her sister was leaving something out, but deciding not to pursue it. "So, the phrase 'supposed cheater' makes me think today wasn't the day you captured your guy in a compromising position."

"If by 'compromising position,' you mean capturing him boring his staff as much as he bored me, then yeah, I busted him real good. Otherwise not so much. What about you? How was your day?"

"Our case involves a likely serial killer," Jessie said, "killing wealthy women alone in their Hancock Park homes. Somehow getting access to their alarm security codes. All our leads so far are dead ends. So, not the best day."

"What about your head?" Hannah asked. "You're squinting when you talk."

"So?"

"You squint when the headaches get really bad," Hannah noted. "Also, you never turned on the light in the kitchen."

Jessie quietly noted her sister's improving skills at observation, even if they were being used on her. "I didn't realize the thing about the squinting," she conceded. "I'm hoping it's just the day catching up with me."

"Did you have any issues with memory or confusion?" Hannah pressed.

"I don't remember having any," Jessie said, trying to smile, "but then again, if I *was* having issues, I guess I wouldn't remember them."

"That's not as funny as you think it is," Hannah said.

Jessie shrugged and sighed heavily, not sure what topics were on or off the table. "The second victim today was a mom," she said quietly. "She had a little boy and a girl. I met them both. When I saw them, and how they're going to grow up without a parent, I couldn't help but think about Callum Reid, about his kids. It made me—"

"I'm sorry but I can't," Hannah interrupted, her eyes welling up with tears. "I know you don't mean to pick at the scab but that just—it's not something I can talk about right now."

"Hannah, I didn't mean to upset you," Jessie said as her sister started toward her bedroom.

"I know," she said. "It's okay. I just need some time to decompress. I'll be out in a bit."

She closed her door before Jessie could reply. She wanted to get up and follow her sister, to apologize for not getting just how tender that wound still was for her, but she resisted the urge. She'd just have to swallow this screwup and wait for the guilt to work its way through her system.

Besides, she wanted to respect Hannah, to let her work this out on her own. After all, she was an adult, not just officially now, but practically as well. She would be attending college in the fall, where she'd be on her own. After everything she'd been through, to think she couldn't navigate her way through this was borderline insulting. And if she needed help, Jessie had to hope she'd come to her.

The garage door opened, signaling Ryan's arrival home. She stood up, turned on the kitchen light, and met him at the door with a kiss.

"That's a friendly welcome home," he said with a smile.

"Just trying to keep my man happy," she said, making sure not to squint as she spoke.

"Mission accomplished," he told her. "How are you doing?"

"Headache. Tired. Just inadvertently hurt Hannah's feelings. Nowhere on the case. Your standard Tuesday."

Ryan looked worried. "You take something for the headache?" he asked.

"Waiting for it to kick in now," she told him.

"Okay, what do you want me to ask about first?"

"Let's get the case out of the way."

"Let's do it," he said. "How about a status report?"

She complied, walking him through all the particulars of the day, including the dashed hopes with suspects Jacob Greeley and Gene Coleman. When she was done, she proposed an idea that she'd been toying with but hadn't even mentioned to Sam.

"I'd like to have an alert sent out," she said, "to anyone who purchased a single-family home in the last nine months within a five-mile radius of either attack, warning of possible home invasion threats, and suggest they change their alarm codes."

Ryan looked at her as if he wasn't sure how best to respond. "Jessie," he finally said, "you know we can't do that. It would set off a panic. That could be hundreds of homes."

"Maybe not," she countered. "We could have Jamil do a search. It's not that big a community. Maybe it's only dozens of sales during that time."

"Either way, we're not calling a large group of citizens and telling them that they are so vulnerable in their own homes that they have to change their alarm codes. They'll freak out. We could end up with neighbors shooting each other because they looked suspicious when they were just getting the newspaper. Plus, we don't even know how the killer is getting access to the alarm codes. What if this person got the new ones too? Then changing them is pointless. It's just not practical. No way Decker would approve it. What I *can* do is recommend increased patrols for the area."

Jessie knew he was right. She hadn't ever really expected him to sign onto the plan, but the idea that she was just sitting here at home, unable to do anything proactive when this killer was out and about, was infuriating.

"The patrols are good," she said in resignation. "And as long as you're asking Decker for them, you should warn him about some trouble brewing in his backyard."

"What do you mean?"

She proceeded to tell him about what she learned from medical examiner Cheryl Gallagher, including a city councilmember's attempt to coerce her into claiming Decker inappropriately showed favoritism to HSS.

"I'll let him know," Ryan promised. "I doubt it will come as a surprise to him. He knows some of them have been gunning for him."

"How did he do today in his testimony?" Jessie asked.

"From what I hear, he held up pretty well," Ryan said. "Plus, there's real momentum for him to become permanent chief now. He's got a solid record to stand on. The rank and file love him. The mayor is behind him. Any councilmembers looking for dirt at this point seem pretty desperate, in my opinion. I mean, you know the guy. He's frickin' incorruptible."

"I wish I was as confident as you that he's going to be okay," Jessie said.

"You've got enough on your plate. Don't add another item that you can't control to the mix," he said before smiling awkwardly. "Speaking of things on your plate, did you happen to give any more thought to the last name question I mentioned this morning?"

For a second, Jessie had no idea what he was talking about. And when she remembered, she realized that it had completely slipped her mind. Whether that was by accident or some subconscious design, she couldn't say.

"I'm sorry, Ryan," she admitted, "but I can honestly say that I have given it almost no more thought."

"That's okay," he said quickly, "don't worry about it."

"Now I feel bad," she replied.

"Don't," he insisted. "I was just checking. It's no big deal."

"I apologize, but it's been a lot with this case. Plus, did I mention that Jamil is acting funny? And these headaches. I mean, why the hell haven't we heard from Dr. Varma?"

"Hey," Ryan said softly, "it's okay. She said she'd call this week. It's still only Tuesday. There's still lots of time. And I didn't mean to rile you up with my question. I tell you what—why don't you go take a nice, long shower and change into something comfy? I'll go grab Hannah and guilt her into helping me make something for dinner. By the time you come back out, it'll be waiting for you. How does that sound?"

Despite the throbbing in her head, Jessie forced a smile. "That sounds nice," she said.

And it did. She gave him another kiss and walked down the hall to the bedroom, telling herself that a shower and a meal would ease the pain in her head, the unsettling sense that bad things were imminent, and the feeling that she was powerless to stop any of them.

***

They were all at the foot of her bed, whispering. She didn't recognize the voices at first because they were overlapping, cascading into each other, and making it impossible to understand what any one person said. Finally, she raised her head off her pillow, looked up, and saw them there in the dark.

Dr. Priya Varma, tall and coolly elegant, was standing off to the left, in her lab coat, holding a clipboard and scribbling notes on her chart. Next to her was Callum Reid, retired LAPD detective, his slight potbelly cresting over his belt. He looked worried as he adjusted his black-framed glasses and conferred with the doctor, who pointed out something on the chart.

On the other side of him was Andy Robinson. She was staring down disapprovingly, in silent judgment over Jessie's choice to use her teenage trauma against her. Her blonde hair was cut and styled to frame her face, and especially her crooked half-smile, just so. She had a nice tan. Her deep, penetrating, blue eyes still had the bright twinkle and playful sharpness that was her most arresting feature. She was wearing a black cocktail dress and high heels, the same dress she'd worn the night she kidnapped Jessie at her wedding.

That detail was what ultimately tipped off Jessie that this was a dream, not the certainty that Callum would never stand next to Andy without putting cuffs on her, or the more glaring fact that both Andy and Callum were dead.

But even once she was aware that none of this was real, Jessie couldn't seem to rouse herself from the nightmare. Instead, she let her head fall back on the pillow and listened as the three of them continued to murmur quietly about her future.

They didn't sound optimistic.

CHAPTER NINETEEN

She wasn't drunk.

Despite what her work friend, Liza, had said when they left the bar, Lauren Pastorini was at most mildly buzzed. But just to be on the safe side, she decided to take a rideshare home.

She could have walked the short distance, but not at this hour and not in this neighborhood. It was both a blessing and a curse to have her condo and her job within about a mile of each other and to have some of the coolest bars and restaurants scattered along the route they shared.

The curse was that there really was no excuse for being late for work, and no one felt bad if she had to stick around a little longer than others at the end of the day. It's not like she had to battle terrible traffic to get home.

The blessings were numerous. One was that her commute, door to door, was about eleven minutes. That included the time required to drive to Sovereign Studios, park in the garage adjacent to the studio, walk through security, then along the backlot street the legendary building where her production company was located.

Another blessing was that the Mexican joint that she was currently being driven away from, Marie's El Barro Restaurant, had some of the best margaritas she'd had north of the border, and she'd done a *lot* of taste tests. And since she was a regular, the staff tended not to skimp on the tequila.

But because Marie's was on Melrose, just north of the invisible line that divided the sketchy part of Hollywood from the more upscale Hancock Park, where she lived, it was inadvisable to make the ten-minute walk to Kensington Green Living, especially at 11:44 at night.

Looking at the time, it occurred to Lauren that every minute of extra sleep she could get might help. After months of working with a pair of writers to hone their screenplay about a secret romance between astronauts on a mission to Saturn, it was finally ready to pitch to talent.

The three of them had a big meeting early tomorrow morning with a star who could guarantee a studio greenlight if he signed on. Maybe that's why, against her better judgement, she'd had that second, buzz-inducing margarita. She was feeling the stress.

But now, she needed some shuteye. The driver pulled up in front of her building, and she got out quick, suddenly deciding that it was essential that she be in bed with the lights out by midnight. She key-carded herself through the doors, hurried through the lobby, and got in the elevator, hitting the button for the fourth floor.

Luckily, at this hour, there was no one else around, and she zipped right up. She took her shoes off before the elevator doors opened and hustled down the hall, careful not to trip on the ridiculously thick carpet. That was one of the many—sometimes too many—accoutrements of Kensington Green, her exclusive condo complex.

When she first moved in, she'd been impressed by the laundry list of amenities they had. Not only were they situated next door to a country club, with views of the golf course, but they also had an on-site concierge, both an indoor and outdoor pool, multiple hot tubs, a fire pit, a rooftop tanning terrace, a 24-hour fitness center, a sauna, and even their own dog park, which didn't do her much good but was still pretty cool. At the time Lauren bought her two-bedroom unit, Kensington Green seemed like it would be one endless party. And since she was young, single, and hot, she figured she had to spend all that film production executive money somehow.

But after living here for four months, some of the features had already gotten to be a bit old. The concierge in the lobby was always up in everyone's business, relentlessly trying to get them to sign up for this event or that social club. The outdoor pool was too cold, and the indoor pool smelled funny.

It seemed like the cleaning crew was always running a vacuum cleaner near her, no matter where Lauren was. The hallway light sconces, meant to look old-world Hollywood, were so heavy and difficult to remove that when a light burned out, it often took days to replace them. And this damn, thick carpet sometimes felt like quicksand, always about to drown her as she walked to her unit.

Lauren unlocked her door and moved over to the alarm panel to punch in her security code. Once that was done, she locked the door again and moved swiftly to the bedroom to start peeling off her work clothes. She glanced at the clock on the wall. It was 11:48.

She tried to calculate what she had left to do tonight and whether she could be under the covers before the clock struck midnight. She still had to change into her night clothes, wash her face, and go the bathroom. Plus, she should probably go to the kitchen and grab a big glass of water to keep beside the bed before turning on the security alarm for the night. She didn't want to deal with cottonmouth at three in the morning.

The thought of that made her change plans. Now in just her bra and underwear, she headed back out to the kitchen to get some water. She would chug a big glass of it first to pre-hydrate ASAP, then pour another one for the middle of the night.

As she filled up the glass, using the filtered water from the refrigerator, she looked out at her living room. It was a mess, with clothes and scripts lying everywhere. She also realized, belatedly, that her curtains were open, and that anyone in the high-rise building across the street who was awake and so inclined, could get a nice eyeful if they wanted.

If they did, she couldn't help but note proudly that they'd be lucky. Lauren did a half turn, checking herself out in the reflection of the window. Her black hair brushed against her bare, ivory shoulders. Just like every other part of her body, the shoulders were well-toned.

After struggling with her weight through much of high school and college, she'd made a commitment to herself in the spring of her senior to turn things around. She started running twice a week, went to the on-campus gym three days a week to do weight training, and while there, became addicted to the rowing machine. She cut out sweets completely and limited alcohol to one night a week. Within six months, she'd lost over twenty pounds and actually felt comfortable wearing a bikini to the beach.

In the six years since then, she'd managed to keep the weight off and replace her cravings for junk food with an equally powerful desire to be the producer of an Oscar-winning film before she turned thirty. She still had fun and had gone on more than a few dates with up-and-coming actors, many of whom clearly liked the way she looked in a tight dress, but she never lost sight of the ultimate prize.

Except, that is, for maybe fifteen minutes tonight when she succumbed to that second margarita. The reality of that decision made Lauren immediately stop with the self-admiration. She was tempted to go over and close the curtains but decided that would cost her valuable time. If she wanted to get to bed quick, it was easier to just turn off the light.

She chugged the water, put the glass down, and went over to the front door to turn off the main lights and activate the alarm for the evening. She flicked off the overheads, leaving only the kitchen light illuminated. She opened the alarm panel and was about to punch in the code when she thought she saw something off to the left, in the area of the coat closet.

She turned that way, and for a moment, she thought that she was drunker than she had realized. Because it looked like there was a shadow, a ghost of some kind, moving quickly toward her. But in a flash, that delusion disappeared, as the shadow came into the light, and it became clear that it was a person coming at her, one wearing all black, including a black ski mask and black gloves.

Lauren felt her entire body explode with fear as she opened her mouth to scream. But before any sound could escape her lips, the black-clad person slammed into her, smashing her into the wall next to the door. She felt all the air leave her lungs as her legs gave out, and she slumped down.

But the black-clad person yanked her up. She was face to face with the person, but her eyes were watering, and she couldn't see anything clearly. And then, before she knew what was happening, the person's gloved hands were around her neck, squeezing, their fingers tightening like ten little vises.

Lauren didn't understand what was happening or why. She didn't have time to process how everything that had seemed so important in her world just moments earlier would be gone in a matter of seconds. Her killer never said a word or gave any indication that they noticed her fluttering eyes or her desperate, final gasps.

When those gloved hands finally let go of her neck and she dropped heavily to the ground, Lauren was long past hearing the security alarm being turned back on or the door closing. She lay there silently, alone in her condo, with the kitchen light casting its distant light on her half-naked body.

CHAPTER TWENTY

Ryan held out as long as he could.

He didn't ask until they were almost to the station, but eventually his curiosity got the better of him, and he couldn't help himself.

"So, I know you slept terribly," he said, "but somehow you still seem to be in a surprisingly chipper mood. I don't want to say anything to upset that, but do you care to tell me why?"

Jessie looked over at him from the passenger seat with the half-smile that had been glued to her face for most of the morning. "It's pretty simple," she told him. "No calls during the night. No calls this morning. That means no new dead body. I was worried that this killer might accelerate their timetable for a new victim, but maybe I was being paranoid. Ellie Hill's murder was Saturday night. Kim Carrigan's was yesterday, on Tuesday morning. That's two and a half days in between. If that pattern holds, we might have until tomorrow night. That gives us a decent window to dredge up some new leads before another attack."

"I hope the window holds," Ryan said, not wanting to puncture her balloon, though he wasn't as optimistic that they would get that long. "Part of me was wishing you'd say that you're smiling because your head feels fantastic today."

Jessie shrugged. "Fantastic might be overstating it," she said, "but it's definitely better than last night. I really think I might have just been overtired. I mean, I did get headaches *before* the concussion, too, you know. It doesn't automatically have to mean my head isn't right."

"Fair enough," Ryan said, not wanting to say anything to get Jessie out of her good mood. "Speaking of heads that aren't right, last night you mentioned something about Jamil acting funny. I let it go because you seemed a little swamped in the moment, but considering that I'm his supervisor, do you want to fill me in on what you meant?"

Jessie's pursed lips suggested that she was having second thoughts about mentioning the researcher in the first place. It took a few seconds for her to reply. "You know, now that I think about it, it was probably nothing. He was most likely just having a bad day. Just because he's a genius doesn't mean he's not allowed an occasional bout of surliness, right?"

"Are you sure that's all it is?" Ryan pressed as he made the last turn before they reached the police station garage.

"I'll let you know if it's not," Jessie assured him before quickly shifting topics. "Don't forget to tell Decker about what Cheryl Gallagher said."

"I won't," he assured her. "I have a meeting with him at nine, and I'll bring it up then. By the way, don't think I didn't notice how clumsily you tried to switch away from discussing Jamil. All that does is make me more suspicious, you know."

Jessie gave him her patented, faux-offended look before replying, "Speaking of discussing things, I know you want an answer on that last name change thing—"

Ryan laughed at the clunkiness of her second effort to change the subject. "My mother wants an answer, not me," he corrected. "I want to be crystal clear on that point. And 'speaking of discussing things?' I think that's the worst segue I've ever heard."

Jessie's offended look looked borderline real this time.

"As I was saying," she replied sharply, "I know you want an answer on that last name change thing, and I don't have one for you yet, but I have been mulling over another name-related idea that that I wanted run by you—"

Ryan's cell phone rang. He glanced down and saw that the call was from Susannah Valentine. A sinking feeling filled his gut. It was 7:54 a.m., and they were less than a minute from the station. Detective Valentine knew that they never arrived after 8 a.m. If she was calling him on his cell anyway, it couldn't be good news. He picked up and put it on speaker.

"Hey Susannah," he said, "Jessie and I are about thirty seconds from pulling into the garage. Can it wait?"

"I'd rather just tell you now so you can figure out a solution on your way up to the bullpen," Susannah said.

"What is it?" Ryan sighed, pulling over to the side of the road just outside the garage, just as he had yesterday morning.

"Karen Bray's son is sick," she said. "He was throwing up all night, and she had to take him into the ER because he was so dehydrated. She said he's going to be okay, but she can't make it in today. But we have to follow up on our interrogation with this fugitive we caught yesterday. Turns out he may have been holding someone captive and we need to get him to fess up. I don't think it's a solo gig."

"Why not?" Ryan asked.

"The first time around we didn't have any success until we started volleying back and forth with alternating questions. It rattled him and that's when he became more responsive."

"What's Jim Nettles doing?" Ryan asked.

"I haven't asked him yet. I wanted to check with you first, and also to see if Jessie was too busy to spare the time."

Ryan looked over at Jessie, who seemed torn. He knew she was committed to catching this security alarm killer, but he could see her wondering if helping with the fugitive would justify taking an hour away from her case.

"I'll get back to you when we get up there," Ryan said, then hung up and asked point blank, "what do you think?"

She didn't get a chance to answer before her own phone rang. They both looked at it. The call was from Sam Goodwin. She put it on speaker.

"Hey Sam," she said. "I'm here with Captain Hernandez. You're on speaker. What's up?"

"Where are you right now?" he demanded.

"We're about to pull into the station garage," she said, frowning.

She had clearly noted the same intensity in his tone that Ryan had picked up on.

"I'm upstairs," he told her. "I'll meet you down there in two minutes. We need to head out. There's been another murder."

CHAPTER TWENTY ONE

Everything about this death was wrong.

As Jessie stared at the body of Lauren Pastorini on the floor of her living room, she noted the ways that her assumptions had been upended. She expected that the next victim would be in her thirties and married. Lauren Pastorini was twenty-eight and single. She expected the victim to live in a large house. Lauren lived in a posh condo complex.

The only things that matched so far, that led the precinct cops to even know to call HSS in the first place, were that she had been choked to death and that the security alarm was on when she was found. What the precinct cops didn't know, which Jessie and Sam learned from Beth Ryerson on the drive over, was that one other thing matched the pattern: Lauren had only bought the place four months ago.

Sergeant Alton Brunson, who had been called in to liaise when it became clear that this was likely an HSS victim, stood silently beside them as they studied the scene, ready to answer any questions they might have. Jessie knelt down next to Lauren's body.

"When does the medical examiner get here?" she asked.

"Expected in the next ten minutes," Brunson said. "Same with CSU."

"I'll be curious to see if they agree," Jessie mused, "but it appears that while she was killed in her underclothes, she likely removed them herself and seemingly wasn't sexually assaulted. It doesn't look like there was any attempt to remove the bra or panties, and there are no abrasions that suggest her clothes were ripped off. The only bruising I see, other than around her neck, is on her back and chest, suggesting she was slammed into the wall."

"It fits," Brunson confirmed. "We found her clothes tossed on her bed. I suppose the killer could have removed them after the fact."

Jessie stood up and glanced into the bedroom where she saw Lauren's outfit from the night before.

"It's possible," she conceded. "We'll have CSU check for glove fibers on the clothes, but I'm skeptical. The collar on her shirt rides pretty high up on the neck. If her attacker had choked her with it still on, the material would have gotten in the way, and we wouldn't see the glove indentations directly on her skin."

"Speaking of the indentations," Sam added, "we won't know without a microscope, but at first glance, they look like a match to what we saw on the other victims."

"I agree," Jessie said, looking around the living room and noting the open, coat closet door. "We should have CSU check in there too. It looks like that's where our killer waited until she got home. Maybe they coughed or sneezed on the backside of the door."

"Will do," Brunson said, making a note.

"The attack probably occurred while she was standing at the alarm panel by the front door," Jessie proposed, "maybe turning it back on for the night. You said it was on when she was found this morning?"

"Yes," Brunson answered, "by her." He pointed to the balcony. Visible through the open curtains was a woman in her late twenties with curly, brown hair, sitting on a patio chair, looking stunned.

"Who is she?" Sam asked.

"Her name is Liza Pritchett," Brunson said. "She's still in shock, but I got a brief statement from her. Apparently, she worked with Pastorini at a production company called Fast Fortune Films just over the way at Sovereign Studios. When Pastorini was late for an important meeting and couldn't be reached, Pritchett said she came by because it was so close. She said Pastorini had given her the code for work stuff, so she felt it was okay to come in. She had security come up with her. Then she opened the door and found her like this."

"She had her code?" Sam confirmed.

"That's what she said," Brunson said. "She also said the alarm was on when they opened the door, and the concierge had to shake her to remind her to punch in the numbers because she completely lost it after seeing the body."

"We need to talk to her," Jessie insisted, "even if she can't offer much right now."

"Good luck," Brunson said.

They stepped out onto the balcony. Once outside, Jessie clocked something that hadn't registered for her when they'd initially arrived at the scene. Kensington Green was only a few hundred yards away from the Beverly Country Club. That was the place where she'd first met Andy Robinson while investigating the murder of another member of the club on her very first case for HSS.

Of course, at that time, she didn't know that Andy was the murderer she was looking for, that the woman would try to kill her, then become obsessed with her, kidnap her, and ultimately have a devoted zealot named Zoe Bradway try to slaughter thousands of people in her name.

The cascade of memories was too overwhelming to deal with, especially under the circumstances, so Jessie chose not to and pushed the thoughts into a corner of her brain as she and Sam introduced themselves to Liza.

She didn't seem to hear them. Jessie sat down in the chair opposite her and grabbed the girl's hand. That appeared to snap her out of her trance.

"Liza," she said quietly. "I know you're struggling, but I need you to set that aside and just focus on my questions, okay?"

Liza nodded unconvincingly. "Okay," she whispered.

"What made you come over here to Lauren's place?" Jessie asked. "That's a pretty dramatic step just because someone was late for a meeting."

"It wasn't just any meeting," Liza said, her voice scratchy, likely from screaming earlier. "She had worked for weeks to set it up. It was with Trent Halsted. He was interested in the lead role in the film she was pitching. If he signed on, we had a top-tier director in the wings and a studio ready to commit to a budget in the $120 million range. There was no way she would be late or even on time. She would have shown up an hour early. This was *the* meeting of her life. I hoped that maybe she was just hungover from last night but even so, I knew something had to be wrong. So, I rushed over and found—" Her voice started to tremble, and she didn't finish her sentence.

"Okay, Liza," Sam said, kneeling down in front of her and giving her a moment to regroup, "we understand that Lauren gave you the code to her security system, so you two must have been really tight."

Liza smiled sheepishly. "We were friends," she explained, "but giving me the code was more for convenience. We worked together. She was the senior executive. I was her junior. I wasn't technically her assistant, but sometimes I'd run work-related errands, drop off scripts, dailies, contracts, that sort thing. She wasn't always around, so she gave me a keycard and the code to the unit."

"Liza," Jessie said, "you mentioned thinking that Lauren might be hungover from last night. Why did you think that?"

Liza shrugged. "We were all at a bar across from the studio last night—Marie's," she explained. "It's literally right around the block from here. She had an extra margarita, and I thought maybe it had hit her a little hard."

"Is that the last time you saw her?" Sam pressed.

"Yeah," Liza said. "She took a rideshare home because she didn't want to walk to her place so late. It was almost midnight."

"And did you stick around at the bar for a while after that?" Sam wondered.

Jessie noted admiringly that while the question came off as simply being curious, it was also a clever way of nailing down Liza's alibi around the time of death.

"Yeah," Liza admitted. "I probably should have left, too, but I wasn't going to be in the pitch meeting, so I didn't feel the pressure to be as ship-shape in the morning."

Something about what she said seemed to upset Liza as tears began to stream down her face.

"What is it?" Sam asked.

"I just realized that I was probably having chips and salsa or doing a tequila shot, completely oblivious, as Lauren was being killed."

She put her head in her hands and began to sob uncontrollably. Jessie briefly considered trying to comfort her but could tell from the woman's heaving body that it wouldn't do much good. She stood up, motioned for the nearby support officer to take her place in the chair, and quietly left the balcony with Sam right behind her.

"I don't think there was anything else we could have gotten from her for a while," she said once they were inside with the door closed.

"Me either," Sam agreed.

Sergeant Brunson walked over purposefully, as if he had new information to share. "Mind if I interrupt?" he asked.

"Please," Jessie said.

"A few more details for you," he replied, looking at his notepad. "We got in touch with the security company. It's a different one from either the Carrigans' or the Hills'. They say that the system was activated for the last time at 11:55 p.m. last night. It was deactivated this morning at 7:37 a.m., which matches the timing we got from Ms. Pritchett."

"So, if the pattern holds," Jessie theorized, "Lauren was likely killed right before 11:55. Then the murderer immediately turned on the alarm and left."

"The pattern *does* hold," Brunson told her. "The building's security just gave us the footage from last night."

He showed it to them on his phone. They watched as someone wearing a trench coat, gloves, and a cap with the brim pulled low over their face walked into the parking garage as the gate opened for a departing car. The timestamp on the video read 9:12 p.m. The person, who appeared to Jessie to be male, got into an elevator, took it to the fourth floor, got out, and walked down the hallway to Lauren's door. With the camera's high angle, the trench coat collar pulled up, and the person's meticulous efforts to keep their head down, it was impossible to discern any facial features. He stood in front of her door for about twenty seconds doing something they couldn't see. Then the door opened, and he stepped inside.

"The security company confirmed that the alarm was deactivated at 9:14 and then reactivated again at 9:15," Brunson narrated as the video clip ended, replaced by a new one.

In this clip, timestamped 11:55 p.m., Lauren's door opened, and someone stepped out. This time, the person was still wearing the trench coat, gloves, and cap, but the coat was open revealing that person, whose build was now clearly that of a man, was wearing all black. He also had a watchcap on under the cap, covering his face. He got into the elevator, took it down to the parking garage, and exited through a side door.

"Can you send that to our research team?" Jessie asked once the clip ended.

"Of course," Brunson said.

"Great work, Sergeant," she told him. "We're going to head back to the station now to break all this down. Please let us know if you find anything else."

They left Lauren Pastorini's condo just as the crime scene unit was arriving. As they rushed down the hall, Jessie thought out loud. "This guy, and I'm fairly confident that it is a guy, is pretty damn brazen," she said. "It takes some serious arrogance to just walk into a building like this, come right up in the elevator dressed as suspiciously as he was, knowing there were cameras everywhere and that he might run into someone at any moment, all to get to a specific resident on the fourth floor."

"In a sick way, it's an impressive accomplishment," Sam said. "The person who did this knew what he was doing."

Jessie couldn't argue the point. As they approached the elevator, she tried to sidestep a wide strip of plastic taped to the hall carpet that extended out from one of the units. Glancing inside, she saw that it was being remodeled, with tarps over all the walls and protective plastic covering the cabinetry.

"Good luck trying to resell that place now," Sam muttered darkly as they waited for the elevator to arrive.

He was right of course. Not only did Lauren Pastorini's death mean a young woman had been cut down in her prime—at perhaps the pinnacle of her professional career—it also meant that property values for every unit on this floor, and maybe all of Kensington Green, would see a steep drop.

She felt dirty for even thinking it. As the elevator doors opened, she resolved to do penance by finding Lauren's killer. When she did, she would rip off his watchcap and shine a light on him so that the whole world could see his ugly soul.

It wouldn't bring Lauren back, but it was something.

CHAPTER TWENTY TWO

Sam tried to hide his frustration.

He would have thought that after two hours they'd have come up with a new lead. And yet, despite all the recent information they had to work with, they didn't seem any further along than they had been yesterday. He glanced over at Jessie, whose desk was across from his in the bullpen, and saw from her crinkled brow that she was as flummoxed as he was. He was about to suggest they take a short break to clear their heads when Captain Hernandez walked into the room. Jessie looked up, and the irritation on her face melted away.

"How did it go with Decker?" she asked as Hernandez walked over.

The captain glanced at Sam before responding. "I passed along your message. He was appreciative, but in general, he was already well aware of the situation," he said cryptically, his words obviously not intended to be understood by the unit's newest member.

Sam didn't take offense. In his short time here, he'd learned to accept that it would take a while for him to be given access to all of HSS's secrets. And with the precinct captain and the unit's profiler now married, he might never know some of them. He decided to let both of them know there were no hard feelings by moving on to another topic.

"By the way, congratulations, Captain," he said. "I heard that while we were out, you were instrumental in helping get that captured fugitive to reveal where he was holding his captive."

"Thanks, Sam," Hernandez said, "But that was mostly Susannah Valentine's doing."

"That's not what she told us," Sam countered.

"How's your case coming?" the captain asked, clearly both unwilling to accept any credit and intent on changing the subject.

"Not great," Jessie said, apparently taking the cue to move on. "You want to update him, Sam?"

"Sure. Jamil and Beth have been reviewing video footage from the latest victim's building. It shows the killer but that hasn't been as helpful as we would have hoped. We know he's male, under six feet tall, and less than 200 pounds. Beyond that, physical details are hard to come by. The building's cameras aren't great, so we can't even determine skin color or age, although based on the man's stride rate, Jamil is confident that he's under sixty years old."

"Okay," the captain said, "that's more than we knew yesterday."

"Yes," Sam conceded, "and we were able to reconfirm some elements of the pattern. For example, there's absolutely no doubt that our killer has access to the victim's alarm codes. And the odds that all three women being recent transplants to Hancock Park are just a coincidence seem increasingly remote."

"But as much as those facts might narrow the pool, others expand it," Jessie noted. "We thought we were dealing with married women, probably in their thirties, in single-family homes. This victim shot all those assumptions out of the water."

"But with her recent move to the neighborhood, that's another property sale," Hernandez pointed out. "Surely that's been a useful data point."

"One would think," Sam said, "but so far, no. Jamil and Beth ran through their database for relationships among the condo sale and both home sales, and there were no statistical links. So, we checked with Vera Steele, the realtor, and Gene Coleman, the loan officer that we briefly suspected, to see if there were connections that might not show up in a spreadsheet. According to both of them, there are zero overlaps among all three sales. They independently told us the same thing: that the people who service the condo market in this community don't intersect with those servicing the single-family home market very often, and in these cases, not at all."

Across the way, Jessie made a noise that sounded somewhere between a sigh and a grunt.

"What's wrong?" he asked.

"Nothing," she said distractedly, "I'm just wondering if we're too fixated on the sale side of things."

"You think so?" Sam asked skeptically. "Don't forget, we also checked the backgrounds of every home inspector and their alibis at the time of the murders. Hell, the Carrigan house had to be tented as a precautionary measure against termites before they moved in, and we looked into everyone involved in that too. I feel like we've been pretty thorough."

"Right," Jessie said vaguely, as if she was only half hearing him. "But as you mention the tenting, it reminds me of all the tarps that were up in that condo that we saw being remodeled today."

"What about it?" Sam asked.

He could tell that Jessie was circling around an idea but that she hadn't quite pinpointed what it was just yet. Looking over at Captain Hernandez, he saw that their boss had the same feeling. In fact, Sam realized that Hernandez hadn't said anything in a while, not since Jessie's sigh-grunt. He seemed to know that his wife was on to something and didn't want to get in the way of it. Sam decided that maybe he shouldn't either.

"Well," she replied, "we've been so focused on the people who had formal access to the home—family, friends, co-workers, the sales staff—that we haven't given much thought to the people who would surely need informal access once the owners moved in. I'm thinking of plumbers, contractors, electricians, carpenters, landscapers, gardeners, that sort of thing. If we gathered a list of every provider who's worked on any of these properties since they moved in, maybe we'd find some overlap there."

"That's a great idea," Sam exclaimed. "Although it might be a challenge to ask two recent widowers and the security office of Kensington Green to give us comprehensive lists of all that."

"You wouldn't need to depend on that alone," Captain Hernandez said. "If you get permission to access the victims' bank records, our research team could sift through payments to providers to come up with a list and see if there are any matches."

All three of them stood up at once and started to walk down the hall. As they did, they called out in unison.

"Jamil!"

CHAPTER TWENTY THREE

Jessie wasn't dragging anymore.

Up until recently, the terrible night of sleep, combined with a new murder and a fruitless morning of hitting evidentiary brick walls, had her fighting droopy eyes, malaise, and a creeping ache in the back of her head that she feared would only get worse as the day progressed. But that had all changed in the last hour, after the adrenaline wave hit.

First, they had gotten approval to access all the victims' bank records. Once that was done, it only took Jamil a few minutes to input everything in the system and generate possible names of service providers at all three properties. It turned out that there was only one who has been to all of them. His name was Wayne Teague.

That was who she and Sam were driving to see right now. Teague was a contractor who did a lot of work in the Hancock Park area. His office was in the mid-Wilshire district, just five minutes west of the Hills' home.

After some digging, Jamil had discovered that Teague had been hired to coordinate cabinetry work on all three homes after the new owners moved in. He ultimately subcontracted all of it out, using the same person for both houses and a different one for the condo. But in all three instances, he had attended the initial homeowner meetings and had visited the properties halfway through the job and again after the work was complete, so he knew the places well.

He might not have had access to the security codes, but it wouldn't have been impossible to watch them being inputted, or to possibly record it being done on his phone while he pretended to be focused on something else.

And though he didn't have any criminal record, he fit the profile physically. He was forty-four, and according to his driver's license, he was five-foot-nine and 170 pounds, all within the parameters that Jamil had predicted.

According to his assistant, Teague was at a job site only two blocks over from the Carrigan home. As Sam pulled up in front of the place, a Spanish-style villa, Jessie saw Teague standing on the front lawn, talking to two other men. He wore jeans and a plaid, long-sleeved, work shirt and was gesticulating wildly, his bald head reflecting the midday sun. He didn't look happy.

"The guy's not big," Sam said as he turned the car off, "but he looks pretty well put together. I know you can handle yourself, but since you're still easing your way back into work, do you mind if I take point on this, in case things go south and he tries to get physical?"

Jessie appreciated the delicate way in which he asked if he could assume the traditional tough guy role. Truthfully, she didn't mind. The last thing she needed right now was another avoidable concussion.

"Go for it," she said. "I'll have your back."

They walked up the path to the house, where Teague, with his back to them, was still lighting into the two men.

"It's going to set us back a week, and they're not going to pay for it," he seethed. "All because you two didn't reconfirm the wood stain before starting the work. I should dock your pay for this. I really should."

The men, who each looked ready to hide under a rock, noticed Jessie and Sam before Teague did. He apparently saw their gaze go elsewhere and turned around. If he was surprised to see two random people standing right behind him, he didn't show it. Mostly, he just seemed irritated.

"Can I help you?" he demanded in a tone that indicated that he would prefer not to.

"Wayne Teague," Sam said, holding up his badge and ID, "I'm Detective Goodwin with the LAPD. This is our consulting profiler, Jessie Hunt. We need to speak to you for a few minutes."

Teague's shoulders slumped before he turned back to the two men, whose mouths and eyes were open wide.

"We'll finish this up in a few minutes," he told them, "in the meantime, go inside and find the *right* stain please."

When they were gone, he turned back to Jessie and Sam. "This is about the women, right?" he said.

Jessie had to work to keep her own jaw from dropping.

"What do you know about that?" Sam asked, admirably keeping his cool.

Teague shrugged. "Well, I know that Kim Carrigan was murdered yesterday less than a thousand yards from here. That was all over the news yesterday. And a guy who sometimes does painting work for me called this morning from Kensington Green to say that a woman I installed cabinets for three months ago, Lauren Pastorini, was murdered last night. He overheard the cops talking about it. I didn't know either woman well, but they both seemed nice. It's awful."

"And you figured that their deaths would lead to cops showing up to talk with you?" Jessie wondered.

Teague didn't look offended by her question.

"I thought it was possible," he admitted. "Two women killed in the same neighborhood, days apart. It seemed suspicious, like they might be connected. And I worked on both their places. I assumed that any exhaustive investigation would lead to people who had been in both their homes, so I prepared myself for the possibility that the authorities might show up to ask me some questions. I also checked my schedule."

"Your schedule?" Sam repeated.

"For alibis," Teague said, "in case you asked where I was when they were killed. The news said that Greg Carrigan found Kim dead when he got home from the gym yesterday morning. I don't know the exact timing on that—it wasn't mentioned on the news—but I was home until about 7:15 a.m. I live over the hills in Studio City, with my wife and two kids. Then I drove to my office. That took just under an hour. You can call my wife to back that up, and I'm assuming you can check my car's location info or something to verify the rest. As to Lauren Pastorini, I don't know when she was killed last night, but unless it was in the window between 5:15 p.m. and 6 p.m., I think I'm in the clear."

"Why is that?" Jessie asked.

"That's when I was supervising a job just a few blocks down from Kensington Green," he explained. "I guess someone could claim I walked to her place from there, although I was around people most of that time. Anyway, I left at six because I had to get back over the hill. My daughter had a symphonic band concert at 7:30, and I wasn't going to be late."

Jessie looked at Sam and could tell that they were thinking the same thing: either they were dealing with a killer who had meticulously covered his tracks or just a guy who was simply so methodically type "A" that he couldn't help coming up with alibis even before he was questioned as a potential suspect in a murder case. They could confirm everything he was saying pretty easily, so she decided to go another way to see if she could throw him off his carefully constructed plan.

"Mr. Teague," she said, "what if we needed your alibi for another night as well?"

For the first time since their arrival, the contractor looked genuinely flummoxed. "I don't understand," he said. "Did I have the times wrong? Was the news off about Carrigan? Because the guy who called me said he specifically heard a police officer say that Lauren Pastorini was killed *last* night."

Jessie watched as he pulled out his phone and tapped it to get to his calendar app. His finger was shaking. When he looked back up at her, his eyes, previously so self-assured, were filled with worry.

But to her, he didn't look like a man who'd been found out keeping a dark secret. He looked like a guy who just had his meticulously organized world upended. Still, she had to be sure. Glancing over at Sam, she saw him nod and knew he was on the same page. So, she went for it.

"Mr. Teague, where were you on Saturday night?"

That was the night that Eleanor Hill was killed, but because it was still officially listed as an accidental death due to a fall, there were no news reports about it, nor any scuttlebutt among painters, contractors, and the like. An innocent man would have no cause to prepare an alibi for that evening.

"What happened on Saturday night?" he asked, simultaneously confused and curious.

"Please just answer the question."

Teague checked his phone. When he looked up, his worry had been replaced by something closer to relief. "I went to dinner and a movie with my wife. Our reservation was at 7 p.m. The movie started at nine. This was in Sherman Oaks. We got home around 11:30, paid the babysitter, and went to bed. I have receipts. What happened on Saturday night?"

There was no point in mentioning it now. If they could confirm his alibi, and Jessie felt sure they would, he wasn't their guy. And if he wasn't, no good could come from telling him what really happened to Ellie Hill. For now, the fewer people that knew the truth, the better.

"Never mind," she said, unable to hide her disappointment.

Once again, they were back to square one, without a good suspect and with a fast-ticking clock. The killer had murdered two women just yesterday. What did he have in store for today?

CHAPTER TWENTY FOUR

Hannah couldn't wait until her lunch break.

Technically, she didn't get a break, as she was still watching Lyman Feller as he went about his ultra-boring, infidelity-free day. But Kat had said that once he went into a lunchtime 12:30 p.m. staff budget meeting in the conference room at his office, they could both take a breather, since he was running the thing and therefore unlikely to use that moment to sneak out to have a minute's worth of phone sex.

"Do you mind if I go grab a bite and just walk around for a bit?" Hannah had asked. "I just need to stretch my legs after being cooped up all morning watching that guy do nothing."

"Go for it," Kat had said, apparently not suspicious that her apprentice intended to use the down time for anything other than what she claimed.

Hannah briefly reconsidered just telling her the truth, but then thought better of it. Kat would think it was too risky for her to be doing this on her own. She'd feel obligated to help out or tell Jessie, who would either shut it down or insist on helping herself. And since the whole point of this, or at least part of it, was for Hannah to do this on her own, saying anything would defeat the purpose. She kept her mouth shut.

So, once 12:30 rolled around and Feller entered the conference room, Hannah was gone, too, away from the hotel leisure lounge that she'd been using to spy on him, and down the street to a small café with a courtyard that had a hidden table in the corner. She'd specifically requested it this morning so she could have a little privacy for the call she was about to make.

Once she sat down, she did one last quick biographical review before dialing. The person she hoped would answer was Lexie Strasser, Sasha Wexler's best friend. Hannah wasn't originally inclined to try to talk to any of Sasha's friends. The circle seemed to have diminished dramatically in the last year, though the number of girls willing to be quoted in news stories as "close friends" of hers had somehow increased in an inverse proportion.

But the one friend who was still in all of Sasha's social feeds, but had notably not spoken to the press, was Lexie Strasser. To Hannah, that likely meant one of two things: either she was a suspect in the disappearance and didn't want to put herself at risk by speaking publicly, or she was a more faithful friend than the others, who had no interest in using their relationship to gain some cheap notoriety in the media.

Hannah doubted it was the former. She would have found some mention of Lexie being questioned in her research if the police suspected her. So, it was much more probable that Lexie was legitimately upset about Sasha's disappearance, and maybe, just maybe, willing to talk to an investigator about what she knew, if she thought it would help get her friend back. At least that was her hope.

Hannah tapped the numbers, hit send, and waited anxiously as one ring led to two and then three. Finally, on the fourth, someone picked up.

"Hello?" asked a wary female voice.

"Hi, is this Lexie?" Hannah asked in the warmest tone she could muster.

"Who is this?"

Hannah had wondered how she would answer this inevitable question. She knew that her response would dictate whether Lexie hung up or gave her a chance. In the end, she decided to simply be straight with the girl.

"My name is Hannah Dorsey, Lexie," she explained. "I work for a private detective agency that's trying to determine what happened to your friend, Sasha. We're concerned that the authorities aren't pursuing all potential avenues, so we've chosen to join the search. I spoke to Keanu Mendoza last night, and he offered some helpful information. I was hoping I could speak with you too."

For several seconds, there was silence on the other end of the line.

"You're a detective?" Lexie asked dubiously.

"I work for a downtown-based agency," Hannah answered, skirting the fact that she wasn't technically a detective herself.

"Who's paying you? I know it's not her parents."

"No one," Hannah said. "We're pursuing this free of charge."

"Why?"

"Because Sasha reminds me of myself a little, and when I saw her story, I knew I had to help. I had to see if I could find her before something terrible happens, assuming it's not too late already."

"How do I know I can trust you?" Lexie demanded. "You could be some tabloid reporter, trying to trick me into revealing stuff about Sasha. I have no proof that you are who you say you are. You're just a voice on a phone."

Hannah couldn't help but smile at Lexie's response. It was exactly what she would have said if she was in that position and hearing it made her even more certain that the girl would be a credible source of information if she could be convinced to talk.

"Totally fair point," she said. "How about this? Let's make this a FaceTime call, and I think I'll be able to prove that I'm legit."

There was another silence, this time briefer. "Okay."

Once they switched over, Hannah smiled as she watched Lexie stare at her and process the fact that she was talking to someone much younger than she expected. As that happened, Hannah studied the girl on the screen. Lexie was cute, with freckles, red hair, and pigtails. She looked almost like Pippi Longstocking, if when she reached her late teens, Pippi had styled herself with lavender lip gloss and a Death Cab For Cutie t-shirt.

"How old are you?" she asked, stunned.

"I'm eighteen," Hannah told her, "just like Sasha, just like Keanu, and just like you'll be on July 17th. I graduated high school last week. That's part of why this case resonates for me. Sasha feels like someone I could have known."

"But earlier, you said you were a detective," Lexie reminded her angrily.

"No, I said I work for a detective agency, and I do—Gentry Investigations. I'm interning there. But don't be fooled by the 'intern' label. I've got access to all kinds of resources. For example, I don't just know your birthday, Lexie. I know everything about you from your driver's license number to your GPA to your social security number."

"Okay, that's scary," Lexie said. "But it still doesn't change the fact that you're a teenager."

Hannah sensed that this could go on for much longer than she could afford and considering that she had to be back at the hotel to spy on Lyman Feller soon, she did something rare for her.

"I'm a lot more experienced than you might think," she said quietly. "Look up my name online—Hannah Dorsey."

She waited while Lexie took herself offscreen and did the search. As she did that, Hannah saw her server, who was standing across the courtyard, attempt to take advantage of the lull in conversation to come over to take her order. But it was too sensitive a moment, and Hannah politely waved her off.

She knew that the girl had hit paydirt when she heard a soft gasp and wondered whether Lexie was reading about the slaughter of her adoptive parents by her serial killer father, her adoption by her criminal profiler half-sister Jessie Hunt, her abduction by a different serial killer, or one of the other horrors she'd faced in just her last two years of high school.

"Oh my god," Lexie finally muttered under her breath, returning to the screen. Her eyes were wet.

"I don't normally volunteer that kind of biographical history to strangers the first time I meet them," Hannah said, cutting to the chase, "but I wanted you to know that I'm for real. I just want to help people, so they don't have to suffer the way I have. That's why I'm spending my summer working at a detective agency. And it's why, when I read about Sasha, I decided I had to do something."

"Okay," Lexie said, "I believe you, but I don't see how I can help."

"It's my job to figure that out. I'm going to ask you some direct questions. I assume some of them may be repeats of what the police already asked you, but I need answers anyway."

"They didn't ask me very many questions," Lexie said.

"What?"

"They just wanted to know the last time I saw her and if she said anything unusual."

"That's it?" Hannah asked in disbelief.

Lexie nodded.

"Okay, then let's start there," Hannah said, pulling out a notepad. "What did you tell them?"

"That I last saw her the day before yesterday, on Monday, here at the house."

"The day she disappeared," Hannah noted. "What time?"

"Around 6:15 or so," Lexie said. "I remember it was right before dinner, which we usually eat at 6:30. My mom asked her if she wanted to stay, but she said no."

Hannah silently did the math in her head. That was almost three hours before she broke up with Keanu at 9 p.m. at Industrial Coffee.

"Why did she come by?"

"To give me a necklace," Lexie said, reaching offscreen and grabbing it. She held it close to the camera, revealing a simple, multi-colored, beaded necklace. "She said it was her favorite but was worried that she wouldn't be able to keep it much longer, so she asked me to take it."

"Wouldn't be able to keep it much longer because she was going somewhere that she wouldn't be able to take it or because she'd have to return it to someone, or maybe that it might be *taken* from her?"

"She didn't say," Lexie replied, looking upset that she couldn't provide an answer.

"That's okay," Hannah assured her. "Is there anything inscribed on the necklace? Does it look valuable?"

"No, none of that. When I showed it to the cops, they said it looked like junk that you might buy in some store in the mall or maybe even make yourself. I was pissed because it sounded so insensitive, but they weren't wrong. If she did buy it, I doubt that it cost more than $10. I assume it had sentimental value, but I don't know why."

"Okay, how did she seem when she came over?" Hannah asked.

"I'd say weird, but she'd been acting weird for a while."

"Weird how?"

"Just really hard to engage, you know?" Lexie said. "She seemed … I don't know if I'd say sad, maybe burdened? She'd gotten more and more that way over the last year. Like something was weighing her down. She seemed especially troubled that night."

"Did you ask her why?"

"Sure I did," Lexie answered, slightly defensively. "I've been asking her that for months. She always says it's nothing, but she's clearly lying. I asked her directly what was wrong and why was she giving me the necklace. She wouldn't say other than that she wanted me to have it, and that everything would be all right."

"Okay," Hannah said soothingly. "I didn't mean to suggest you weren't concerned. I just have to ask these questions."

"I get it. Go ahead."

"All right. Did she say anything recently about going somewhere or running away, even in what sounded like a joking way?"

"Not that I remember," Lexie said.

"Did she ever say or hint that she was being forced to leave?"

"No. I would definitely remember that."

"What's her relationship like with her parents?" Hannah asked. "There were no comments from them in the news stories, and she barely mentions them on her social feeds."

Lexie laughed bitterly. "There is no relationship to speak of," she said. "They wouldn't do anything to harm her, if that's what you're thinking, but that's mostly because they don't care enough to hurt her, at least not physically. That's how I knew it wasn't them paying you to investigate."

"What do you mean when you say there's no relationship?" Hannah pressed.

"First of all, they're married, but Sasha described it as the most loveless union in America. They're more like roommates. And as to their relationship with her, maybe this will give you an idea. She told me that they once went a whole week without saying a single word to her. When her mom finally broke the silence by asking her to get a roll of paper towels from the garage, she almost fell off her chair in shock."

Hannah, suddenly feeling the aching loss of the parents who adopted her as a baby and gave everything, including their lives, for her, chose not to delve into that topic any deeper.

"Did she have any enemies that you were aware of?" she asked. "Any bullies at school?"

"I don't think so," Lexie said. "To be honest, she had retreated so far into herself that there wasn't really anyone to beef with. How can you have enemies if you don't interact with anyone?

Hannah sighed to herself. She was out of specific questions, so she went with a general one. "What do you think happened to her, Lexie?"

Now, it was the other young woman's turn to sigh. As she did, her pigtails flopped around her shoulders, like even they were depressed by the question.

"I don't know," she said quietly. "It's like she had a whole inner life that she never told me about. Sometimes I worry that something in that life went bad, and she got desperate—made a terrible choice. Other times I worry that she was abducted; that some guy in a van grabbed her, tossed her phone in the trash, took her out to the desert, raped her, killed her, and dumped her body for the animals to pick clean. That's what I think when I stop being busy, even for a minute."

"Don't go there," Hannah said with all the authority she could marshal. "There's a saying among the really good detectives: have hope until there's no hope left to have."

"I'll try," Lexie said. "Did anything I said help?"

"I think it just might have," Hannah told her. "I'm going to find out once we say goodbye."

"Good luck," Lexie said.

"Thanks," Hannah replied and hung up.

She sat quietly at the hidden table in the corner of the café's courtyard, thinking about how she had been honest with Lexie up until the very end. She wasn't at all sure that anything the girl had said would help. And there was no well-known detectives' saying about having hope until there was no hope left to have. She had made it up on the spot to ease Lexie's pain. It was a good line, but she wasn't sure she believed it herself.

This time when the server came over, she gave her order, but asked for it to go. She wasn't in the mood to sit around anymore. While she waited, she reviewed her notes so far.

Sasha had gone to Lexie's house to give her an inexpensive but personally significant necklace, almost like a goodbye gift. Later that night, she met Keanu to break up with him, though she didn't seem to want to, then went on social media to say he'd dumped her. She had no meaningful interaction with her parents. She had months of ever more troubling online posts.

Per Keanu, she made a stab at exploring the faith of her youth but got little support for her efforts, even from him. She had no obvious enemies, according to the one friend she seemed to have left. And based on the police report that Hannah had surreptitiously read using Ryan's department access code, there was no obvious sign of struggle where her phone was found in the trash can—no blood, no torn clothes, no other missing items, no tire marks from a van peeling out, nothing.

Hannah looked at the photos on her phone that she snapped last night when she had her rideshare driver go by the street where the phone was found in the trash can. She imagined herself in Sasha's place, standing by that trash can late at night, feeling the weight of the world collapsing down on her. What had happened next?

Hannah had a gut feeling, but she tried to remember what Jessie always warned against in cases: making assumptions. Her sister had shared many cautionary tales about how incorrect assumptions sent her down rabbit roles that cost her valuable investigative time.

But a gut feeling wasn't necessarily a wrong assumption. It was a hunch. Jessie had also followed her hunches many times, and there were lots of people who might not be alive if she hadn't.

Hannah's hunch told her that this didn't feel like an abduction. The police might believe it was. They seemed to suspect that Lexie's fears about finding a body in the desert were more than reasonable. But to Hannah, based on what she knew, it felt like Sasha had left. It felt like she made a choice to go away.

But if her hunch was right, it still left a key question unanswered, one that might hold the key to finding her: was Sasha simply running away from home, or was she running away from something else—something much worse?

CHAPTER TWENTY FIVE

Jessie felt like a junkie.

The adrenaline of late morning, when they'd discovered Wayne Teague, had given way to the stagnation of mid-afternoon, and she worried that without another blast of clue-inspired energy, she was going to crash hard.

She already sensed the lack of sleep tugging at the edges of her brain, trying to fuzz up her thoughts. Luckily, the headaches hadn't returned, but she doubted they were far behind. It was after 3 p.m., and she, Sam, Jamil, and Beth had spent the last three hours in the research office together, reviewing every lead again, in the hopes that they might have missed something the first time around. But they hadn't, which left the cupboard bare.

Ryan, who was stuck in a meeting down at headquarters, called briefly to check in. After they updated him, which didn't take long, he did his best to keep their spirits up.

"Don't worry," he said enthusiastically, though Jessie could hear the well-masked tinge of disappointment hidden beneath the positivity, "something will pop up. It always does."

Jessie knew she was really in trouble when she started to entertain a theory that immediately filled the back of her throat with bile. As she watched Jamil hunched over his desk, typing at his keyboard violently, mostly monosyllabic in his communication, she wondered again what could have caused such a dramatic shift in his personality of late.

And then her mind, without her conscious consent, pried open the possibility that he might have done something to turn him into this other person. Could he have committed an act—be continually committing acts—that would shroud his entire being in darkness?

It seemed inconceivable, and yet if anyone had the technical expertise to uncover these people's alarm codes, it was Jamil Winslow. And because no one knew the algorithms used to sift through the evidentiary data as well as him, not even Beth, he could easily fudge the results they were receiving, then send them off to pursue red herrings while covering up his involvement.

That was the how. But it didn't clarify why. And no amount of speculation could bring Jessie to an explanation for why the young man who had helped save so many lives would suddenly start taking them. That's when she decided she needed a break.

"I have to clear my head," she said, standing up. "I'm going on a little walk. I'll be back in a few minutes."

Beth, along with Sam, who had set up shop on the research office couch, both nodded absently. Jamil didn't even acknowledge her words. She stepped outside, shaking her head in self-disgust.

Whatever was going on with Jamil, it did *not* involve him suddenly turning into a serial killer. The idea was absurd, and she was ridiculous for having permitted it to consume any of her valuable time. She needed to focus her attention on theories that actually made sense.

She headed half a mile northwest to Pershing Square, the closest area of any size with walkable green space. She moved at a brisk clip, hoping that each footfall would force the guilt out of her system so that she could more clearly concentrate. When she got to the square, she found it less crowded than expected on a June afternoon.

Pershing Square, a combination of green spaces and hardscapes, was often used for outdoor concerts and political rallies. But it was also common to see people eating lunch on the benches or having picnics under the shade of the trees. Right now, she joined a collection of folks that included a woman pushing a stroller, a young couple aggressively making out on a bench, and a father showing his pre-teen son how to operate a drone.

She remembered how, when she was that age, her adoptive father had taken her to a huge park in Las Cruces, New Mexico, where they lived, and taught her how to fly a kite. Because the terrain included both desert and mountains nearby, there were often huge, gusting winds that could send the kite skyrocketing high in the air, only to quickly plummet back to earth mere moments later.

Now fathers were teaching variations on these lessons to their kids with drones. Things had changed a lot in just a few generations. Suddenly, she felt much older than thirty-one, and not just because the man who had taught her to fly a kite was now in the ground, another victim of someone who intended to hurt Jessie by making her loved ones suffer. It seemed to happen a lot.

She shook off the thought and did her best not to be irked by the latter two groups, even though the guy in the kissing couple appeared to be intermittently using his tongue like a Q-tip inside his girlfriend's ear, and the dad was buzzing the drone much lower than Jessie considered safe. She walked to the far end of the square to avoid either getting knocked in the head or inadvertently slobbered on.

As she got away from the murmuring voices and the drone's buzz, she found herself able to think more clearly, and she re-focused on the case. They knew three things for sure: the killer was male, he had access to the victims' alarm codes, and he chose victims who had moved recently. She was sure that those last two facts were somehow connected, and that if she could figure out how, it would quickly lead to the murderer.

She tried to let her mind relax, to create space to find that connection, but something was preventing it. She suddenly felt like she was being watched. She turned around but didn't see anyone suspicious.

Am I losing it?

And then it hit her. The buzzing of the drone was audible, not loud, but it was there. She looked up and saw it hovering about forty feet above her. Glancing across the square, she made eye contact with the father, who was pointing at her and giggling with his son. Apparently, he thought another great lesson to teach him was how to be a creepy techno stalker.

Jessie froze in place. Her whole body tensed up at once as her brain was flooded with a tumbling series of thoughts. She remembered her theory that Wayne Teague might have covertly recorded the homeowners inputting their alarm codes on his phone. Why couldn't a drone be used for the same purpose?

Woozy with excitement, she reached out for the trunk of a nearby palm tree to steady herself. There was no reason that it couldn't if it got close enough. She flashed back to each of the three victims' homes and recalled something that hadn't registered for her at the time. In each one, at least one alarm panel faced a large window or a glass door with open curtains or blinds.

She doubted that it would be hard for a good drone operator to get quality video of the code being inputted and magnify it later. And with the windows and doors closed, the victim would never hear the drone buzzing as it hovered just outside their home, violating their private space and their security.

Using a drone, the killer could also get a sense of the layout of the house or condo complex for future infiltration. He could track the victims' movements over time from afar, to see when their husbands went to the gym, when their families left town for the night, or when they returned from a bar.

But why choose people relatively new to the neighborhood? Who would even know these people were recent arrivals? And then an obvious answer became clear: someone who was paid to know these things, like a drone photographer assigned by a realtor to take exterior shots of properties for sale.

How did I miss that?

Jessie didn't remember when she started running. But at some point while she was thinking her theory through, her legs had simply taken over, leading her back in the direction of the police station. She was sprinting full speed now. There was no point in calling Sam or Jamil or Beth. She'd be back with them to explain in a matter of minutes.

She put her head down, pumping her arms and legs even harder, happy that the pain she felt in her body this time wasn't a mystery, but a means to an end.

CHAPTER TWENTY SIX

Jessie was still catching her breath.

She, Sam, and Beth all stood near the doorway of the research office, not wanting to distract Jamil as his fingers flew across the keys and the screen in front of him changed rapidly.

Jessie had explained her theory through panted gasps the moment she returned. They were all—minus Jamil—as enthusiastic about it as she was, though he did start typing even before she finished talking. Even though she no longer harbored questions about his involvement in these killings, Jessie remained befuddled by his demeanor. Since there was nothing to do now but wait for Jamil's results, she decided that it was time to get answers.

When she was finally able to inhale and exhale at a normal rate, she tapped Beth on the shoulder and motioned for her to come out into the hall. Then she led her a few steps away from the office and leaned in close.

"I know Jamil isn't your responsibility," she whispered. "He's your boss, and you shouldn't have to explain his behavior, but you're also his friend, right?"

Beth nodded silently. Her expression, normally a picture of sunny calm, was downcast. She seemed to be shaking slightly.

"Okay," Jessie continued, "then even though it's not fair to put you in this position, I'm going to do it. I have to assume you know what's been going on with him lately better than most. You're with him every day in a small office. From where I stand, he's been erratic, moody, and borderline contentious. He isn't as proactive as usual and seems to need to be pushed to tackle leads that he'd normally pursue on his own. Plus, he looks exhausted, like he hasn't gotten decent sleep in forever. I'm really worried about him. If you know what the issue is, please tell me."

Beth's face scrunched up like she was trying hold back tears. It was clear from the distraught look in her eyes that she was torn, and that she considered talking to be a betrayal of some sort. After a moment, she seemed to regain control and took a deep breath.

"He doesn't want me to tell anyone because he thinks he can handle it on his own," she said, her voice barely audible, "but he can't. He's consumed by guilt, and he's starting to spiral."

"Guilt over what?" Jessie asked, refusing to jump to any conclusions.

"The twenty-seven people who died in the Operation Z attack back in April," she muttered, "he views their deaths as his fault."

"What?" Jessie asked, shocked but doing her best to keep her voice low. "He was essential to uncovering Zoe Bradway's identity. I know we couldn't get to the customers at the Corner K convenience store in time to save them, but without his work, so many more could have died. There were nearly 2,000 people in that movie theater that night. If even a tenth of them had eaten Zoe's poisoned popcorn, it could have been so much worse."

"He doesn't see it that way," Beth said. "He feels like he should have figured out her identity sooner, and that if he had made different, better decisions, they'd *all* be alive. He says he feels haunted by them. He told me that any time he laughs, it's like he's spitting on their graves. That's why he's been burning the candle at both ends, so that there's no time for anything else. He doesn't want to let himself have a moment to feel good or free. He's punishing himself. I don't know what to do for him."

Beth couldn't prevent herself from softly crying this time. Jessie felt her own cheeks burn as tears streamed down her face. She pulled Beth into a hug, squeezed her tight, and whispered in her ear. "I'm so sorry you've had to deal with this on your own," she said, "but not anymore. We're going to get him help. I promise. I think I know someone who might be able to reach him."

She felt Beth squeeze her even tighter. Neither of them said anything as they stood in the hall, hugging each other, ignoring the cops who walked by, trying to awkwardly avert their gaze.

Sam poked his head out of the office. He looked briefly startled at the two women embracing in front of him but got over it quickly.

"Jamil says he found something," he told them.

They both quickly wiped their eyes and followed him back in. Luckily, Jamil never glanced back at them, so he didn't see their wet eyes and get suspicious.

"Go ahead," Sam said. "They're back."

This time, Jamil had the courtesy to project the image from his screen onto the wall in front of him as he spoke. "The reason none of us picked up on this lead before," he said, diving in as if they'd already been in the middle of a conversation, "is that even though these drone shots were taken for realty companies, the realtors don't have the drone contract. The neighborhood homeowners association does. So, they hire the drone photographer, and the realtor for the seller pays the HOA a fee to use their services."

"But shouldn't that still show up as a line item when the house is sold?" Sam asked.

"It does," Jamil said, pulling up a screen and circling one line among dozens. "As you can see, the line item is listed only as 'HOA services,' so there's no way that we'd know it meant aerial drone photography."

"How many photographers do they contract with?" Beth asked.

"That's what I was about to look up," Jamil said, pulling up a page in the HOA's annual budget. "It looks like they just have one: Morgan Presser. I'll see what I can find on him."

He typed for a few seconds that seemed to drag on interminably. "No criminal record," he said. "I'm getting the driver's license to see if the physical description matches. Here we go."

The license popped up on the screen, and Jessie's heart immediately sank. Morgan Presser was female. No one spoke as they all stared at the image of the pleasant-looking, twenty-something woman who had crushed their collective spirits.

"I don't get it," Beth finally muttered. "It made perfect sense."

Jessie didn't get it either. She thought for sure this was the lead that would pay off. She knew they had to start over, but in that moment, she didn't feel up to it.

"Hold on a second," Sam said, not sounding totally defeated. "Jamil, can you pull up a still image from one of the victims' homes?"

A few finger flicks and mouse clicks later, they were staring at an overhead shot of the Hill family's Tudor-style mansion. Jessie tried to see what had sparked Sam's interest but was at a loss.

"There," he said, pointing at the bottom right corner of the screen. "I knew something wasn't right. Jamil, can you magnify the corner of the image?"

Jamil did, and Jessie saw what had her partner so amped. In the corner, in tiny letters, she read the words "B.D. Aerial Photography."

"Good catch, Sam," she said. "Unless someone can explain why Morgan Presser's initials seem to be 'B.D.,' I think we need to make a call."

Jamil punched in the number for the HOA and put the call on speaker. A charming older-sounding lady named Clara answered on the second ring. After explaining who he was, Sam got to the point.

"Does Morgan Presser still have the contract with you to do aerial photography for local realtors?"

"Oh my, no," Clara said. "Morgan left us a little under a year ago. She got an offer to go work for a film production company, one she couldn't refuse. That's a little film joke."

"It's a good one," Sam lied charmingly. "But your website still has her listed as your photographer."

"Oh dear, we really should update that," Clara admitted. "We're a little slow with that sort of thing. In any case, the new photographer is named Barney Doyle. He's a real sweetheart."

Even as Sam was extricating himself from the conversation, Jamil was punching the name into his databases. When Sam got off the phone, the researcher was ready.

"Barney Doyle moved here a year ago," he said. "He got the HOA job ten months back."

"That's just before the first victim's house was purchased," Jessie pointed out. "The Carrigans moved in eight months ago."

"He doesn't have a record here, but he used to live in Nevada, and it looks like he does have one there," Jamil said as Doyle's file appeared on the wall. "He was charged with voyeurism twice. The second time, the victim claimed he was taking photos though no camera was ever found. He pleaded down to trespassing both times and got probation in each case. The last incident was eight years ago."

"Didn't the HOA do a background check?" Beth asked.

"Both charges were misdemeanors, so it looks like his record was sealed after a year," Jessie noted. "Assuming the HOA even cared enough to check. Even if they did, they don't have access to sealed records."

"If his last incident was eight years ago, are we sure it's him?" Jamil asked, showing more interest in the case than Jessie had seen in days. "Maybe he's reformed."

Sam shook his head. "I worked the vice unit for a long time," he said. "In my experience, it's less likely that he reformed than that he just got much better at spying, so he didn't get caught."

Jessie started for the door, anxious to get moving.

"I think it's time we find out the truth for ourselves, Sam, don't you?" she said, and then added without waiting for his reply, "let's go!"

CHAPTER TWENTY SEVEN

Jessie hopped out of the car before it had even come to a complete stop.

According to Clara, the HOA had Barney Doyle assigned to do a photoshoot of an older apartment complex called The Sullivan on North Rossmore Avenue, the same street where Lauren Pastorini's body had been found this morning.

Jessie knew The Sullivan well. She'd actually interviewed a witness for a case here last year. Like many of the old-school apartment complexes on this stretch of the street, it looked like it was right out of a 1940s film noir.

It was pure glamour on the outside, complete with art deco design and palm trees out front. But personal experience had taught her that it was a mirage. The lobby smelled stale and visible dust rose up off the boysenberry-colored carpet with every step. She hoped they wouldn't have to go inside.

Jamil confirmed that Doyle's car GPS location had him parked in front of The Sullivan. In fact, when they walked down the sidewalk toward the building's entry path, they discovered that Sam had parked on the street just a few spaces behind it. Once they got to the front door, they stopped.

"How do we find out exactly where he is right now?" Sam asked, perplexed.

Jessie wondered the same thing. But it only took a few seconds to get her answer. A familiar buzzing sound tickled her ears, and she looked up to see a drone high above, circling over the roof of the building.

She was just pointing it out to Sam when the drone stopped circling, moved across the street, and disappeared on the roof of the building directly across from The Sullivan. A moment later, a man who had been previously blocked by a pillar stepped into view. It was Barney Doyle. He bent down to pick up the drone before examining it.

"Want to go say hi?" Jessie asked her partner with a smile.

Sam nodded. They crossed the street, entered The Catalonia, which was slightly newer than The Sullivan, but that still meant it was almost a hundred years old and didn't have elevators. They took the stairs six stories up to the roof. The rooftop door was held open with a cinder block. After catching their breath, they stepped outside.

Barney was still in the same spot on the roof where they'd seen him before. But he was no longer standing or holding the drone, which had been placed in a case beside him. Now he was crouched by the edge of the roof, facing away from them, with what looked like a video camera perched on the flat, brick, parapet wall. He was peering through the eyehole. His pants were down around his ankles.

Jessie looked over at Sam and muttered. "You can take point on this one."

Sam grimaced and stepped forward, removing his weapon. "The more things change, the more they stay the same, huh Barney?" he called out.

The man's head whipped around, though not his body. Barney Doyle looked older than his forty-one years. He had a hunched, worn-out frame. His hair, currently being buffeted by the rooftop wind, was almost completely gray. The wrinkles on his face were clearly visible, even from this distance. And he looked stunned. Sam didn't give him time to get his bearings as he approached him.

"Barney Doyle," Sam continued, "we're with the Los Angeles Police Department, and we have a few questions for you. But first, would you please be so kind as to put your trousers back on?"

"It's not what you think," Doyle told them as he pulled up his pants.

"Not like in Nevada?" Sam asked, getting closer.

"Who are you exactly?" Doyle demanded, turning to face them as he buckled his belt.

"I told you," Sam said, holding up his badge with his free hand, "LAPD. I'm Detective Goodwin and this is our criminal profiler, Jessie Hunt."

Jessie noticed that Doyle didn't seem as interested in the answer as in desperately scoping out the roof, as if looking for some means of escape.

"That's a bad idea, Barney," she called out. "There's nowhere to go. This door is the only way back down.

She had no idea if that was true and hoped Doyle didn't either. She just didn't want him to run. But after giving her a long, panicked look, he did anyway. Turning away from Sam, who was now less than ten feet from him, he made a break for the lower level of the tiered roof. Jessie heard Sam curse under his breath as he chased after him. She did the same.

Doyle got to the edge of the top roof level and leapt the four feet to the one below. But he landed awkwardly, yelped as his ankle turned, and stumbled, careening out of control toward the parapet wall. His stomach slammed into it, sending his upper body teetering precariously over the edge. Jessie gasped silently, sensing what was to come, helpless to prevent it, even as she dashed over.

And then, after one second that felt like five, his legs rose off the ground and began to follow his body over the side. His hands flailed desperately, trying to grab the edge of the brick wall, but his fingers scraped the top without getting a grip. His torso disappeared over the side of the wall, and his legs were about to as well when Sam lunged, reached out, and grabbed the man's left calf in his hands.

The weight of Doyle's body forced his leg to rip downward through the detective's fingers until somehow the momentum stopped at his ankle, just above his shoe. But the sheer force of bulk and gravity was yanking Sam toward the edge now too. As his body slammed into the wall, he managed to yell out one word. "Jessie!"

But he didn't need to. She had already dived off the top level, making sure to keep her balance as she hit the lower one. She dipped into a roll as she moved toward them, coming to a stop at Sam's legs, which she bearhugged from behind as she bent into a deep crouch, forcing every ounce of her weight into the rooftop gravel.

She felt Sam's momentum come to a stop. Looking up, she saw that he had braced his hip against the wall and was wincing as he attempted to drag Doyle back.

"I'm going to pull you from behind," she said, standing up, wrapping her arms around Sam's ribs, and leaning backwards as she tugged at him.

The extra force seemed to do the trick, as their collective weight suddenly propelled everyone into reverse, and Doyle shot back over the wall onto the rooftop, like a cork finally popping free from a wine bottle. The three of them landed in a crumpled heap, where they all lay still for a few seconds, trying to catch their breath and process what had almost just happened.

Jessie, who had endured the least daunting physical experience, recovered first. She wriggled out from under Sam, pulled out her handcuffs, and slapped them on Barney Doyle's wrists.

She did a quick self-check. Her head was swimming slightly, and she felt winded and marginally nauseated. Was that an after-effect of her concussion or just the result of an extremely intense physical experience that stressed her muscles and cardiovascular system at the same time? She didn't have to study the issue.

"When he's able to speak again," she told Doyle, "my partner is going to read you your rights and then we're going to have a conversation."

***

But the conversation didn't happen.

Jessie should have anticipated problems, but she'd allowed herself to hope things would come easier once they had Doyle in custody.

Instead, as soon as Sam read the man his Miranda warning, he clammed up. He didn't say a thing on the way down the apartment building stairs or on the drive back to the station. When they cuffed him to the metal table in interrogation room two and began asking questions, he did offer one word: lawyer.

As they waited for his attorney to arrive, she called Ryan to update him. He did his best to offer her a bit of optimism.

"At least he's off the streets," he said. "Now that he's in custody, we can track his recent movements. We won't need a confession to nail this guy."

"I hope not," Jessie said. "While we wait for his lawyer to show up, I'm actually going to look through the footage from the video camera he had with him. Maybe it'll have something incriminating."

"I'm surprised you haven't looked already," Ryan said.

"It's old school," she explained. "Jamil had to find the right cord to hook it up to a monitor. It's a bit of a treasure hunt situation."

"Speaking of Jamil," Ryan replied. "Are you ready to really tell me what's up with him. I know you were covering earlier."

"Yes, but not now," she told him. "Maybe tonight, when we have a little more privacy."

"Okay," he said. "I'm not sure when I'll be back though. I'm still stuck at headquarters. The mayor wanted Decker to do a department organizational review to make sure all his interim appointments are panning out. I've been helping set that up. We're almost done, but I might be stuck here a little longer."

"Okay," she said, Keep me posted. I love you."

"I love you too," he said. "Also, did you notice how I didn't ask you any last name-based questions in this conversation?"

Jessie couldn't help but laugh. "I noticed that pointing out that you didn't ask any questions is basically the same as asking a question."

"Hey!" Ryan said, trying to sound hurt.

Jessie's phone buzzed. A text from Hannah appeared.

"I've got to go," she said, "to be continued."

They hung up, and she looked at the text. It was short and concise: *Wrapping up here but may make a pit stop on my way home. Tying up some loose ends. See you later.*

Jessie noted that the text was awfully vague about the nature of the pit stop and the loose ends that needed tying up. She didn't know if that was due to some confidentiality issue related to the case or if her sister's previous, notorious habit of using ambiguity to hide questionable choices was rearing its ugly head again.

She was tempted to call her on it or even to reach out to Kat to see if she could shed any light on things. But then she reminded herself that she was supposed to be giving her sister more latitude in light of her age, impending start of college, and recent good judgment. So, though it pained her to do so, she texted back with a simple: *Okay. Keep me posted.*

With that done, she headed back to the interrogation room to find out if Doyle's lawyer had arrived. But as she did, she got a text from Jamil that he'd found the needed cord to access the video camera footage. She went to research instead. When she arrived, Beth wasn't there. Jamil stood up.

"Where are you going?" she asked.

"I'm going to step out for this," he said. "I'm not comfortable being here while you review footage from a peeping Tom, especially one who might be using it to plan murders."

She couldn't argue with his logic and was actually happy to see a glimmer of the easily embarrassed, hyper-courteous guy she had such affection for. Once he left, she closed the door for a little privacy and turned on the camera.

The footage was clearly from The Sullivan, the building across the street from where they'd found him, and the timestamp—3:57 p.m.—indicated that it was taken just before they arrived. It showed a woman in an apartment on the fifth floor. She was younger than the victims, probably late teens or early twenties, and she was in her living room, doing some kind of workout while watching an instructor do the same on the screen in front of her. Blonde and attractive, with a curvy figure, she was wearing workout leggings and a sports bra and seemed to be oblivious to anything other than the routine.

Jessie turned her attention from the girl to the apartment, scanning for an alarm panel, but she couldn't see one. After a few minutes, the screen went black, which she guessed was when Doyle turned it off upon their arrival on the roof.

She rewound the footage to the beginning and found video he'd previously taken of three other women, each as beautiful as the first, all either barely clad or completely naked. She guessed that none was older than twenty-five.

She noted several other things. From what she could tell, each video session showed a woman in an apartment building or condo. None of them were in stand-alone houses. And while one apartment seemed to have a visible alarm panel, the other two didn't, which she found odd. When she'd seen all the footage, she returned to the bullpen, where Sam was at his computer.

"Any word on his lawyer?" she asked.

"He just got here," Sam said. "I think they'll be chatting for a while before we know whether he'll let him talk to us. I'm not holding my breath."

"Okay," Jessie said. "Hey, I just watched the footage from Doyle's camera."

"You didn't wait for me?"

"Sorry," she said. "I guess I was just anxious to check it out and forgot."

"That's all right," he said. "Depending on what it was, I'm not sure we needed to have a watch party for the stuff. Besides, I was working on getting a search warrant for Doyle's place."

"Good thinking. But you should check out the video when you're done with that," she told him. "I'd be curious to get your thoughts. I had some … reservations."

"What do you mean?"

"Something about the footage just doesn't sit right with me," she said. "All of the women in it are younger than our victims, and they don't fit the same profile. These girls all look like models or actresses.

Plus, in the footage I saw so far, they all lived in apartments—no houses—and only one of the four had a visible alarm panel."

Sam leaned back in his chair, clearly pondering her concerns. "Okay," he said. "I guess that is a bit off. But it's such a small sample size. Maybe when we check his place, we'll find footage of older women or ones who live in houses. Or couldn't it be that he was checking out these women, saw that they weren't good options for attacks, but kept recording just for the lascivious pleasure of it."

"Entirely possible," Jessie conceded, though she wasn't convinced. "Anyway, I know you're prepping that warrant request, but look when you get a chance. Meanwhile, since we're in a holding pattern until Doyle finishes with his lawyer, I'm going to check something out."

"Care to share?"

"Not just yet," she said. "Maybe if it turns into something,"

She walked back down the hall to research, sifting through her apprehensions, trying to decide if she was making too much of them. Maybe Sam was right, and a search of Doyle's home would show a library of footage of other women, maybe even of their three victims. Maybe the guy had simply decided that even if these younger model-types weren't future targets, he might as well do some peeping.

Maybe, but maybe not. But if it turned out that Doyle wasn't their guy, that meant a killer was still out there. And if he was, how the hell was she going to find him when the only thing she was sure of was that the man had a drone?

She looked at her phone. It was after 5 p.m. now. If the murderer was still out there, she doubted the day would end without another victim, and the day was fast slipping away.

She stepped into the research office, where Jamil and Beth were both sipping coffee, looking fried. They glanced up as she entered.

"Hey guys," she said, "what can you tell me about drones?"

CHAPTER TWENTY EIGHT

Hannah hadn't lied exactly.

But she definitely wasn't completely forthcoming in her text to Jessie. When she wrote that she "may make a pit stop on my way home" and that she was "tying up some loose ends," she had been purposefully ambiguous. She was actually surprised that her sister didn't call her on it, but she wasn't going to question her good luck.

The pit stop on the way home, after another day of watching Lyman Feller do nothing remotely illicit, was back to the West Los Angeles street where Sasha's phone had been found. Now that she was working off the premise that Sasha had run away rather than been abducted, she wanted to retrace the girl's steps with that in mind. So, with that in mind, she had her rideshare driver, an amiable twenty-something surfer dude with long, blond locks named Kellen, circle the block where the phone was found, while she imagined that she was Sasha.

Where would I go if I was her?

As an eighteen-year-old girl living in the modern world, Sasha knew that as long as she had that phone, she could be tracked. So, getting rid of it was a sure sign that she was going somewhere that she didn't want to be found. But where could she find a place like that around here, on the relatively cushy west side of Los Angeles?

As Kellen made increasingly large concentric circles around the block with the trash can, Hannah scanned the area. When they got four blocks out from the trash can, they finally found themselves on a non-residential street, Pico Boulevard. She had to assume that Sasha had picked this area for a reason and not just on a whim. Maybe this street had something to do with it.

Again, Hannah attempted to project herself into Sasha's mindset. If she'd dumped her phone to avoid being found, then she would have taken other precautions, too, like avoiding cameras whenever possible, and using cash instead of credit cards. And since she was still missing, her evasive measures had clearly been successful so far.

"Pull over there," Hannah told Kellen when she saw a Best Western across the street.

Once they stopped near the front entrance, she hopped out and walked into the lobby. There were security cameras everywhere. Everything about the hotel felt wrong.

There's no way she'd risk coming here and being seen. Besides, this place is nicer than she'd want. They'd likely require a credit card to reserve a room.

No, Sasha would want a more out of the way place, one that took cash, and scrupulously avoided questions. She returned to the car and did a search on her phone. Most of the other hotels nearby were equally reputable.

But there was one motel, just three blocks north, that might fit the bill. It was still technically in West L.A., but in a less desirable area, right next to a tow yard and a payday loan outfit. According to online reviews, it was seedy, smelled bad, had bars on the windows of the rooms, and was popular with drug addicts and folks who used it on an hourly basis. It apparently also took cash.

***

"Are you sure you don't remember this girl," Hannah asked, holding up a picture of Sasha on her phone for a second time to the manager of the Hollywood Motor Court, which, despite its name, was nowhere near Hollywood.

"I told you I don't," said the scrawny guy, whose long beard seemed intended to make up for the lack of hair on his head. "Besides, in case you couldn't tell from looking around, this is the kind of place where *not* remembering anyone is kind of part of my job description."

"Could you check your security cameras?" she asked.

"What security cameras?" he half-laughed, half-snarled.

She turned around, worried that engaging with the guy any more might increase her frustration and cause her to say something she regretted. At least she knew that as an establishment without cameras that took cash, the motel might appeal to Sasha.

Looking out through the barred reception window, she noticed a minibus parked next to Kellen's car that hadn't been there before. Written on the side was "HHM Transport."

"Don't tell me that the Hollywood Motor Court offers transportation to the airport?" she said to the manager, pointing at the vehicle.

"Are you kidding?" he said, amused at the idea. "That's a church rehab bus. It comes by all the time to pick up addicts who want to try to get clean."

Upon hearing his words, an idea popped into Hannah's head.

"How often does it come?" she asked. "Every day?"

"I don't know, girlie," the manager said, annoyed. "Why don't you leave me alone and ask the driver?"

Hannah saw an older man with thinning, slicked back hair walk out from behind the back of the bus. He was wearing black slacks and a white, button-down shirt. She went out to meet him.

"Are you from the church rehab place?" she asked.

"I am," he said warmly. "I'm Alvin from Have Hope Ministries. Are you looking for help? We can offer a free ride to our facility."

"How often do you come here?" Hannah asked, ignoring his question.

The man smiled, not at all put off by her refusal to answer. He was clearly used to it.

"We make stops at the Motor Court every Monday, Wednesday, and Friday at noon and 5 p.m., give or take. Jester in there should have handed you a brochure with our schedule. If you like, we can take you to the Ministry and when you feel you're ready, bring you back, free of charge."

"Jester didn't mention anything about times or days unfortunately," Hannah said. "So, to be clear, if someone missed the Monday bus at 5 p.m., the next available one would have been earlier today at noon, correct?"

Even before he answered, she calculated the potential math in her head. If Sasha had arrived here at the motel late on Monday night after first dumping Keanu and then her phone, she would have had to hole up in a room for a day and a half until catching the HHM minibus.

"That's right, I did that drive myself," Alvin said, still smiling but now mildly perplexed by the intensity of her questioning. "You seem a little troubled, young lady. Are you interested in visiting the Ministry? We're here to help."

"I'm not," Hannah said politely. "I don't take drugs but a friend of mine does. She's fallen on hard times, and I know she used to come here sometimes to score. I was looking for her. But when I saw your bus, I hoped that she might have taken you up on the offer."

She showed him the same photo that she'd just shared with Jester the motel manager.

"I'm trying to find her to make sure she's okay," she continued. "Do you remember taking her on her your noon trip today? She might have been wearing a hoodie or a cap pulled down low over her face."

Alvin looked at the picture, squinting in the hopes that it might help jog his memory.

"I don't specifically remember this young person," he admitted. "I make multiple stops and the bus gets pretty full, but I do feel like I remember someone getting on wearing a cap. I couldn't say for sure though. It all starts to run together after a while."

"What time would you have arrived at the Ministry?" she asked.

"I couldn't tell you exactly, but we usually pull in around 2:30."

"Do you have cameras on your bus that I could check, or do you maybe use them back at the Ministry?" she asked.

Alvin gave her a sympathetic half-smile. "No cameras on the bus," he said. "We do have them back at HHM for security purposes, but you should know that the administrators there are reluctant to share that sort of thing out of respect for the privacy of folks who come to us for aid."

"I understand," Hannah said. "Still, I might like to talk to them. Where is the Ministry located?"

Alvin gave her the address, and she hopped into the back of the car. She was about to share it with Kellen, but he beat her to the punch.

"I already plugged it in," he told her. "I couldn't help but listen in through the window. You're my most interesting customer in weeks."

"Interesting enough to risk a speeding ticket for?" Hannah asked. "Because we need to get to this place ASAP."

***

Hannah knew that Have Hope Ministries was a bust even before she got out of the car in their main parking lot.

A different minibus was currently parked out in front of the large, squat industrial-looking building on South Alameda Street at the edge of the Downtown Arts District. Newcomers were filing into the building slowly. None of them seemed to notice what Hannah saw immediately.

The facility was equipped with half a dozen security cameras affixed to the walls above the various doors. That didn't account for the cameras near the gated entrance to the parking lot. She could only guess how many there were inside the building. There was no way Sasha would have entered this place.

Still, it might have been a useful means to an end. After staying out of sight at the cash-accepting Hollywood Motor Court from Monday night until midday today, she could have taken the free ministry bus here and then simply walked away to her real intended destination.

Hannah pulled out her phone again, looking to see what landmarks within walking distance of HHM might appeal to Sasha. The answer was immediately obvious. Two and a half blocks away, on East 7th Street, was the Greyhound Bus Station. She held out the map to Kellen.

"We're going here," she said.

***

"Are you sure?"

"I'm positive, Kellen," Hannah said. She was speaking to him over the phone as he sat in the bus station parking lot, and she stood in the middle of the crowded bus station waiting area. "This is the end of the line. If she's already caught a bus to Canada, that's seriously outside your expected driving area. I'll find another way to catch up to her. You've gone above and beyond. Don't worry. You'll be getting a great tip."

"Don't worry about it," he said. "This was the most fun I've had in days. I hope you find her."

After hanging up, Hannah took stock of the situation. There was no guarantee that Sasha had come here. After all, this place was crawling with cameras too. But there was nothing else in walking distance that made any sense. As a bus station employee walked by, she tapped the woman on the shoulder.

"Excuse me, do you know if bus tickets can be purchased with cash?"

The woman nodded yes without speaking and continued on her way. That seemed to clinch it. This had to be the place. If it wasn't, Hannah was out of luck. It was 6:32 p.m. on Wednesday night, nearly forty-eight hours after Sasha had first disappeared. If this lead didn't pan out, then it was almost certainly too late to pick up the trail again.

She walked over to an empty chair, sat down, and did a search on the website for buses that had left any time after 2:30 this afternoon. No destinations jumped out at her. There were no buses going to Canada.

There was one that left for San Diego at 3 p.m. Sasha could have conceivably tried to get over the border into Tijuana, Mexico, from there. But the authorities were on the lookout for her, which she had to know, and it wasn't clear to Hannah why she would want to leave the country anyway. Other than that, nothing seemed plausible.

Hannah closed her eyes, again trying to put herself in Sasha's shoes. She didn't know where the girl was going or why, but she felt certain that she planned to use this place as a first stop on any journey, whether to escape her past or pursue her future.

She stood up and walked over to the main board showing departures that had yet to leave tonight, along with corresponding times. Her eyes passed over city after city. None held any significance for her, not Phoenix, not Nashville, not Las Vegas, not Denver, not Salt Lake City, not Seattle.

She paused for a moment as a faint recollection teased her, like a wisp of smoke she could see briefly before it disappeared. She wanted to grab at it but knew from conversations with Jessie that it was better to let it go and wait for it return on its own schedule. And then it did.

Hannah smiled. She wasn't sure if the theory that had sidled into her consciousness just now was correct, but it made sense, and she intended to follow it. She walked up to the ticket window with the shortest line. After a few minutes, she was at the front.

"Destination?" the clerk, a middle-aged woman with extremely thick glasses, asked disinterestedly.

"Does the 7:30 bus to Denver make any stops?"

"Do you want to purchase a ticket to Denver?" the clerk wanted to know.

"Can you answer my question please?" Hannah pressed.

The clerk looked briefly appalled, as if she was being asked for nuclear codes, before reluctantly typing on her keyboard. "There are fifteen-minute stops in San Bernardino, Barstow, Kingman, then a thirty-minute stop in Flagstaff, and one last fifteen-minute stop in Durango before arriving in Denver. Do you want a ticket or not?"

"Not," Hannah said giddily, walking away.

Durango, Colorado—according to Keanu, that was where Sasha had gone to Jewish summer camp as a kid, where she had some of her best childhood memories. Was it so crazy to think that she might return there to recapture some of the joy from that earlier time?

Hannah turned around. The Denver bus left at 7:30. That was almost an hour from now, which meant that, if her hunch was right, Sasha was still here at the bus station, waiting to board. It would be daunting to walk around the entire waiting area, checking out everyone with a cap or hoodie without drawing attention to herself in the time she had left.

But then she realized she didn't need to do any of that. There was no way Sasha would sit out here, with all the security cameras around, among the hordes of people, any of whom might recognize her. No, she'd want to keep a low profile. She'd want to stay out of sight. Hannah walked to the women's restroom.

***

She did her best not to look suspicious.

It was a little difficult, considering that she'd been standing at the restroom mirror, pretending to touch up her makeup for over fifteen minutes. But it proved to be worth the mild discomfort.

That was because, as women filed in and out of the restroom, the stall farthest from the door remained occupied. Whoever was in there wore hiking boots, the kind that might prove useful in rural Colorado.

When the restroom eventually emptied completely, other than the two of them, Hannah grabbed a "temporarily closed for service" sign from the maintenance closet, hung it on the outside of the door, and closed it. Then she walked over to last stall, stepped into the one next to it, gulped hard, and spoke.

"Hi Sasha," she said quietly.

CHAPTER TWENTY NINE

She prayed that all her desperate travels around the city hadn't led her here only to accost some random woman minding her own business in a bathroom stall.

No one spoke, but she did hear a small gasp from the other side of the stall door and saw the heels of the hiking boots rise nervously.

"It's okay," Hannah continued quickly. "You don't know me, and no one knows I'm here. My name is Hannah Dorsey. Can I talk to you for a second?"

There was an eternity of silence from the other stall, then finally one unexpected word. "Why?"

Hannah felt a flood of relief. She recognized the voice instantly from her online videos. It was Sasha.

"Because a lot of people are worried about you, Sasha. Keanu is. Lexie is. I don't know if you're following the news, but half the city is. I know that you must have a really good reason for what you did, dumping your phone and making it look like you were abducted. I was hoping you could tell me what that is."

After several more seconds of silence, Sasha replied, "Why should I tell you anything? I don't even know who you are."

"Maybe that's the reason to tell me—because you don't know me. You don't owe me anything. I don't have any expectations of you. Sometimes it's easier to speak honestly to strangers. But if it helps, I'm a lot like you. I'm eighteen. I just graduated from high school. But I also work for a detective agency, which is how I found you. I read about your case, and you reminded me of myself. I've been through a lot of stuff myself lately, and it seemed like you were going through a lot of stuff, and I wanted to see if I could help you. That's why I'm here."

There was another endless stretch without words.

"I didn't mean for Keanu to get in trouble," Sasha finally said.

"What do you mean?"

"That's why I said he broke up with me on social," she said. "I was worried that he'd come looking for me, try to get me back, and he'd discover that I was gone or worse, that he wouldn't have an alibi for when I went missing. But I figured that if I blamed him for the breakup, he'd be pissed at me and stay away—stay home, and then he'd have his family to say where he was and he wouldn't be a suspect. But I read that they questioned him really hard anyway."

"He's okay," Hannah said. "He just wants to make sure you're alright. *Are* you alright?"

She could hear sniffling from the next stall. Then it turned into muffled sobs. Hannah got out of her stall and knocked softly on the door.

"Are you alright, Sasha?"

She heard the door unlock. After a moment of internal debate, she gently pushed it in. Sasha was sitting on the seat with her head in her hands. Her brown eyes were red and puffy, and her long, brown hair had started to escape from under the baseball cap she wore.

"No," she said through her tears. "I'm not alright."

"What's wrong?"

Sasha shrugged. "Everything was already on a knife's edge, you know? My parents don't give a crap about me. I didn't get good grades. I barely graduated. I didn't have very many friends. My boyfriend was sweet but super deep. And then last fall, a friend of mine that I used to go to summer sleepaway camp with—her name was Marnie—killed herself."

She paused, temporarily unable to speak.

"I'm sorry, Sasha," Hannah said quietly.

Sasha nodded, swallowed hard, and pressed on. "We'd talked just the week before, and I didn't see it coming," she said. "After that, I just couldn't keep it together anymore. Stuff that sucked but seemed manageable just wasn't anymore. I tried to get back into my faith, thinking that would help, but no one really got on board with that, and even though that shouldn't have mattered, I gave up on it. I started thinking of doing what Marnie did. And then last week, I found this necklace that she made me one year at camp, and it seemed like a sign that maybe I should start fresh. I figured what better place to do that than where I had my best memories, back at camp. I thought I would just make everyone think I was dead, that something bad had happened to me, and then no one would come looking. I gave Lexie the necklace because I wanted someone to have something of me to hold onto. And then I did … all the things that led me here."

She stopped talking and let out a huge sigh of relief, as if all the weight she'd been carrying had been released from her body with one giant breath. Suddenly, she seemed freer, but smaller, too, and more vulnerable.

Hannah took a step forward and extended her arms. Sasha, still crying, stood up, reached out, and embraced her, squeezing tight, her body heaving as the sobs broke free from her chest. They stayed like that for a while.

As they hugged, Hannah couldn't help but be overcome by her own swirl of emotions. Just a minute ago, she'd told Sasha that they were a lot alike because they were both eighteen, had just finished high school, and had been through "a lot of stuff lately." And while that was all true, it wasn't completely honest.

She probably would have been on the same path as Sasha—feeling hopeless and utterly alone, about to take a bus to oblivion or choose an even darker route from which there was no return—if not for one thing: Jessie.

At the darkest moment in her life, when her adoptive parents had been murdered and she was being tortured by her serial killer father, Jessie Hunt showed up to save her, and not just that night, but countless times since then. Jessie took her in, became her guardian, then sacrificed her own well-being, health, and even risked her life for her.

What would have happened if Jessie hadn't come along at the moment when Hannah needed her most? Where would she be now? Institutionalized? In prison? Dead? Had she ever really thanked her sister for what she'd done for her? For just being there when she needed her? For being her rock? Sasha didn't have a rock. She didn't even have a frickin' pebble.

"Are you going to make me go back?" Sasha eventually asked between tearful gasps, her head burrowed in Hannah's neck.

Maybe it's time for me to be the rock.

"Sasha," she whispered, "I've been through a lot in my life. I lost both my parents less than two years ago. I've been kidnapped. I admitted myself to a facility because I was worried that I might hurt people. Just a few months ago, I watched a good man die right in front of me, sacrifice his own life to save hundreds of others, leaving his children fatherless. And after all that, I'm still standing here, bent but unbroken."

She paused for a moment, unsure if she could go on. But then she reminded herself that, of course, she could. That was the whole point, after all.

"So, I can tell you honestly that if you come back, there is hope for you," she said quietly. "And if you let it in, there is help for you too. But no, I'm not going to make you go back. I'm not going to make you do anything. If you want to get on that bus to Durango, I'll leave here, go home, and never say a word to anyone about finding you. Your secret is safe with me. But if you do come back, I'm here for you. It's your choice."

CHAPTER THIRTY

"We'll never get through this list in time," Beth said.

Jessie knew she was right. It was after 7 p.m., and they hadn't made a real dent.

Things had seemed so promising when they first started. First, they began with the premise that their killer owned a drone. After getting a crash course in the devices, Jamil was the one, despite his guilt-stricken exhaustion, who had come up with the lead that re-invigorated them all.

"With very few exceptions," he had explained, "almost all drones are required to be registered with the FAA. That means that in addition to information about the device itself, the owner has to provide their name, address, phone number, e-mail address, and credit or debit card details."

"So," Beth had said excitedly, "we use the FAA database to note any registrants in the immediate vicinity of the crimes with criminal records. That can form our suspect list."

And it did. Based on Jamil's recommendation, they selected anyone registered as a drone owner who lived within five miles of any of the murders and who had a felony conviction in the last ten years. Unfortunately, that list was eighty-six people long. And after more than an hour of poring through their files, they'd only gotten through two dozen names.

Beth had nailed it. At this rate, they'd never get through the list in time to help the next victim. They had to shake things up somehow. Jessie was about to suggest an idea when Sam walked in.

"The judge just approved the warrant for Barney Doyle's place," he said. "Ready to head out?"

"Actually, do you mind taking some uniformed officers on this one instead, Sam?" Jessie asked. "I'm still following up on that thing I mentioned earlier."

The detective looked mildly disappointed but didn't say so.

"No problem. I'll let you know what we find."

He left without another word.

"Is he upset that you don't believe that Doyle is the guy?" Beth asked once he was gone.

"Maybe," Jessie said, "but that's not my concern. If Doyle's guilty, then this exercise harms no one. If he's not, then what we're doing is crucial to saving a life, maybe several. That's why we need to shake things up."

"What do you mean?" Jamil asked nervously.

"We have to change the search parameters," Jessie said. "I know you wanted to cast a wide net to start, Jamil, but it's *too* wide. I want to narrow it. Let's reduce the range for residency to anyone living within two miles of one of the victims. And let's change the criminal considerations. Instead of felony convictions in the last ten years for *any* crime, let's make it convictions *or* arrests on felony *or* misdemeanor charges, with no date restrictions, but *only* for crimes of a sexual nature. That means everything from rape or murder down to peeping or indecent exposure."

"But if we only go with sexual crimes, we might be leaving out a huge pool of potential suspects," Jamil objected, wincing. "What about home invasions or traditional assaults? What about murders?"

Jessie understood his real, unspoken concern: that by shortening the list, they would remove the culprit from it, and that he would end up feeling responsible for another death in addition to all the Operation Z victims that already weighed on him. But her gut told her that for this killer, these murders were an escalation of a sexual need, and that was where they needed to focus. If she was wrong, the guilt would be hers to bear, not Jamil's, though she doubted he'd see it that way.

"I hear you," she told him. "But this isn't working. We need to try something new. It might work. It might not. All we can do is try our best and deal with the consequences. Please change the parameters."

Jamil glanced over at Beth, who nodded her agreement.

"It's time to start trusting yourself again," she said quietly.

He looked down at his hands then back up at the two of them. Then, despite his obvious misgivings, he started typing. A new list popped up, revealing twenty-nine names.

"That's much better," Jessie said. "Let's get to work."

***

"So, nine then?" Jessie reconfirmed a half hour later.

"I think so," Jamil said.

"Me too," Beth agreed.

"Then it's decided," Jessie said. "Let me call Sam."

She dialed his number, and he picked up on the first ring.

"How's it going?" she asked him.

"Not great," he admitted. "We're still looking, but so far, all we've found are more videos like the ones from the video camera: lots of model/actress types changing, working out, or in the middle of having sex with someone. But they're all in apartments, they're all young, and we haven't found a thing connected to our victims. I'm starting to think you were right."

"Can the uniforms who are with you finish up the search?" Jessie asked.

"Why?"

"Jamil, Beth, and I have been pursuing a lead involving the drones. We got a list of all registered drone owners in the general area, then reduced it down to men with relevant records who live near the victims. We just finished narrowing it down to just guys who match the physical description from the video at Lauren Pastorini's building: under sixty years old, under six feet tall, under 200 pounds. That left us with nine suspects. I was hoping we could split them up and go check them out, like right now."

"Absolutely," Sam said without hesitation, "but won't that take a while? Can we enlist the rest of the team to help?"

Jessie looked over at Beth, who shook her head. "Susannah and Nettles are on a stakeout," she said. "I don't know all the details, but Captain Hernandez said it has something to do with a city councilmember. They have strict instructions not to leave. And Karen Bray is at home with her son. He was released from the hospital this afternoon, but there's no way she's going anywhere tonight."

"So, I guess it's just a matter of who takes four suspects and who takes five?" Sam said.

"I guess so," Jessie agreed as her phone buzzed. It was a text from Ryan: *Finally done at headquarters. Heading home. See you there?*

She looked up at the two researchers, smiling.

"Actually, Sam, how do you feel about splitting up the list three ways?"

CHAPTER THIRTY ONE

Jessie ordered herself not to get discouraged.

Just because the first two names on her section of the list had been total busts didn't mean the whole theory was ill-conceived. Still, despite her best efforts at positive self-talk, she could feel doubt creeping in.

What if Jamil's apprehensions were right? What if they shouldn't have removed everyone convicted of a non-sexual felony from the list? Should she have really reduced the residential radius from five miles to two? What if the killer lived 2.1 miles away from one of the victims? As she and Officer Louden Burrow approached the house of their third and final suspect, she stopped and literally shook herself.

"Are you okay, Ms. Hunt?" asked Burrow, a slim, fresh-faced, young officer with short-cropped, brown hair and friendly eyes that hadn't yet been hardened by too many years on the job.

"Yeah," she said. "I'm just gearing up. Remember, let's stay on our toes. Just like with the last two guys, we don't know what we'll find in there."

"You mean, we might find a wheelchair-bound gamer or a software developer who's been out of the country for the last week?" Burrow asked, clearly disappointed at the underwhelming nature of their prior two visits.

"Every eliminated suspect gets us closer to our killer," Jessie reminded him. "Let's try to stay positive, Burrow."

"I'm sorry," he said. "Have the other teams had any better luck?"

"Not so far," Jessie told him, not mentioning that neither Sam nor Ryan were part of a "team." They were both investigating their leads solo. In fact, Ryan had balked at letting her pursue her three names at all unless she brought a uniformed officer along, using phrases like "you're not a detective" and "you're still recovering from head trauma." Officer Burrow didn't need to know any of that.

Unlike the gamer, who lived in a fancy, high-rise building just down the block from Lauren Pastorini's condo, or the software developer, who had a mini mansion a few doors away from Gregory and Kim Carrigan, the last guy on their list didn't even live in Hancock Park.

Barry Millstead lived in Hollywood, just north of Melrose Avenue, the dividing line between the two communities, in a tiny house on a run-down stretch of Lillian Way. Still, it was less than a half mile from Lauren Pastorini's apartment and barely over a mile from the Carrigans' place.

Despite his proximity to two of the victims, Millstead was last on her list of suspects for a reason. At fifty-three, he was on the older side. That, coupled with a string of recent, documented health issues, suggested he might not be physically able to attack several younger, healthier women.

Beyond that, his one criminal conviction, twenty-six years ago, was non-violent. He broke into a woman's home, took her panties out of a drawer, laid them on her bed, and proceeded to pleasure himself to them right there in her bedroom. Unfortunately for him, the woman's boyfriend had dropped by that day to return some clothes she'd left at his place, found him there, and beat him to a pulp. Ever since, Millstead had kept his nose clean, at least officially.

They walked up the short path to the house, and Jessie noted the weeds reaching across the walk, trying to lick her at her ankles as she passed by. As she got closer, she saw that the house was in serious disrepair. Multiple shingles were missing. Whole sections of paint were gone. Some of the window shutters looked to be hanging on by a thread.

Jessie knocked on the door and waited. Next to her, Officer Burrow stood anxiously, shifting from foot to foot, his hand resting uneasily on his holster. After a few seconds, the porch light came on, further highlighting the home's rough shape. It was almost 8:30, and the sun had set a half hour ago, masking the fact that termites had eaten away at chunks of the door frame's wood exterior. The light laid that truth bare.

They heard the door unlock, and Jessie tensed up, her own hand rising to her right hip as a precaution. When the door opened, she found herself facing a small, elderly woman with white, curly hair, deep wrinkles, and squinting eyes. She wore a nightgown and slippers modeled after Dorothy's ruby red ones from *The Wizard of Oz*.

"May I help you, dear?" she asked.

"Yes ma'am," she said, trying to hide her surprise, "we're looking for Barry Millstead."

"That's my son," the woman said enthusiastically.

"Is he around?" Jessie asked. "We'd like to speak with him."

"Not right now," the woman said. "I believe he's at work. Would you like to come in and wait for him?"

"That would be great," Jessie replied, stepping inside immediately. "Do you expect him back soon?"

The woman's face scrunched up in uncertainty. "I don't really know," she admitted. "I get a bit forgetful these days. Barry keeps telling me it's called dementia, and I keep telling him I've always been a little scatterbrained. In any case, he'll be home at some point, and you're welcome to wait. So is your handsome young friend."

"Thank you, ma'am," Burrow said, stepping inside as well and closing the door.

The living room behind her was small and messy, with just a loveseat and one chair around a rickety coffee table covered in mugs, glasses, and plates littered with leftover food. The loveseat cushions were split in sections and stuffing had started to escape. A lamp in the corner looked like it might topple over at any moment. The house smelled damp and musty.

"Both of you should call me Dot," the woman insisted.

"Like Dorothy?" Jessie asked. "Is that why you have those slippers?"

Dot looked down at her feet. "I suppose so," she said unconvincingly. "I was just about to put on my robe. Will you join me?"

"Of course," Jessie said, before quietly whispering to Burrow, "stay alert."

They followed her to the room just off to the right, which was apparently her bedroom. She shuffled in and picked up a robe off the bed. Jessie noticed that there were arm and leg straps tied to bottom of the mattress and an absorbent pad on top of it.

"What are those for, Dot?" she asked.

The woman looked at the bed and shrugged resignedly. "I guess I sometimes walk away at night. Barry said that he's found me wandering the street a few times. So, he puts those on me at bedtime, for my own safety and protection. And since I can't get up to go to the bathroom, the pad is there, just in case, you know, something happens."

She said the last part in a quiet, embarrassed voice. Jessie glanced at Dot's wrists and noticed they were rough and scabbed over in parts. So were her ankles.

"You don't walk away in the day?" she asked, quickly moving on from the talk of pads.

"I guess not. Just when the sun goes down it seems, like a vampire," Dot cackled. "Plus, I sometime have an aide in the day to help."

"Not today though?" Officer Burrow asked.

"I think she left a little while ago," Dot said. "That's how I know Barry will be back. He always comes home to strap me in before bedtime."

Jessie wasn't sure if Barry Millstead was a serial killer, but at the very least he seemed like a terrible son and absentee caretaker. She was seriously considering having him brought up on charges of elder abuse. In the meantime, despite the slight ickiness she felt at doing it, she decided to take full advantage of Dot's welcoming personality.

"While we're waiting for Barry, do you mind if I take a look around your lovely home?"

"Be my guest," Dot said happily.

"Thanks," Jessie said. "In the meantime, Louden is going to hang out with you."

She left the room and walked along the short hallway to the only other bedroom in the small house, which was clearly Barry's. It looked like it had been frozen in amber sometime in 1987, which would have been around the year he graduated from high school.

There were multiple baseball trophies on the bookshelves, which were lined with books by Stephen King and Robert McCammon. The walls were covered with posters of the hair metal bands Ratt, Warrant, and Quiet Riot. Interspersed among them were pages of models that had been ripped out of various Sports Illustrated Swimsuit issues and taped up wherever space allowed.

She sat down at his desk, which was neatly organized with a stapler, a tape dispenser, a full pen and pencil holder, and letter opener. What it lacked was a computer, or any sign that Barry Millstead was into tech at all, much less drones.

She sighed and looked at the sad, mostly unoccupied homemade bookshelf next to the desk. The only things sitting on top of it were a row of ten Rubik's Cubes. This guy really seemed to have a serious case of arrested development.

Jessie picked up one of the Cubes and considered giving it a twist, then thought better of it. She started to put it back when she noticed a small sliver of light shining through the wall, right above the bookshelf in the spot where the bottom edge of the Cube had been. Had she not picked up the Cube, she wouldn't have noticed it at all.

Curious, she picked up the Rubik's Cube next to the one she'd already grabbed. The sliver of light extended along its length as well. Jessie stared at the shard of illumination as a thought clawed its way to the front of her brain. It was almost as if Barry was using the Cubes to hide the light from anyone who might come into the room.

She stood up. Quickly, she removed all of the remaining Cubes from the shelf, revealing one long, unbroken, barely visible line of light. But there was something more. Just behind the very last Cube, there was a small notch protruding from the wall. It looked a bit like an imperfection in the paint job, only it was too perfectly rounded to be accidental. She pushed on the notch.

There was soft click and a portion of the wall from the bookshelf to the floor, about four feet wide, popped open and inward, away from the bedroom. It was a hidden door leading into what appeared to be dead space behind the drywall.

Jessie, her heart beating fast, knelt down and looked inside. The dead space amounted to a small, secret room about the size of a broom closet. It was dim, but there was enough light for her to see what was inside: multiple computer monitors spread across a wide desk that took up the whole room. It reminded her of Jamil's set-up in research.

She stepped into the room, moved over to the monitors, and tapped the keyboard. The screensaver disappeared, and she was asked for a password. She moved the mouse over to the other monitors but couldn't get beyond that initial screen on them either.

Frustrated that she couldn't access whatever Millstead had on the computer and worried that time was slipping away, she decided it was time to let the others know what she'd found. Then she saw the notepad.

It was lying next to the keyboard with a pen on top of it. The pad was blank. Hoping against hope, she stepped out of the secret room, grabbed a sharpened pencil from the holder on the desk, and returned. She gently rubbed the tip of the pencil across the pad, praying that her intuition would bear out.

Sure enough, midway down the page, the outline of a name emerged: *Antonia Reston.* Below it was an address, which was much harder to discern, but that didn't matter. The name was enough.

She stepped out of the secret room again and grabbed her phone as she walked out toward the living room of the house. She made a group call to Ryan, Sam, and Jamil. When they were all on the line, she filled them in.

"I think I found our guy," she said, keeping her voice down so as not to freak out Dot in the bedroom nearby. "His name is Barry Millstead. Burrow and I are at his house right now, but he's not here. His elderly mother is home, and she doesn't know where he is. But I found a secret room in his bedroom. It has a whole setup with multiple computers. I couldn't access the data, but I found a notepad that he wrote a name on. Jamil, can you tell me where Antonia Reston lives?"

"Hold on," he said, and after ten seconds told her, "there is an Antonia Reston who lives in Hancock Park. She's thirty-two and married. I'm sending you all the address now."

"I'll meet you both there," Jessie said, about to hang up.

"Hold on," Ryan told her. "Detective Goodwin and I have got this covered. You and Officer Burrow need to stay there to secure Millstead's house."

Jessie felt a surge of fury rise in her gut as her cheeks flushed with mortification. No one else on the line spoke.

"May I speak to you privately, Captain Hernandez?" she said through clenched teeth.

"Of course," he replied. "Sam, get to that address now. I'll see you there. Jamil, have dispatch send a unit to patrol the area. No lights, no sirens. Just have them observe unless instructed otherwise."

Once they hung up, Jessie made her point. "I'm the one who uncovered this, and you're freezing me out."

"That's not true. You don't need to be there, Jessie," he replied. "Why would you put yourself in harm's way unnecessarily?"

"Why are *you*?" she countered. "Sam's a good detective. He can go without you, especially with a patrol nearby. If I'm such a delicate flower, why don't you come over here and secure the scene with me?"

"Jessie, you're not being fair," Ryan pleaded.

"I'm sorry, I've got to go now," she said, unable to keep her voice from curdling. "I have to stare at a bunch of computers and make sure an old lady doesn't wander out into the street. You have fun though."

She hung up before he could reply.

CHAPTER THIRTY TWO

The hardest part was staying calm.

Even though he had worked on cultivating a steel will, the closer he got to the big moment, the harder it was for Barry to keep from letting his excitement get out of hand.

He'd been looking forward to this all day—since last night in fact. The thrill from choking the life out of Lauren Pastorini had faded quicker than he expected, and it had been a struggle to concentrate at work. Of course, it was always a struggle to concentrate when your job was to work front desk security at a self-storage facility.

But after the crap-fest that his life had become in the last year, it was the best job he could get. First, he had to leave Indianapolis nine months ago and move back into the dingy little house where he grew up to take care of his mother. Yes, he got payments from the state for it, but it wasn't nearly enough to deal with the near-constant set of demands from her.

She often forgot to eat, get dressed, or shower. She would mistake him for his dead father and berate him for misdeeds he hadn't committed. She never thanked him for anything he did for her. She woke him up in the middle of the night because she got scared or had an accident or got lost. That's why he lied to her about her having a problem with sleepwalking out into the street at night and convinced her that she needed to be strapped down. It was the only way he could get any decent sleep.

And then a few weeks ago, the heart trouble started. He collapsed at the electronics store and thought it was a heart attack. But when they brought him to the ER, they told him it was congestive heart failure, which made sense in retrospect. He'd been having trouble catching his breath for a few years now. Every time he climbed a flight of stairs, it was an ordeal. But he'd never thought to get checked out, maybe because he didn't have any insurance.

Now the doctors told him that unless he got a transplant, an unlikely proposition, he likely had less than four months to live. Very soon, probably in about two months, they warned that he would be unable to do normal tasks like walk the length of a self-storage building corridor or go grocery shopping. Then, after a particularly bad night with his mother, while cleaning up her carpet the next morning, he had a moment of clarity: he would make the most of the time he had left.

He always loved using his drone to peek in on how the other half lived. Ever since he'd moved in with his mom, he'd have Itty-Bitty, as he called the drone, circle the fancy Hancock Park neighborhood to the south, looking for people just moving in. Then he'd track them over the following months, seeing how they settled in, how late they woke up, what services they procured, what furniture they bought, what kind of parties they threw.

But now, with nothing to lose, he decided to use Itty-Bitty for more gratifying purposes. For years, he'd followed society's rules, controlling the urges that bubbled inside him, never letting them come to the surface, except online in the darkest corners of the web.

But he knew these families' habits. He knew when they came and went. He knew the layouts of their homes. He knew when the ladies he liked were alone. He knew, because of Itty-Bitty, the codes to their alarms. He could pay them visits. He could make his fantasies real.

As a middle-aged, bland-looking fellow, he could walk by their homes or apartments and see what kind of locks they had on their doors, so that he could return later to pick them. And if he could get in their homes without their knowledge and take them by surprise, he didn't have to be in great shape to get the upper hand. He was bigger than them, and in short spurts, he was stronger.

If he did it right, he could get the adrenaline rush he wanted. And so far, it had worked. He had already done it three times in four days. Tonight would be the fourth. And after that, if the schedule he'd made held up, he had seven more women to visit in the next week and a half.

He didn't have much of a plan beyond then. That was partly because he didn't realistically expect to make it that long without getting caught. It was also because he wasn't sure his heart would hold out another ten days with all this extra activity and excitement. If not, at least he'd go out on a high note.

Barry pulled onto Antonia Reston's street and eased his car along slowly, looking for a spot to park. He found one just across from her house, turned off the car's lights, and looked at the time. It was 8:46. If everything was as it should be, her husband, Tate, would be at his weekly Wednesday softball game. It always started at 8 p.m. and usually ran until 9:30, sometimes 10.

Antonia typically took advantage of his boys' night to drop off their three-year-old daughter, Cleo, at her mom's place for the night and have some solo time. Typically, that meant a long bath, followed by settling in for a sexy thriller with some popcorn and Chablis. Tate would usually get home in time to shower and join her for the tail end of the thriller. Then they'd retire to the bedroom for some sexy time of their own.

Barry's timing was perfect. Antonia typically ran the bath from about 8:45 to 8:50. He would use the noise of the water filling the tub to mask when he entered the house and disabled the alarm. But he needed to move quickly. In about four minutes, she'd be shutting off the water.

He was just about to get out of the car when he glanced over and saw something unexpected in the kitchen window of the house: Antonia Reston. She was in her robe, and she was not alone. Speaking to her was a tall man, well over six feet, with unruly, brown hair. Whatever he was saying, Antonia was listening intently. Her hands were clasped together in front of her mouth, and she looked tense.

Barry felt the rage begin to bubble up inside him. After everything he'd been through with his mother, with his health, and with his crappy job, he'd been looking forward to tonight, and now it wasn't going to happen. His special evening with Antonia was ruined. He deserved this, and it was being taken away from him. He gripped the steering wheel tight in frustration.

Just then, Barry saw a police car pull onto the street ahead of him and come slowly in his direction. He bent over as low as he could and waited until the headlights passed him by. After a while, he raised his head slightly and watched in his side-view mirror until the police car eventually turned right at the end of the block. Then, he turned on his own lights, pulled out of his parking spot, and left.

He didn't know what he would do next, but he did know one thing: this wasn't over. Someone was going to pay tonight. If it wasn't Antonia, it would be somebody else. He could almost taste their pain now, and it was delicious.

CHAPTER THIRTY THREE

"You don't think I should at least try?" Jessie asked.

"No, I don't," Jamil said forcefully.

She was sitting in Barry Millstead's secret room, staring at his main computer monitor, hoping that her resident research genius could help her unlock the system's password and access evidence of what he had already done and planned to do in the future.

"Why not?" she asked. "We have all kinds of biographical information on him. Maybe we'll get lucky."

"And maybe he's got lockout protocols," Jamil countered. "If we try to access his system with the wrong password, it could lock us out completely, or worse, delete all his data. Let's just wait, Jessie. There are professionals whose whole job is to break into unbreakable systems. I'm not one of them. And you definitely aren't. Me trying to talk you through this over the phone is a recipe for disaster."

"But what if Millstead isn't at Antonia Reston's?" Jessie pressed, "or what if Sam and Ryan got there first, he saw them, got spooked, and moved on to his next target?"

"Jessie," Jamil said hesitantly, "please don't kill me for saying this, but is it possible that you're still pissed off at Captain Hernandez for holding you back from going to the Reston house, so you're desperately looking for some other way to make a difference, instead of sitting in that house twiddling your thumbs while you wait for the backup team to arrive?"

Though she was loathe to admit it, the second Jamil said it, she knew he was right. She was bouncing off the walls being stuck here. And while her theory about Millstead getting spooked and moving on wasn't absurd, the idea that she should try to crack his password was.

"Point taken," she said. "I will not kill you at this time. But can you please tell me when the family services people are supposed to arrive to get Dorothy Millstead? Burrow is doing yeoman's work out there with her, but he's not trained for this."

"They should be there in the next fifteen minutes," Jamil said, before adding, "if you feel so bad for Burrow, then maybe you could help him out a little?"

Though his reply was a little snarky, Jessie didn't mind. She'd rather have a snarky Jamil than a sullen one. And he made a good point. It wasn't fair to leave the rookie officer out there to handle Dot all on his own.

"Fine," she said, a little sullen herself, "text me with *any* updates, and I mean any."

She hung up and left the secret room, determined to focus on helping the person she could impact right now. That meant Dot.

"How's it going out there, you guys?" she called out as she stepped into Millstead's bedroom and shoved her phone back in her pocket.

Someone replied, but the words were barely audible.

"What was that?" she asked as she headed toward the bedroom door, "I couldn't really hear you."

She heard another response, but it was equally muffled. Something about the tone of the voice, its intensity, sent a prickling sensation up the back of her neck. Without stopping to think, she simultaneously started to move to the side of the door and unsnap the holster of her gun.

As she did, a man darted out of Dot's bedroom and charged at her. She recognized Barry Millstead from his driver's license photo: his pudgy, stubbly face, his thinning, black hair, and his watery blue eyes. He was less than five feet away, and Jessie barely had time to process his identity, much less do anything about it.

She was just pulling out her gun when he slammed into her, knocking her backward. She didn't know where she was going and had no time to brace herself. A moment later, she felt her body land on his bed, his full weight on top of her. Her gun flew out of her hand. Air shot out of her chest.

As she gasped, trying to regain her breath, Millstead wrapped his hands around her throat and started to squeeze. She tried to wriggle loose, but despite his small stature and advanced years, he was surprisingly strong. She could feel his fingers digging into her throat and knew that no help would be coming. Burrow was almost certainly dead. Unless she did something now, she would be too.

Ignoring her burning chest, she extended her arms out, balled her hands into fists, and brought them together fast and hard, boxing the man's ears with as much force as she could muster. He looked startled, and his own breathing seemed to get raspy, but he didn't stop squeezing.

She extended her arms again and punched his ears a second time and then a third. After the fourth, she felt his grip loosen slightly. After the fifth, he released his right hand from her neck and held it to his ear briefly, then clutched at his chest for a moment before returning his attention to her.

As she sucked in air, he looked down at her with furious, wet eyes and lifted his hand. She saw that he was about to hit her in the face and literally beat him to the punch, thrusting the palm of her right hand up toward his nose as he swung downward. She made contact before he did, and she heard him screech in pain. His swing glanced off her ear as he slumped to the side, doing more damage to his mattress than to her.

She used the moment to push him away and roll off the bed, landing stomach-first on the floor below. It was still hard to breathe, but she scurried away on her hands and feet, trying to scramble to her feet. There was no point in looking for her gun. She just needed to get out of this room.

She was almost upright when he tackled her from behind, sending her to the ground again, flat on her stomach. She was just pushing herself up when she felt his right arm wrap around her neck, trapping it in the crook of his elbow. He was lying on top of her back, pinning her down. She could hear him wheezing loudly in her ear.

Unable to move and feeling her windpipe start to close again, she did the only thing she could think of—bracing herself with her left forearm, she took her right hand, reached around, and started jabbing her fingers back toward her left shoulder in the direction of Millstead's face, hoping to make contact with his eyes.

Instead, she hit hard bone and knew it was his skull, that he'd turned his head to the side to avoid just such an attack, as if he'd experienced it before. So instead, she grasped at his hair and yanked, ripping out what little he had left. He yowled, and his grip seemed to weaken considerably but he still didn't let go. It was now the sheer weight of him on top of her, with her neck trapped between his torso and his arm, that was crushing her windpipe. Jessie's eyes started to water.

His yowls had been replaced by low, plaintive moans, as if *she* was the one pressing down on him instead of the other way around. And in that moment, as her thoughts began to jumble, it hit her: he was having a heart attack.

The realization gave her a spark of renewed energy, which she used to fling her body upward, in the hope that it would force him off her. It didn't, though it did slightly loosen his arm's tight clamp around her neck. But not enough.

I have to try one more time. I have to find the strength.

In the doorway, shadows began to swim before her eyes. Her grip on his hair loosened. She found it harder to gasp for breath and decided to let go of him entirely as she pressed her palms into the floor, ready to give one final desperate heave.

One of the swimming shadows in front of her seemed to loom especially large. It moved forward menacingly. The shadow was close now, extending a leg out, as if it was kicking at her face, then just past her face.

And all at once the pressure around her neck eased. She felt Millstead's arm release its grip completely. Suddenly, the shadow was above her, murmuring. She blinked through her wet eyes and saw that it wasn't a shadow at all. It was Ryan. His murmurs were replaced by words. "… you understand me? You're going to be okay."

She tried to nod to indicate that she understood him, but her neck hurt.

"Don't try to move," he said. "I'm just going to put you on the bed. Then I'm going to cuff this guy, all right?"

She didn't try to nod that time.

***

It was about three minutes before she was able to speak. "Burrow?" she asked hoarsely.

"He's going to be okay," Ryan assured her. "It looks like Millstead knocked him out with a lamp, but he's breathing."

"Dot?"

"The old lady?" Ryan said. "She's alive and conscious. She'd been gagged and had her wrist strapped to the mattress, but otherwise she's unhurt."

Jessie tried to smile but it hurt her neck muscles too much.

"The woman?" she asked. "Reston?"

"She's fine, too," Ryan assured her. "Sam's with her. We think Millstead may have seen him there and come back here because he couldn't get to her."

"Millstead's having a heart attack," she muttered.

"Oh," Ryan said, surprised. "I didn't realize. I knocked him out when I kicked him in the face, but I'll let the EMTs know."

"How did you know to come here?" she pressed, though it was painful to speak.

Ryan smiled. "I didn't," he admitted. "You just made me feel so guilty that I decided I should stop by to help you secure the scene."

Jessie gulped hard before responding, "Good."

CHAPTER THIRTY FOUR

Mark Haddonfield walked down toward the boat slip as if he belonged.

He'd scouted the marina so often in recent days that it felt like he did. When he got to Woody Garnett's boat, the classily named "Double D," he glanced around to make sure there was no one around, then stepped onboard.

Mark might have looked suspicious wearing a dark hoodie in June elsewhere in L.A., but not late at night right on the water. The temperature was hovering around 60 degrees, and there was a brisk breeze, so he fit right in.

He knew that Woody would be alone. The young woman that he'd left his wife for a few months ago had recently dumped him, and he'd spent most of his evenings of late on board his boat, drinking rum and coke while watching old westerns on the DVD player he used because the Wi-Fi in the immediate area was so spotty.

He moved quickly across the boat's deck and down the companionway into the cabin, confident that Woody wouldn't hear him. There had been complaints from boat owners in adjoining boats about him playing his movies so loud late at night, so he'd recently invested in headphones and was oblivious to just about everything around him.

Sure enough, he didn't stir when Mark stepped down onto the creaky floor. He was seated in an easy chair with his back to the companionway, wearing a sweatshirt and pajama pants, his gray hair greasy and unwashed, watching some movie with John Wayne and Jimmy Stewart that Mark was unfamiliar with.

He reached for his nearly half-empty glass and took a healthy swig. Mark saw the bottle of rum on the table to the man's left, walked over, and with his gloved hand, slid it a few feet away, just enough so that Woody would have to stand up to get it the next time he wanted to refill his glass. Then he stepped back into the corner, out of sight.

One would have thought that after suffering a near-death experience at the hands of a serial killer, Woody would have changed his ways at least a little. If he didn't reconcile with his wife, at least he might have considered adopting a healthier lifestyle rather than diving headfirst into the booze. But he didn't seem interested in that. Then again, that's why Woody was Mark's first choice; that's why he was here.

He pulled out the knife—the same hunting variety that Harper Grey had used on Woody in the hotel a few months back—and waited. He felt a strange brew of emotions: excitement, yes, but also anxiety and something bordering on nausea.

Was he really going to do this? Was he actually going to take a human life, even one as offensive as Woody Garnett, in order to teach Jessie Hunt a lesson, to make the world see her hypocrisy and corruption? Was that who he was now? Was he sure he was willing to become that person? Was he that certain of the righteousness of his mission?

Woody Garnett glanced over and saw his bottle too far away to reach. He appeared briefly perplexed by how it had moved, but got over it quickly, and stumbled to his feet. He scuffled around his chair and picked up the bottle to refill his glass.

In that moment, all the doubt fell away. Mark slipped out of the darkness of the corner, took two steps forward, and just as Woody looked up and met his eyes, he plunged the knife deep into his stomach.

The metal slid in easily, no trouble at all. As it plowed through Woody's insides, Mark's brain exploded with a giddy thrill, like fireworks on the 4th of July and New Year's Eve combined. He thought he might faint from the sheer joy of it.

The older man gasped and started to slump, but Mark pulled him in, refusing to let him fall. He stared into the older man's blue eyes, noting the crow's feet that extended out from them like tiny, dried-out creek beds.

Then he pushed the knife in harder until it hit something solid in the back that might have been the spine. He twisted the blade back and forth, giggling at the sound of blood gushing onto the wooden floorboards between them. Woody groaned softly.

Mark held him upright as he maneuvered him back around his chair and then eased him down into it, before pulling the knife out in one beautifully violent, swift motion. Blood sprayed everywhere.

As Mark leaned over and wiped the blade on Woody's sweatshirt to clean it off, the old man's eyes dulled. He seemed to be trying to form the word "why," but he couldn't get it out. Mark answered the question for him anyway.

"Because you deserve it."

But Woody was dead before he finished the sentence.

That was okay. Woody didn't need to understand. The person who did would ask why soon enough. And when she did, Mark would decide what she could know and when.

Jessie Hunt was no longer in charge. He was. And it felt amazing. More than that, it felt right.

CHAPTER THIRTY FIVE

"I'm just worried about him," Jessie said.

"To be clear," Dr. Lemmon replied over the phone in her best "are you sure this is what you mean?" tone, "after nearly getting choked to death, being hospitalized overnight for observation, and having your neurologist come see you this morning, the first thing you want to discuss with your psychiatrist is a guy who works in the research department at your station?"

"He's not just a guy," Jessie insisted, grateful for the medication that made it possible for her to speak without pain as she sat upright in the hospital bed at Cedars-Sinai Medical Center. "Jamil Winslow is the twenty-four-year-old head of research for HSS, he's a legitimate genius, and he's tearing himself to pieces because he's consumed by misplaced guilt over deaths he couldn't have prevented. I'm really concerned that he's at a breaking point."

There was a long pause before Dr. Lemmon responded, "so you're telling me that this person is placing unreasonable blame on himself because he made tough choices that saved some lives at the expense of others?" she confirmed.

"That's right," Jessie said.

"Almost like a criminal profiler who keeps castigating herself for doing what she had to do to survive when she was held captive in an isolated mine by a mentally unstable woman who threatened to kill her?" Lemmon noted.

"It's not the same," Jessie said.

"You're right, it's not the same. He's a twenty-four-year-old kid. *You* should know better," Lemmon replied. "I'll talk to him. Just know that you and I aren't done discussing your need to damn yourself for using every tool at your disposal, even a psychopath's childhood trauma, to outwit said psychopath. But we can save that chat for another time. You mentioned that Dr. Varma came by earlier today. What did she say about your test results?"

Jessie leapt at the chance to change topics. "Mostly good news," she answered. "All my tests show improvement—memory, spatial awareness, concentration, general mental acuity. My scans look better too. She said that the headache symptoms I'm having now sound more related to stress, anxiety, and exhaustion than to concussions. They don't present as migraines. There's no nausea anymore, and I don't have light or sound sensitivity the way I used to. She sounded optimistic, though she strongly recommended that I avoid situations where I might incur another concussion, and she suggested I pursue additional therapy to reduce my stress load."

"Now, there's an idea," Lemmon said with mock surprise.

"I'm talking to you now, aren't I?" Jessie reminded her.

"And I'm very pleased about that. Have you told Ryan and Hannah about the results yet?"

"Not yet," Jessie said. "I figured I'd give them the good news tonight. Actually, I see them about to come in the room right now. Can we finish this up later?"

"Not *too* much later," Lemmon said, before hanging up.

Hannah opened the door and Ryan came in pushing a wheelchair.

"Are they really going to make me leave in that thing when it's my neck that's sore?" Jessie asked incredulously.

"Hospital policy apparently," Ryan said. "Besides, if you're in the chair, it'll be easier for you to carry those."

He nodded at the giant vase of flowers that had been sent over from Gregory Carrigan. Jessie smiled at the sight of them. If Carrigan was able to order flowers, it meant he was at least somewhat functional. She hoped the Hill family would get there at some point too. Thinking of that family, now motherless, reminded her of two other orphaned children, and of a glimmer of hope she'd found amid the darkness.

"Hey," she said, sitting up straighter in the bed. "I started to mention this to Ryan yesterday but got sidetracked. I'm glad because now I can tell both of you at the same time. I have an idea."

"For what?" Hannah asked.

"For Callum Reid's family, specifically for his kids."

Hannah's face fell. "You know I don't like to talk about—"

"Just give me a second," Jessie interrupted. "I get that he's a painful topic for you. He is for me too. We both know what he sacrificed and what his children will be missing without him there in the years to come. We can't give them that back. But I thought we could give them something."

"What?" Hannah asked quietly.

"You know that between my divorce and what my parents and Garland Moses left me in their wills, I have more money than I know what to do with. A lot of that is tucked away as a safety net, in case things ever go so sideways in a way that only large sums of cash will help with. But I thought, why not put some of that safety net to better use? That's why I've decided to set up the Callum Reid Memorial Scholarship Fund. It will ensure that both his kids can go to college, free of charge. And with a little fundraising and department support, I think we can turn it into an annual thing, helping pay for college for other children of fallen police officers. What do you think?"

"I think it's a great idea," Ryan said, smiling.

Hannah was quiet. When she did speak, her voice sounded shaky, "I think I need to borrow your bathroom for a moment," she said, lowering her head so that Jessie couldn't see the tears that she knew were streaming down her face. "I'll be out in a minute."

"I think she likes it," Ryan said, after the bathroom door closed. "Speaking of big, positive news, I thought you'd want to know: Harold Gore, the city councilman who was trying to pressure Cheryl Gallagher to burn Chief Decker, was arrested last night on charges of criminal intimidation, among other things."

"That's what Susannah and Nettles's stakeout was about?" Jessie asked.

"I can't officially confirm or deny that," Ryan said. "But I can tell you that earlier this morning, while you were in morphine-induced sleepyland, Decker's interim designation was removed. He's now officially the full-time Chief of the LAPD."

"That's fantastic!" Jessie said.

"It really is," he agreed. "And you should know that you and Goodwin catching Barry Millstead certainly didn't hurt when it came time to make the final decision. Stopping the man who killed Greg Carrigan's wife has been a real good news story."

"That's not the only person he killed," Jessie said quietly.

"I know, Jessie. But it's a win, and we should take them where we can get them," Ryan said. "And if you're still in the mood for good news, I have a little more."

"What's that?"

"You want personal or professional first?" he asked.

"Let's go with professional."

"Jamil texted me a little while ago," Ryan said. "The cyber unit cracked Millstead's computer. They found tons of files for all three victims, more than enough to convict him, if he even survives that long. The doctors aren't sure he'll even regain consciousness after suffering that heart attack while assaulting you last night."

"I hope he makes it," Jessie replied. "Those families deserve their day in court."

"I hope so, too," Ryan agreed. "But at least he won't be hurting anyone else. The cyber unit also found comprehensive files on at least half a dozen other women he'd been tracking. He had a detailed schedule for when he planned to attack them, all within the next two weeks. He wasn't going to stop. You saved a lot of lives."

Jessie felt a wave of relief wash over her. "I'm glad," she said quietly. "What about the personal news?"

"Oh yeah," Ryan replied. "I told my mother to kick rocks."

"Excuse me?" Jessie asked.

"I mean, I was a little more polite than that," Ryan said, "but I realized that it wasn't right for me to let a woman who hasn't been a part of my life for years pressure me into asking the woman who defines my life to change anything about herself, especially her name, out of some misguided need to carry on a legacy I don't even feel a part of. So, sorry about that."

"I appreciate that, Ryan," Jessie said as a second, less intense wave of relief rolled through her system, "because I didn't want to hurt you, but Hunt was the name of the people who raised me and died for me, and I'm not giving it up for anyone. No offense."

Only as she said the words did she recognize that this had been the issue eating at her all along, and that if she'd come to the realization earlier, she could have saved them both a lot of time.

"None taken," Ryan said with his sweet-natured grin. "I fell in love with Jessie Hunt. I don't need Jessie Hernandez. And if that's our biggest issue, then we're good."

"We actually do have a bigger issue," Jessie noted reluctantly. "And it has to do with our ongoing boss and employee, husband and wife dynamic. Specifically, it has to do with you sending a detective to a potential victim's house and leaving me to tread water with a rookie cop at a home you thought would be risk-free. You keep trying to sideline me, Ryan."

She waited for an apology but was surprised when he shook his head instead.

"I understand how you feel," he said, "and maybe I didn't handle things perfectly. But you have to look at things from my perspective too. You're my wife. You're also my employee. Both of those people had serious head trauma recently. And in neither of those roles did you need to be at Antonia Reston's house last night. I made a judgement call, and I stand by it."

"Well, I'm telling you as both my husband and my boss that we need to get clarity on those roles, or this is going to undo us. Somehow, we have to find a way to resolve that."

"Resolve what?" Hannah asked, emerging from the bathroom.

Jessie and Ryan exchanged a look before he answered.

"Resolve what is taking so long to get your sister discharged," he said. "It's after 1 p.m. already. You should have been cleared to leave an hour ago. I'm going to the nurse's station to find out what the holdup is. Be right back."

"He's obviously lying," Hannah said once he left the room, as she took a seat near the bed, "but I guess a couple has to have some secrets."

Jessie wasn't feeling especially forthcoming, and since she didn't want to lie to her sister, she decided to change the subject entirely. Glancing at the muted television on the wall, she did her best to offer a distraction.

"I'm glad *that* worked out," she said, nodding at the screen.

"What?" Hannah asked, turning to look.

The local news was on, and a reporter was standing in front of a west side house with a chyron that read: *teenaged girl once feared dead returns home unharmed.*

"The girl that was missing," Jessie said. "I thought she was dead for sure. But I guess she just planned to run away. Apparently, she didn't have the greatest home life. Supposedly, she's going to live at her friend's house for a while. Did you know she's the same age as you?"

"No," Hannah said with a disinterested shrug, "I haven't really been following the story. But I'm glad to hear that she's safe. I hope it works out for her."

"Me too," Jessie said.

Neither of them spoke for a moment, then she heard her sister sigh nervously and looked over. "Hey," Hannah muttered quietly, her eyes on the floor, "did I ever tell you that you're a pretty great big sister, and that I appreciate how you've turned your life upside down to make room for me, and that I love you?"

For a second, Jessie feared that she'd suffered a concussion she wasn't aware of and was having a new side effect: hallucinations. She was about to make a crack along those lines but stopped herself at the last second. “No,” she answered. “I don’t think you ever have.”

“Well, I’m telling you now,” Hannah said, finally looking up. Her eyes were damp.

“Thank you,” Jessie said, still stunned, though that feeling was quickly being overtaken by a giddy warmth. “Where is this coming from?”

Before Hannah could reply, Ryan poked his head into the room. “Okay, we’re going,” he said.

Hannah popped up out of her seat and moved quickly to grab the wheelchair. It was clear that she didn’t want to continue the conversation they’d been having.

“I’m discharged?” Jessie asked, deciding to let it go.

“No, they can’t find the doctor, and they don’t seem to be in any rush,” he replied, clearly annoyed, “but I figure that if we put you in that chair and start wheeling you out, they’ll get their butts in gear.”

It sounded like a good plan to Jessie, who happily settled into the wheelchair. A minute later, the vase of flowers was in her lap, and they were rolling down the hallway. She could hear a nurse calling after them as Ryan pushed faster, and Hannah giggled beside him.

“Please hold on, sir,” the nurse said, when she finally caught up to them in the lobby. “We’ve paged Dr. Minnette and expect him down here any moment.”

“Bring the car around, Hannah,” Ryan said, before turning to the nurse, “you’ve got until she pulls up and then we’re out of here.”

“Please sir, don’t be difficult,” the nurse pleaded. “If you’ll just come over to the desk, we can get everything settled.”

“Do you mind waiting here for minute?” Ryan asked Jessie, making a big show of it.

“I suppose not,” she replied, playing along.

He eased the wheelchair to the side of the lobby, away from the hustle and bustle, and walked over to the desk. Jessie watched him pretend to be angrier than he really was, amused at his inability to really sell being a jerk. He might fool strangers, but he was just too nice of a person to be truly mean, unless you were a murderer, of course.

Jessie’s phone rang and with the big vase of flowers in her lap, she fumbled to grab it. When the caller ID appeared on the screen, her blood went cold.

CHAPTER THIRTY SIX

The call was coming from the Western Regional Women's Psychiatric Detention Center. There was only one person currently being held there that held any significance for her: Zoe Bradway.

Zoe was Andy Robinson's final acolyte, the person responsible for the Operation Z attack that caused twenty-seven deaths and nearly resulted in thousands more. Jessie had tried to speak to her multiple times in recent weeks to get answers about that attack specifically and to finally close the loop on the questions she had about Andy's larger, multi-year plan to destroy her. But Zoe always refused to meet with her. Now, *she* was the one calling.

"Collect call from Zoe Bradway," said an automated voice. "Will you accept the charges?"

"Yes," Jessie said, gulping hard.

She heard a click, followed by multiple voices echoing in what was clearly a busy institutional hallway. She imagined Zoe on a payphone with multiple women lined up behind her, waiting for their turn to talk.

"Hi, Jessie," the young woman said, her voice somehow meek and confident at the same time. "Thanks for taking my call."

"Frankly, I'm surprised to get it," Jessie admitted, pleased that her own voice sounded stronger and more assured than she felt.

"Well, I saw what happened to you on the news, and I felt like I should reach out to make sure you were doing okay," Zoe said.

"I appreciate the concern, but I'm fine," Jessie replied. "I tried to reach out to you several times, and you didn't seem all that receptive."

"I was making my peace with my new situation," Zoe said quietly. "You have to understand that I'd spent months working on this involved plan and then, in one moment, it was all over. I needed some time to mourn."

Jessie decided not to comment on the fact that Zoe considered failing to kill thousands of people mourn-worthy.

"But you're through with that now?" she asked, sensing that the young woman wasn't being entirely forthright with her.

"I have to admit that it's hard, Jessie," Zoe sighed, "especially when I feel like I still don't have the whole truth. I keep seeing occasional stories on the news about how Andy is still out there, hiding in caves in the desert. But I've got to tell you—I have my doubts. I'm starting to wonder if maybe Andy didn't make it after all; if she was actually killed by you or one of your lackeys, and you've been maintaining the fiction that she's still alive, initially to keep me from activating Operation Z, and now, just to keep me guessing. Am I wrong to be suspicious about that, Jessie?"

Zoe was *not* wrong. That was exactly what was going on. They'd planted false stories of Andy's survival in the press because they knew that Zoe was supposed to put Operation Z into effect if Andy died and pretending that she was still alive was a way to forestall that outcome. Since then, they'd kept the lie going because as long as Zoe believed Andy lived, she was potentially vulnerable to manipulation. They held out hope that she might reveal additional details of Andy's grand plan. But it looked like that jig was just about up.

"I don't have any answers for you about that," Jessie said, trying to avoid a direct lie. "If anybody could survive in a mine in the desert, it's Andy Robinson. And you would know better than me if she had other hideouts besides the place where she took me. But is that really why you called?"

"No, it's not," Zoe conceded. "I guess I'll have to live with my doubt about Andy's fate. But that discomfort is eased a little by what I have to tell you."

"One minute remaining," an automated voice interrupted, letting them both know that their call was nearing an end.

"Sounds like you better hurry," Jessie noted.

"You think this is over, but it's not," Zoe said simply.

Jessie felt a cold surge rush up her spine at the words. "What do you mean?" she managed to ask without choking on the words.

"I almost feel bad saying this when you're in such a vulnerable state," Zoe said, not sounding like she felt bad at all, "but I thought you deserved to know."

"Know what?"

She heard Zoe inhale with excited anticipation before responding, "Do you really think that after all those months of organizing, I would have embarked on the final stage of Operation Z without making sure that I had planned for every contingency? Do you think that Andy would have left me unprepared for any scenario that might play out?

I'm sure she told you that Operation Z was two-fold. Part one was a mass casualty event, designed to kill as many citizens of this city as possible. That didn't go as well as I would have hoped, due to the efforts of you, your husband, and the rest of your annoying HSS friends. But that wasn't the only part of the operation, was it? Do you recall part two?"

Jessie did, but she was unwilling to say it out loud. Zoe didn't seem to mind doing it for her.

"Part two was your family, Jessie. I was tasked to kill the people you care about: Ryan, Hannah, and Kat. I was told to make them suffer, to make sure you felt the depth of their suffering and understood that it was all happening because of you, because *you* refused to be with Andy. I may be locked up in this place, Jessie, but do you really think I can't get to them? I assume that none of what I'm saying is news to you, but I wanted to make it crystal clear. Do you really think I haven't already set part two in motion?"

Jessie waited for the rest of the threat, but it didn't come. Only then did she realize that the minute was up, and the call had been cut off.

She sat in her wheelchair, trying to shove the fear down so she could make sense of what she'd heard. She wasn't even sure if Zoe was for real. These could just be the desperate rantings of a woman hoping to salvage lost relevance.

But Jessie couldn't quite convince herself of that. Even as she'd listened in horror, part of her brain was homed in, hoping that Zoe might inadvertently reveal some detail that could lead to how she planned to make part two of Operation Z a reality.

Don't spin out. Think your way through this. Even if the threat is credible, that doesn't mean it's imminent. Stay calm.

Maybe they could bug Zoe's future phone calls. Maybe they could track her visitors. Maybe they could check her bank accounts to see if there was any unusual activity. Zoe might just be playing head games, but there was no harm in bringing the resources of HSS to bear to find out whether this threat was legitimate or not.

There's no reason to panic. Don't panic.

"Finally," Ryan said, walking over. "Imagine how long it would have taken to get you discharged if we hadn't pulled that whole charade."

He grabbed the handles on the back of the wheelchair and steered her out through the automatic doors into the sunlight. Hannah was parked and sitting on the hood, a bored look on her face, oblivious to the peril she was apparently in. Ryan leaned over the chair with a broad smile on his face, equally clueless to the threat he faced.

"Let's get you in the car," he said happily, before his smile faded. "Hey, what's wrong? You're so pale all of a sudden."

Jessie saw Hannah glance over at them, her bored expression replaced by one of concern.

"Nothing," she said quickly, realizing she needed to get her act together. This wasn't the time or the place to deal with what she'd just heard. "I was just thinking of something, but we can talk about it later, maybe tonight?"

"Sure," he said, not entirely convinced but apparently willing to let it go for now. "Let's just get you home and worry about everything else after that."

He eased her into the passenger seat and walked around. Hannah took the flowers from her, got into the backseat behind her, and gave her shoulder a gentle squeeze.

"You'll feel better once you're back home in your comfort zone," she promised.

"I'm sure you're right," Jessie said, then asked as casually as she could, "hey, how's Kat doing?"

"She's fine," Hannah said. "Working that Lyman Feller case solo today, for obvious reasons. She said she'd stop by tonight. I almost feel bad that we're taking Feller's wife's money. The only cheating that guy does is on the rent his company charges his clients."

Jessie wanted to ask more about what security precautions Kat was taking about but knew it would raise her sister's curiosity, so she let it go for now. When Ryan got into the driver's seat beside her, he was looking at a text and shaking his head.

"What's wrong?" she asked.

"I just got an update from Nettles," he said. "Do you remember a guy named Woody Garnett?"

"Of course," she said. "He's a real charmer—left his wife after three decades of marriage, right in the middle of a therapy session. More importantly, he was Harper Grey's last intended victim. She stabbed him in the stomach in a hotel room and was going to finish him off until we got there and stopped her. Why?"

"He was found murdered on his boat this morning."

Jessie blinked in surprise. "How did he die?" she asked.

"He was stabbed in the stomach," Ryan said.

"That's kind of weird," Hannah noted from the back seat.

Jessie couldn't disagree. "Can you have whoever's looking into it send me a copy of the case file?" she asked Ryan. "I want to take a peek at it."

"Sure, but you don't mean now?" he asked, borderline appalled.

"No," she assured him. "I'm exhausted. I'm sore. I'm heavily medicated. I'll look into it but not today."

"Good," Ryan said. "You can worry about it later. Besides, it'll probably turn out to be nothing."

NOW AVAILABLE!

THE PERFECT VENEER
(A Jessie Hunt Psychological Suspense Thriller—Book Twenty-Six)

When a wealthy couple is found dead in their home's high-tech panic room, Jessie Hunt is summoned to the crime scene. In this room designed to be safe from all harm, how has the killer managed to kill these people? Why? And which opulent home will he strike next?

"A masterpiece of thriller and mystery."
—Books and Movie Reviews, Roberto Mattos (re Once Gone)

THE PERFECT VENEER is book #26 in a new psychological suspense series by bestselling author Blake Pierce, which begins with *The Perfect Wife*, a #1 bestseller (and free download) with over 5,000 five-star ratings and 1,000 five-star reviews.

Jessie must enter the killer's mind, his traumatic past, to decode the clues at the crime scene.

Can she stop him before he strikes again?

A fast-paced psychological suspense thriller with unforgettable characters and heart-pounding suspense, the JESSIE HUNT series is a riveting new series that will leave you turning pages late into the night.

Future books in the series will be available soon.

"An edge of your seat thriller in a new series that keeps you turning pages! ...So many twists, turns and red herrings… I can't wait to see what happens next."
—Reader review (Her Last Wish)

"A strong, complex story about two FBI agents trying to stop a serial killer. If you want an author to capture your attention and have you guessing, yet trying to put the pieces together, Pierce is your author!"

—Reader review (Her Last Wish)

“A typical Blake Pierce twisting, turning, roller coaster ride suspense thriller. Will have you turning the pages to the last sentence of the last chapter!!!”
—Reader review (City of Prey)

“Right from the start we have an unusual protagonist that I haven't seen done in this genre before. The action is nonstop… A very atmospheric novel that will keep you turning pages well into the wee hours.”
—Reader review (City of Prey)

“Everything that I look for in a book… a great plot, interesting characters, and grabs your interest right away. The book moves along at a breakneck pace and stays that way until the end. Now on go I to book two!”
—Reader review (Girl, Alone)

“Exciting, heart pounding, edge of your seat book… a must read for mystery and suspense readers!”
—Reader review (Girl, Alone)

Blake Pierce

Blake Pierce is the USA Today bestselling author of the RILEY PAGE mystery series, which includes seventeen books. Blake Pierce is also the author of the MACKENZIE WHITE mystery series, comprising fourteen books; of the AVERY BLACK mystery series, comprising six books; of the KERI LOCKE mystery series, comprising five books; of the MAKING OF RILEY PAIGE mystery series, comprising six books; of the KATE WISE mystery series, comprising seven books; of the CHLOE FINE psychological suspense mystery, comprising six books; of the JESSIE HUNT psychological suspense thriller series, comprising twenty-eight books; of the AU PAIR psychological suspense thriller series, comprising three books; of the ZOE PRIME mystery series, comprising six books; of the ADELE SHARP mystery series, comprising sixteen books, of the EUROPEAN VOYAGE cozy mystery series, comprising six books; of the LAURA FROST FBI suspense thriller, comprising eleven books; of the ELLA DARK FBI suspense thriller, comprising fourteen books (and counting); of the A YEAR IN EUROPE cozy mystery series, comprising nine books, of the AVA GOLD mystery series, comprising six books; of the RACHEL GIFT mystery series, comprising ten books (and counting); of the VALERIE LAW mystery series, comprising nine books (and counting); of the PAIGE KING mystery series, comprising eight books (and counting); of the MAY MOORE mystery series, comprising eleven books; of the CORA SHIELDS mystery series, comprising eight books (and counting); of the NICKY LYONS mystery series, comprising eight books (and counting), of the CAMI LARK mystery series, comprising eight books (and counting), of the AMBER YOUNG mystery series, comprising five books (and counting), of the DAISY FORTUNE mystery series, comprising five books (and counting), of the FIONA RED mystery series, comprising five books (and counting), and of the new FAITH BOLD mystery series, comprising five books (and counting).

An avid reader and lifelong fan of the mystery and thriller genres, Blake loves to hear from you, so please feel free to visit www.blakepierceauthor.com to learn more and stay in touch.

BOOKS BY BLAKE PIERCE

FAITH BOLD MYSTERY SERIES
SO LONG (Book #1)
SO COLD (Book #2)
SO SCARED (Book #3)
SO NORMAL (Book #4)
SO FAR GONE (Book #5)

FIONA RED MYSTERY SERIES
LET HER GO (Book #1)
LET HER BE (Book #2)
LET HER HOPE (Book #3)
LET HER WISH (Book #4)
LET HER LIVE (Book #5)

DAISY FORTUNE MYSTERY SERIES
NEED YOU (Book #1)
CLAIM YOU (Book #2)
CRAVE YOU (Book #3)
CHOOSE YOU (Book #4)
CHASE YOU (Book #5)

AMBER YOUNG MYSTERY SERIES
ABSENT PITY (Book #1)
ABSENT REMORSE (Book #2)
ABSENT FEELING (Book #3)
ABSENT MERCY (Book #4)
ABSENT REASON (Book #5)

CAMI LARK MYSTERY SERIES
JUST ME (Book #1)
JUST OUTSIDE (Book #2)
JUST RIGHT (Book #3)
JUST FORGET (Book #4)
JUST ONCE (Book #5)

JUST HIDE (Book #6)
JUST NOW (Book #7)
JUST HOPE (Book #8)

NICKY LYONS MYSTERY SERIES
ALL MINE (Book #1)
ALL HIS (Book #2)
ALL HE SEES (Book #3)
ALL ALONE (Book #4)
ALL FOR ONE (Book #5)
ALL HE TAKES (Book #6)
ALL FOR ME (Book #7)
ALL IN (Book #8)

CORA SHIELDS MYSTERY SERIES
UNDONE (Book #1)
UNWANTED (Book #2)
UNHINGED (Book #3)
UNSAID (Book #4)
UNGLUED (Book #5)
UNSTABLE (Book #6)
UNKNOWN (Book #7)
UNAWARE (Book #8)

MAY MOORE SUSPENSE THRILLER
NEVER RUN (Book #1)
NEVER TELL (Book #2)
NEVER LIVE (Book #3)
NEVER HIDE (Book #4)
NEVER FORGIVE (Book #5)
NEVER AGAIN (Book #6)
NEVER LOOK BACK (Book #7)
NEVER FORGET (Book #8)
NEVER LET GO (Book #9)
NEVER PRETEND (Book #10)
NEVER HESITATE (Book #11)

PAIGE KING MYSTERY SERIES
THE GIRL HE PINED (Book #1)

THE GIRL HE CHOSE (Book #2)
THE GIRL HE TOOK (Book #3)
THE GIRL HE WISHED (Book #4)
THE GIRL HE CROWNED (Book #5)
THE GIRL HE WATCHED (Book #6)
THE GIRL HE WANTED (Book #7)
THE GIRL HE CLAIMED (Book #8)

VALERIE LAW MYSTERY SERIES
NO MERCY (Book #1)
NO PITY (Book #2)
NO FEAR (Book #3)
NO SLEEP (Book #4)
NO QUARTER (Book #5)
NO CHANCE (Book #6)
NO REFUGE (Book #7)
NO GRACE (Book #8)
NO ESCAPE (Book #9)

RACHEL GIFT MYSTERY SERIES
HER LAST WISH (Book #1)
HER LAST CHANCE (Book #2)
HER LAST HOPE (Book #3)
HER LAST FEAR (Book #4)
HER LAST CHOICE (Book #5)
HER LAST BREATH (Book #6)
HER LAST MISTAKE (Book #7)
HER LAST DESIRE (Book #8)
HER LAST REGRET (Book #9)
HER LAST HOUR (Book #10)

AVA GOLD MYSTERY SERIES
CITY OF PREY (Book #1)
CITY OF FEAR (Book #2)
CITY OF BONES (Book #3)
CITY OF GHOSTS (Book #4)
CITY OF DEATH (Book #5)
CITY OF VICE (Book #6)

A YEAR IN EUROPE
A MURDER IN PARIS (Book #1)
DEATH IN FLORENCE (Book #2)
VENGEANCE IN VIENNA (Book #3)
A FATALITY IN SPAIN (Book #4)

ELLA DARK FBI SUSPENSE THRILLER
GIRL, ALONE (Book #1)
GIRL, TAKEN (Book #2)
GIRL, HUNTED (Book #3)
GIRL, SILENCED (Book #4)
GIRL, VANISHED (Book 5)
GIRL ERASED (Book #6)
GIRL, FORSAKEN (Book #7)
GIRL, TRAPPED (Book #8)
GIRL, EXPENDABLE (Book #9)
GIRL, ESCAPED (Book #10)
GIRL, HIS (Book #11)
GIRL, LURED (Book #12)
GIRL, MISSING (Book #13)
GIRL, UNKNOWN (Book #14)

LAURA FROST FBI SUSPENSE THRILLER
ALREADY GONE (Book #1)
ALREADY SEEN (Book #2)
ALREADY TRAPPED (Book #3)
ALREADY MISSING (Book #4)
ALREADY DEAD (Book #5)
ALREADY TAKEN (Book #6)
ALREADY CHOSEN (Book #7)
ALREADY LOST (Book #8)
ALREADY HIS (Book #9)
ALREADY LURED (Book #10)
ALREADY COLD (Book #11)

EUROPEAN VOYAGE COZY MYSTERY SERIES
MURDER (AND BAKLAVA) (Book #1)
DEATH (AND APPLE STRUDEL) (Book #2)
CRIME (AND LAGER) (Book #3)

MISFORTUNE (AND GOUDA) (Book #4)
CALAMITY (AND A DANISH) (Book #5)
MAYHEM (AND HERRING) (Book #6)

ADELE SHARP MYSTERY SERIES
LEFT TO DIE (Book #1)
LEFT TO RUN (Book #2)
LEFT TO HIDE (Book #3)
LEFT TO KILL (Book #4)
LEFT TO MURDER (Book #5)
LEFT TO ENVY (Book #6)
LEFT TO LAPSE (Book #7)
LEFT TO VANISH (Book #8)
LEFT TO HUNT (Book #9)
LEFT TO FEAR (Book #10)
LEFT TO PREY (Book #11)
LEFT TO LURE (Book #12)
LEFT TO CRAVE (Book #13)
LEFT TO LOATHE (Book #14)
LEFT TO HARM (Book #15)
LEFT TO RUIN (Book #16)

THE AU PAIR SERIES
ALMOST GONE (Book#1)
ALMOST LOST (Book #2)
ALMOST DEAD (Book #3)

ZOE PRIME MYSTERY SERIES
FACE OF DEATH (Book#1)
FACE OF MURDER (Book #2)
FACE OF FEAR (Book #3)
FACE OF MADNESS (Book #4)
FACE OF FURY (Book #5)
FACE OF DARKNESS (Book #6)

A JESSIE HUNT PSYCHOLOGICAL SUSPENSE SERIES
THE PERFECT WIFE (Book #1)
THE PERFECT BLOCK (Book #2)
THE PERFECT HOUSE (Book #3)

THE PERFECT SMILE (Book #4)
THE PERFECT LIE (Book #5)
THE PERFECT LOOK (Book #6)
THE PERFECT AFFAIR (Book #7)
THE PERFECT ALIBI (Book #8)
THE PERFECT NEIGHBOR (Book #9)
THE PERFECT DISGUISE (Book #10)
THE PERFECT SECRET (Book #11)
THE PERFECT FAÇADE (Book #12)
THE PERFECT IMPRESSION (Book #13)
THE PERFECT DECEIT (Book #14)
THE PERFECT MISTRESS (Book #15)
THE PERFECT IMAGE (Book #16)
THE PERFECT VEIL (Book #17)
THE PERFECT INDISCRETION (Book #18)
THE PERFECT RUMOR (Book #19)
THE PERFECT COUPLE (Book #20)
THE PERFECT MURDER (Book #21)
THE PERFECT HUSBAND (Book #22)
THE PERFECT SCANDAL (Book #23)
THE PERFECT MASK (Book #24)
THE PERFECT RUSE (Book #25)
THE PERFECT VENEER (Book #26)
THE PERFECT PEOPLE (Book #27)
THE PERFECT WITNESS (Book #28)

CHLOE FINE PSYCHOLOGICAL SUSPENSE SERIES

NEXT DOOR (Book #1)
A NEIGHBOR'S LIE (Book #2)
CUL DE SAC (Book #3)
SILENT NEIGHBOR (Book #4)
HOMECOMING (Book #5)
TINTED WINDOWS (Book #6)

KATE WISE MYSTERY SERIES

IF SHE KNEW (Book #1)
IF SHE SAW (Book #2)
IF SHE RAN (Book #3)
IF SHE HID (Book #4)

IF SHE FLED (Book #5)
IF SHE FEARED (Book #6)
IF SHE HEARD (Book #7)

THE MAKING OF RILEY PAIGE SERIES
WATCHING (Book #1)
WAITING (Book #2)
LURING (Book #3)
TAKING (Book #4)
STALKING (Book #5)
KILLING (Book #6)

RILEY PAIGE MYSTERY SERIES
ONCE GONE (Book #1)
ONCE TAKEN (Book #2)
ONCE CRAVED (Book #3)
ONCE LURED (Book #4)
ONCE HUNTED (Book #5)
ONCE PINED (Book #6)
ONCE FORSAKEN (Book #7)
ONCE COLD (Book #8)
ONCE STALKED (Book #9)
ONCE LOST (Book #10)
ONCE BURIED (Book #11)
ONCE BOUND (Book #12)
ONCE TRAPPED (Book #13)
ONCE DORMANT (Book #14)
ONCE SHUNNED (Book #15)
ONCE MISSED (Book #16)
ONCE CHOSEN (Book #17)

MACKENZIE WHITE MYSTERY SERIES
BEFORE HE KILLS (Book #1)
BEFORE HE SEES (Book #2)
BEFORE HE COVETS (Book #3)
BEFORE HE TAKES (Book #4)
BEFORE HE NEEDS (Book #5)
BEFORE HE FEELS (Book #6)
BEFORE HE SINS (Book #7)

BEFORE HE HUNTS (Book #8)
BEFORE HE PREYS (Book #9)
BEFORE HE LONGS (Book #10)
BEFORE HE LAPSES (Book #11)
BEFORE HE ENVIES (Book #12)
BEFORE HE STALKS (Book #13)
BEFORE HE HARMS (Book #14)

AVERY BLACK MYSTERY SERIES
CAUSE TO KILL (Book #1)
CAUSE TO RUN (Book #2)
CAUSE TO HIDE (Book #3)
CAUSE TO FEAR (Book #4)
CAUSE TO SAVE (Book #5)
CAUSE TO DREAD (Book #6)

KERI LOCKE MYSTERY SERIES
A TRACE OF DEATH (Book #1)
A TRACE OF MURDER (Book #2)
A TRACE OF VICE (Book #3)
A TRACE OF CRIME (Book #4)
A TRACE OF HOPE (Book #5)

Made in the USA
Columbia, SC
25 February 2023

12963650R00126